CONAN DOYLE
AND THE CRIMES CLUB

The Creator of Sherlock Holmes and his Criminological Friends

STEPHEN WADE

FONTHILL

Fonthill Media Limited
Fonthill Media LLC
www.fonthillmedia.com
office@fonthillmedia.com

First published 2013

British Library Cataloguing in Publication Data:
A catalogue record for this book is available from the British Library

Copyright © Stephen Wade, 2013

ISBN 978-1-78155-194-3

The right of Stephen Wade to be identified as the author of this work has been asserted by him in accordance with the Copyright, Designs and Patents Act 1988.

All rights reserved. No part of this publication may be reproduced, stored in a retrieval system or transmitted in any form or by any means, electronic, mechanical, photocopying, recording or otherwise, without prior permission in writing from Fonthill Media Limited

Typeset in 10 pt on 14 pt Sabon
Printed and bound in England

Connect with us
facebook.com/fonthillmedia   twitter.com/fonthillmedia

Contents

	The Court of Criminal Appeal, 30 July 1908	5
	Introduction: Tales of the Criminous and Clubmen	9
1.	Arthur Lambton: The Fight for Legitimacy	25
2.	Conan Doyle: Good Fellowship and Sleuthing	33
3.	John Churton Collins Investigates	45
4.	Samuel Ingleby Oddie and Dr Crippen	58
5.	Henry Brodribb Irving and Remarkable Criminals	66
6.	George R. Sims: Justice Campaigner and Celebrity	76
7.	Max Pemberton	93
8.	Fletcher Robinson and *The Hound of the Baskervilles*	99
9.	A. E. W. Mason: Writer and Spy	104
10.	A Lord, a Knight, and a Medical Man	112
11.	Trials and Theories: Atlay and Diosy	124
12.	William Le Queux: Landru and the Crumbles Bungalow Murder	131
	Conclusions	145
	Acknowledgements	153
	Bibliography and Sources	154
	Index	159

The Court of Criminal Appeal, 30 July 1908

It could have been simply another day down in the law courts for the professionals working in the law machine of Edwardian Britain. Normally, they would have donned their gowns and wigs, chatted in the dressing room, ready to walk into their space and assume their roles in the drama of the court of law where issues were decided and closure applied.

Yet it was nothing like an ordinary day in the courts. It was a momentous day. In 2012, it is not an event one might find in a calendar of important centenaries. A more likely candidate for that might be Selfridges, which less than a year later, would be ready to open its doors.

No, this was a fateful day, and beneath the professional veneers, the men of law on that day knew the significance of one of the many cases before them very well. Some of the cases would be minor matters, to be sorted out almost as easily as going down a list of minor repairs – jobs to do, no less. But one man, due to stand before them, would make them pay full attention. Why? What was so special about that summer day in the pride and leisure of good King Edward's reign, with London still at the heart of a vast Empire?

It was the first time that a murder case had come up before the judges at the new court. Barristers were keen to finger through, one more time, the clauses of the new statute, to be sure that they were well informed. There was so much to remember, and a life depended on their getting it right. A man stood there in the dock, no doubt with a sense that his heart was beating at his ribs with an intensity he was fighting to control.

A jury had found James Jefferson guilty of murder. Now he was standing in the dock in another court room, wondering whether he would leave the court to the gallows, or back to his cell, or even whether his destination would be Broadmoor Asylum. He had been convicted at Leeds Assizes, and there, the issue had been whether or not he was actually fit to plead. After the usual legal debates and discussion of possible precedents, the jury found Jefferson to be capable of planning a murder, and that he was of sound mind. His offence had suggested anything but sanity.

The man in the dock had been found in the act of cutting off the head of a woman lying in the road, using a table knife. The man who found him tried to talk to him, and then ran for help. When he came back with other people, Jefferson was now with the body in a field, cutting off an arm. One man had a crowbar and threatened him. They all told him to stop immediately, and Jefferson was escorted away from the scene, but he took with him the woman's umbrella, hat, and corsets, talking about what cash he would get for them. If he had been of sound mind, then what version of sanity was this behaviour? The first court to hear the tale was not troubled by the issue.

The body in the field was almost naked, with twenty-eight wounds in it, from a knife. Jefferson had come out of prison in Newcastle a few months before this attack, and during his time behind bars, he had been seen as quite sane. Clearly, bearing in mind his actions on that horrendous day, his defence at the assizes argued that he was insane. But a Dr Edgerley from a local asylum testified that Jefferson was sane when he killed. He based this opinion on impressions gleaned after two long interviews with the prisoner. Two prison doctors, who had watched Jefferson closely during his remand period, agreed with Edgerley. But they did add, 'He did not know how wrong the thing was, nor did he know the quality of the act or appreciate it.' However, one aspect of their patient that all medical men agreed on was the fact that he had hallucinations and delusions. This last fact should have proved his state of unsound mind.

The jury in Leeds were convinced that Jefferson knew what he was doing when he killed the woman. He was given the death sentence. At the appeal court, Jefferson's brief argued that the jury were wrongheaded on the issue of sanity, specifically that Jefferson had not been fit to plead in the first case. But even the new Criminal Appeal Act made no allowance for that in terms of a ruling being made. But there was a clause relating to medical evidence of mental condition. The counsel for defence was astounded that the Leeds jury had disagreed with the medical statements. Fortunately for Jefferson, the clause in question allowed for an argument that the conviction was unsatisfactory.

The judge presiding was the celebrated Lord Justice Darling, along with Judge Lawrance, and they decided that, as Lawrance put it, 'in the opinion of the court, the verdict of the jury ought to have been that the appellant was insane at the time he committed this act'.

The sentence was quashed, and under the Trial and Lunatics Act, Jefferson was sent for the rest of his life to the asylum for the criminally insane. This replaced what should have been a special verdict back in the assize trial. He walked out dazed, led and guided by the efficient and professional arms of the court ushers and the prison warders. He was to join the lunatics in Broadmoor; the people labelled criminally insane until changes made over forty years later. His life would now be regulated for every moment of every day, from communal eating, to steady gardening and supervised leisure. He was one of the casualties of that increasingly common condition of mental chaos, accelerated by the breathless modernity of the new cities, and the rush for power and status. He would be forgotten, but not deprived of his life.

That Jefferson did not walk to the gallows and swing at the end of the hangman's rope was partly because of the investigations into miscarriages of justice undertaken by some members of the Crimes Club, among them, George R. Sims, writer and journalist, and his friend, the man who had just a few years before, resurrected his hero, Sherlock Holmes – Dr Arthur Conan Doyle.

Introduction:
Tales of the Criminous and Clubmen

They were a fair proportion of the literary and legal elite of their generation. They had excelled in the professional worlds of authorship, commerce, the bar, and the higher journalism. They loved to meet in convivial and relaxed clubs, and they enjoyed parading their conversational talents in front of gaggles of like-minded men, perhaps at ease with brandy and a cigar, or sometimes giving a learned and entertaining talk about a topic of general interest. Peter Costello, in his book *Conan Doyle: Detective*, wrote that 'the members were [...] so many students of contemporary crime. But they kept their affairs secret, so that even today [...] little has been divulged about them. The club still exists and remains, as ever, exclusively secret'.

They were at first named Our Society, but later became The Crimes Club. They first assembled at the Great Central Hotel in London on 17 July 1904, after meeting for an informal talk at the home of the son of the great actor Sir Henry Irving, Harry Brodribb Irving, the year before. This followed a dinner at the Carlton Club in December 1903, and from that it is certain that the more formal conditions and guidelines for activities were formed. Although members wanted the club to remain easy and chummy, with chats about fascinating criminal memorabilia, or talks on infamous cases by professional members who were in the legal profession, word got around, and others wanted to join in.

They were an assortment of mainly university men, many from Oxford, where they had learned the importance of networking. But back then, the word used for this was simply *society*. They had all acquired the gentlemanly accomplishments expected of men of letters who wanted to stay in favour among their peers in the publishing world of the time. Most of them could hardly be called, in the parlance of the twenty-first century, movers and shakers. No, they had merely a common interest, and they saw the benefits of sharing knowledge and experience.

The meetings soon attracted all kinds of members, and in 1909, one of the original members, Ingleby Oddie, resigned. He was miffed at the new identity of the club; something more streamlined and rather academic than at first conceived. The other founding members were from the more celebrated persons: Sir Arthur Conan Doyle, Churton Collins, James Beresford Atlay, Lord Albert Edward Godolphin Osborne, George R. Sims, Max Pemberton, Fletcher Robinson, Harry Irving, C. A. (Lord) Pearson, and A. E. W. Mason. From the less well-known, there were Arthur Lambton, and a medical man from Norwich called Dr Herbert Crosse.

There were many other personalities on the fringe of the club, also with profound interests in legal and criminal matters. There was George Ives, who started a vast collection of press cuttings in 1892. His archive of such material was destined to run to 6,000 pages after sixty years of collecting. Many of his cuttings concerned criminal matters, and as his editor Jeremy Brooks noted in an anthology taken from the Ives cuttings, the man hated injustice, and he wrote books on penal reform too. Ives never joined the Crimes Club, but he did join Conan Doyle in another club: the Authors' Cricket Team, along with J. M. Barrie and P. G. Wodehouse. Here is yet another example of Conan Doyle being gregarious in a world of clubs and societies. He was always, since the time of his first real successes in literature, eager to be seen in society, and to mix with his peers.

In some ways, in its first identity as Arthur Lambton wanted it, the club was as much a source of play and relaxation as the charity cricket matches many of them played. Conan Doyle had even bowled out the great W. G. Grace. Conan Doyle and Alf Mason put on their whites alongside stars of the music hall and the theatre. That was the spirit of the club in 1903. But it was soon to transform itself into yet another exclusive group with an interest in a very topical theme: the nature of the criminal, and the challenge of understanding the nature of the most heinous or astounding crimes.

The members typified the authors of their generation: creative minds coming into full powers of narrative and commercial know-how in an age of vast expansion in their readership. The 1890s had brought them new possibilities and new markets as the popular journalism encouraged by George Newnes and Alfred Harmsworth expanded. One of the club members, Arthur Pearson, was of that breed, with his magazine *Pearson's Weekly*. Matthew Arnold referred to this popular writing, with a strong literary impulse mixed together with informative, didactic work, as 'the new journalism'. With this came the rise of literary agencies (the first had appeared in 1875 with A. P. Watt), and the arrival of net book agreements for retail. The profession also had the Society of Authors, which began to organise advice, legal help, and dissemination of information. In short, being a writer at the turn of the nineteenth century was becoming more of a career choice, although it was tough on those, such as George Gissing, who insisted on literary standards related to classic literature. For men like Conan Doyle and George Sims, the opportunities widened, such was the demand for popular storytelling. In that literary climate, the notions of brotherhoods of writers were extensions of professional attitudes. The working lives of writers became topics of intense interest, so much so that *The Idler* magazine ran a long series of interview pieces with the title, 'Lions in their Dens.'

Were they a clique in an age of cliques? That is, did they preserve their difference by being notably insular and exclusive? G. K. Chesterton saw a clique as a group with 'a tendency not only to talk shop, but to talk workshop. Like talkative art students, they show each other their work before it is finished; and like lazy art students, they often find this an excellent excuse for not finishing it at all'. Well no, the members tended to see their projects through.

The years around 1900 were a time when writers generally took a very profound interest in crime and law in all its manifestations. Arnold Bennett, always keen to learn material for his craft, perhaps typifies this. In 1899, he sat on a coroner's jury at Fulham and heard four cases. He reflected in his journal on something that was always centrally important in the crime writers around Conan Doyle: 'The dramatic quality of sober fact. In two instances, the deceased persons had died from causes absolutely unconnected with the superficial symptoms. Thus a woman who had brought on a miscarriage and died, had died from heart disease.' In that brief note, Bennett encapsulates the allure of crime and transgression for the writer: the crime story has muddled interpretations and a variety of sources behind the act itself. The Crimes Club met in order to enjoy and maximise the delight in digging for cause and effect in the confusion and mystery of human actions.

The first Crime Club members were out to celebrate amateur sleuthing, but it was far more than fun and relaxation. They enjoyed analysing cases, but even more challenging and absorbing was the inquiry into unsolved crimes, and into the mysteries of motivation in criminal matters. The meetings were initially intended to be the kind of occasions in which professional men put their feet up, and over a brandy and a cigar, discuss a transgression and all its human complexity. Before the real professionalisation of the social and psychological sciences, they explored deviant behaviour. In the infancy of criminology, they went deeply into the social and relational contexts of celebrated crimes, and at a time when the police had only just begun to question the validity of the influential work of Cesare Lombroso, whose notions of physiognomy as a guide to criminal types had been accepted by many for some time since the publication of his *L'Uomo Delinquente* in 1889, although to be fair to the man, he did take an interest in a range of subjects related to criminal behaviour.

In this book, I am answering my own questions about who these men were, why they assembled to talk crime, and what else they had done in life. The more I looked into their experiences and achievements, the more I saw that most of their stories have never been told. Apart from Conan Doyle himself I discovered, the only other member whose life has been recounted in great detail is Henry Brodribb Irving, son of the great actor manager, and even then, his criminological interests have not been examined. In some cases, previous biographers have admirably undertaken thorough and ground-breaking work, yet their subjects are still not widely known. I am thinking here in particular of Bertram Fletcher Robinson and William Le Queux. Telling their stories will inevitably involve recounting some of the infamous cases they studied and talked about.

Arguably, the most well-known image of the fascination with crime in the late Victorian period comes from the iconic figure of Sherlock Holmes and the arrival of *The Strand* magazine. The concept of this new publication came from George Newnes, who wanted a British magazine with a picture on every page. The editor received two stories from Arthur Conan Doyle: 'A Scandal in Bohemia' and 'The Red-Headed League', and his excitement at reading them led to the employment of Sidney Paget to provide the illustrations. A massively influential literary creation was born. Holmes was not only an amateur forensic student, but also a meticulous preserver of criminal profiles and biographies, and this cultivation of an interest in the deviancies of his world made him entirely representative of a trend amongst men of letters at the time. True crime, as we would call it in the twenty-first century, was becoming something worthy of serious attention.

In addition to the Holmes stories, *The Strand* carried features such as 'Smugglers' Devices' and 'Her Majesty's Judges'. A little later, the *Harmsworth* magazine went even further into this market, having a similar format to *The Strand,* but having even more curious and fascinating criminal topics such as 'Poison Devices: conceived by the grim and ghastly ingenuity of our forefathers', and 'The Medical Detective and His Work'. The magazine succeeded *Harmsworth*'s very popular 1887 publication, 'Answers to Correspondents on Everything Under the Sun'. By the mid-1890's, mainly due to the advent of Jack the Ripper in the Whitechapel murders, interest in all things criminal had burgeoned in the mind of the reading public.

The whole subject of crime and criminals was, to these literary and legal minds, one strangely existing in a world separate from their book-lined studies and elegant legal chambers. A murder case was fascinating to them because it presented a riddle, a mystery, and the narrative of the whole nasty affair was akin to a work of fiction to their minds. Ever since Thomas de Quincey, back in the 1820s, had written his tongue-in-cheek account of the study of murder, *Murder Considered as One of the Fine Arts*, crime had offered something especially attractive to the intellectuals and aristocrats in the higher circles of debate and conference: information on human motivation of an extreme and deviant nature. Before 1868, felons had been hanged in public, and writers such as Dickens and Thackeray had joined the throng to watch murderers dance on the end of a rope at Newgate, or earlier than that at Tyburn, where Marble Arch stands today. But as that open spectacle of suffering ended, so the subject of murder became again something confined to the courts.

The 1880s and 1890s saw a plethora of books on exciting criminal cases, with the Old Bailey or the assize courts at the centre of the story. There was R. Storry Deans' *Notable Trials: Romances of the Law Courts* (1896) and Peter Burke's *The Romance of the Forum* (1899), for instance. Lawyers began to write their memoirs to feed the hunger for sensational criminal tales, but they were not true crime in the sense that the penny dreadfuls were. In the 1880s, the famous *Newgate Calendar* was republished anonymously, with engravings, produced on cheap paper as chapbooks for the readers who wanted their crime stories in tabloid English with plenty of action and fear. In contrast, the books and periodicals aimed at the middle class readers aspired to present crime stories with more of a literary feel. There was more interest in such social issues as the causes of crime and the effectiveness of efforts of reform for habitual criminals.

There was always the sense of drama, and many of the members were men of the theatre. Max Beerbohm, writing in 1893, told his friend, 'I am spending a great deal of my time in the music halls, theatres, and courts of law.'

The real world of detectives was accelerating at the time too, largely due to fingerprinting and the beginnings of proper forensics. The Crimes Club met in very exciting, if not revolutionary, times for the criminal justice system. Partly this was in forensics, and partly in the establishment of the first Court of Criminal Appeal (1907).

In this context, the advent of a proper, official Fingerprint Bureau at Scotland Yard in 1901, under the management of Assistant Commissioner Edward Henry, did much to increase the general interest in forensics among literary men and journalists. It was a branch of forensics that had obvious appeal to storytellers and purveyors of popular sensational fiction.

One of the most celebrated detectives of the twentieth century, Fred Cherrill ('Cherrill of the Yard') explained his early fascination with fingerprints by telling the tale of his going to an old mill with his father in a storm. The miller was ill, and someone was needed to grind the corn to meet demand. In the mill, flour was sprayed everywhere, putting a white film over every surface, and young Fred found himself grabbing an eel his father threw across the room at him, with orders to put it in a sack. His hands were caked in eel slime, and then he writes:

> Startled, I put out a hand to steady myself. For just a moment my slime-covered fingers rested on the wooden chute, which had become highly polished by all the flour and meal which had passed over its surface [...] I was gazing at the chute in awed fascination [...] There, by the agency of nature alone, were my fingerprints!

Cherrill's story accounts for the long history of the knowledge of fingerprints, long before they were used in forensics. There had been various academics who had done work on prints, but nothing had come of it: a professor at Breslau University in 1823 had read a Latin thesis on fingerprints in a lecture, and the artist Thomas Bewick had done wood engravings of fingerprints, using them as identifying signatures on his works. In China, for many centuries, thumb-prints had been used in documents for identity purposes in ratification. Similarly, these impressions had been used in India with illiterate members of the population. When the scientist Francis Galton got to work on the subject, he wrote a book-length study, simply called *Fingerprints*, published in 1892. In some ways, the introduction of fingerprinting into police work is similar to the rivalry to reach the South Pole: while Sir Edward Henry was using fingerprints in India for crime investigation, the same work was being done in Argentina by Francesco Rojas. But after Henry had introduced fingerprinting into the repertoire of detection methods at the Yard, it was to affect a revolution in detective procedure.

The prototype scenario, and first conviction by the use of prints, came in 1902, when the Yard had around 100 fingerprints in their first small volume of records. It was a murder case, and it took place at Chapman's Oil & Colour store in Deptford. An old couple, Thomas and Ann Farrow, ran the shop, and they had an assistant called young William Jones, who along with Louis Kidman, found Thomas' corpse, and later the still breathing Ann Farrow.

The old man had been brutally beaten, with a broken cheekbone and a fractured skull; the doctor said that the man had died around 90 minutes earlier. When Ann Farrow had been taken to hospital and the scene was ready for some inspection, Chief Inspector Fred Fox arrived to do his work with two photographers. Crime scene investigation, in something close to the modern sense, was being born that day. No less a figure than Melville Macnaghten came to assist and then take charge. The killer had not forced an entry; that was the first important detail established. There had been a frenzied search of the whole shop and house, but after going upstairs and hitting Mrs Farrow, the scene suggested that they had come downstairs and fought the old man again, as he had recovered from their first blow.

There were no witnesses. Three masks were found abandoned in the shop, so now Macnaghten knew he was looking for three killers, and that made the murder all the more savage and reprehensible. There was no indication as to what weapon had been used in the murderous attacks either. The question now on the detective's mind was whether Ann Farrow would recover and give descriptions. What was particularly unhelpful in the course of following the usual tracing procedure in pawn shops and similar outlets, was that the killers had only taken money. That created a dead end in the normal line of enquiry. It was looking desperate for Chief Inspector Fox; another shopkeeper had been killed in London the same day. Then, the final blow came: Mrs Farrow died.

Macnaghten went back to the bloodbath that was the sitting room of the Farrow household. Casting his eye across the room and the pools of blood, he thought of the surface prints that had just been used in smaller scale arrests. Would the Farrow murder be the first opportunity to try this new device? He established that none of the police personnel at the shop had touched the cashbox, then he covered his fingers with a handkerchief, and showed his team the print on the box. Collins, of the new fingerprint branch, was a sleuth with a scientific bent. He had been working on other types of basic forensics and was excited about this new technique. It was a matter of magnifying glasses and intense study at that time; he had a small collection of filed prints from known criminals, and that was that. There had been a long-established method of filing basic records of habitual offenders, so there was some hope of a result. But the print on the cash box had no match in Collins's shelves.

Basic police work however, provided the lead that would eventually take the investigation back to the cash box. A milkman at work on the day of the killing had seen two men leaving the shop, and he gave a description of them. The milkman saw that they had left the door open and told them so, but they took no notice, as they said there was someone behind them. To tally with this, three men had been seen in a local pub very early that day, and they answered the descriptions. It was when a certain Ellen Stanton came forward that things accelerated; she had seen two men running at the right time, and they had the same appearance as two suspects, and Ellen knew one of them. Macnaghten was now searching for one Alfred Stratton. The man was taken in Deptford. The identification parade failed, but Collins took the prints of Stratton and his brother. One print matched that of Alfred.

What happened then is a pattern for almost all succeeding scientific forensic advances when it came to actually implementing the knowledge and seeing it take part in a process of law in the courts. In other words, this new detective force, with its fingerprints and other types of records, was going to find it hard to convince judge and jury about the new methods of detection. But the Stratton brothers went to the gallows; hangman John Billington officiated at Wandsworth. The judge Mr Justice Channell had said in court that the men should not be convicted on fingerprint evidence alone, and that was the case. But the first trial involving fingerprint evidence had happened. From that point on, the concept would be a little more familiar, and the newspapers played their part in ensuring that.

What was happening in the closing years of the nineteenth century and the first years of the new century, was that Scotland Yard was acquiring a much more sophisticated records department than ever before, and fingerprints were beginning to play a major part in that. Edward Henry initiated the Central Fingerprint Bureau, and together with the Register of Habitual Criminals, the Criminal Records Office was created. Three CID men, Stedman, Collins, and Hunt, were to run the new section.

The Court of Criminal Appeal suddenly gave the general reader a sense of the dramatic in the life-or-death tale of murder to rival the Old Bailey sensations of the Regency a century earlier. Here was a court at which men sentenced to hang had one last chance of a commutation of the sentence to life imprisonment, or even acquittal. The hearing was like a one act play, with a conclusion that led either to the gallows, or back to the cell. Even if anyone missed the trial and the newspaper reports, the cases were reported in depth in collected volumes each year.

In this stimulating and thought-provoking climate, the writers and intellectuals of the club met. Of course, several infamous murders and notorious crimes took place at the time of their first meetings too: the years from 1899 to 1905 saw the imprisonment and release of Oscar Wilde, the hanging of the baby-farmers Amelia Sachs and Annie Walters, the reign of terror of George Chapman, the Moat House Farm murder, and the fingerprint case of the Strattons.

The kind of talk and discussion the Crimes Club enjoyed is best illustrated by the word criminous – a term coined by William Roughead, seen by many as the doyen of the higher, more literary crime fact genre. I need to explain this by giving a short profile of Roughead, who, although he was never directly involved in the Conan Doyle circle, did occasionally write to Sir Arthur. They also knew of each other's work of course, Roughead having begun his voluminous writings on murder cases and trials in 1906. Later, they did actually meet at a dinner, and catch up on their passions in criminology. Roughead was very much a specialist in Scottish criminal history, and naturally, his writings on Edinburgh cases would have made him known to Conan Doyle.

In 1913, Henry James wrote to his friend William Roughead after receiving the latter's volume on Scots trials. James wrote:

> Most interesting and attaching is the book, which has held my attention charmed, and your manner of presentation is so strong and skilful that one casts about with open appetite for more such outstanding material into which you may be moved to bite – or at least to make *us* bite.

That sums up the appeal of the writer whom many true crime writers regard as the master of their genre. James had expressed what is apparent in a reading of any of Roughead's narratives of crimes and courtroom dramas: that he draws the reader into the intrigue and raises irresistibly complex questions about serious crime throughout history.

In his busy and productive career, Roughead became much admired as an editor of case books on several of the most celebrated trials in criminal history. He was fascinated by the specific insights given to us by crime history – ways of understanding the nature of transgression in human communities. Perhaps because he took the cases so seriously, and deepened the nature of the crime writer's enquiry into motivation and circumstance, he became that rare instance in the genre, the true stylist. This is what attracted Henry James to his writing, and it is what has confirmed and maintained Roughead's reputation. When New York Review Books published *Classic Cases* in 2000, the first move was made to bring Roughead back into print. The editor Luc Sante pointed out that there is another element in a Roughead crime case book: 'Virtually all the hallmarks of the classic British mystery appear here, the apparent originals of those overly clever poisonings, those horrors in sleepy priories and drams set against majestic Highland backdrop.' In other words, there is a strong storyline in Roughead's recreations of extreme transgression; a quality that lifts the writing to the level of the best crime fiction.

His most effective and comfortable form in his extensive body of work was surely the extended essay. At a length of around eighty pages, the ingredients were generally a mix of reflection, summary of facts, and interpretation of the central story. It was Roughead who did much to popularise and promote the classic Scottish horrors of the body-snatchers Burke and Hare, and Deacon Brodie, the killer with the double life who was the inspiration for R. L. Stevenson's Dr Jekyll and Mr Hyde. When Roughead edited and assembled such large-scale cases, he had the power and skill to elucidate all the elements of the scene, from the legal professionals to the investigation process.

It was in 1906 that he began his career as a crime writer. The word he concocted to explain his subject was criminous, and one writer has described Roughead as 'the recording angel of Scottish matters criminous'. Scotland and Scottish criminal history provided his main material, but his range extended to such locations as the island of Ireland's Eye, near Dublin, the scene of a complex and fascinating murder, and even to Pennsylvania to investigate a crime from 1832.

As with other much admired classic crime writers, such as F. Tennyson Jesse, and Joan Lock, Roughead was aware of the seminal essay *On Murder Considered as one of the Fine Arts* by Thomas de Quincey, and he wrote his own explanation of the appeal of true crime, and of murder stories in particular. In his essay 'Enjoyment of Murder' he has much to say on the compelling nature of the murder trial; one of the key elements of a true crime story. He wrote of such a trial: 'Every foot of ground should be stubbornly contested, the issue of the fight be uncertain, and the fortunes of the combatants vary from day to day.' He understood the heady fusion of terror and professionalism at the heart of a court drama.

In explaining his art, Roughead was modest, saying simply that all he claimed to do was 'Tell a tale of crime well and truly; to provide the psychologically minded with reliable grist for their recondite mills'. What he hoped for was that he was taking the reader on his mental adventures into the actions of monsters, and also into the fateful wrong decisions of the sad, feckless people who end up in the dock, facing retribution.

William Roughead was born in Edinburgh in 1870. His father was a drapier in Princes Street. But when his father John Carfrae Roughead drowned at sea off the Scilly Isles in 1887, the business was sold. William began his studies at Edinburgh University, taking up law, but not completing the degree programme. He had been articled to a law firm in George Street, and William, having a comfortable income from the sale of the business, had no pressing need to follow the normal route into a professional career. He had acquired an interest in the dramatic criminal trial, and this became his primary concern, forming the basis of his future success in writing.

Despite the aborted course of his legal studies, Roughead entered the law by another route: he became a writer to the signet. The word writer here was just a very dated term for lawyer, and the post was linked to the status of the private seal of Scottish kings, and so Roughead was basically a solicitor, his name appearing in the official Scottish Law List. From his time as a student through to the year 1949, three years before his death, he was there in the Edinburgh High Court whenever there was a trial for murder.

He married Janey More in 1900, and they had a daughter Winifred, who had down's syndrome and died in 1929, and also three sons. William was destined to lose another child – his son Frank – who died in a train accident in 1947. As for the future crime writer, he began his writing life as a poet and editor, but his entrance into the criminous world as an author was from the springboard provided by the company that has been forever linked with high quality and scholarly publishing of crime records: Hodge. To the *aficionado* of crime and courtroom analysis, the *Notable Trials* series is a template of excellence. Hodge was a friend of Roughead's, and together they started *Notable Scottish Trials* with a volume on Dr Edward Pritchard, a Glasgow doctor who poisoned his wife and mother-in-law. Roughead's role was to be editor of the volume, which would have to cover the process of the trail in detail. It set the standard for what was to follow, such was Roughead's expertise and depth of knowledge of the trajectory of a high-profile trial. He also had the research skills to back up the local knowledge.

A collection of the *Notable Scottish Trials* with Roughead as editor would have to include ten volumes in total. His subjects were mostly cases that turned out to be some of the most infamous and thoroughly explored criminal cases in the whole of true crime literature, including the volume on Oscar Slater (1910) and John Merrett (1929). The distinctive red bound volumes from Hodge were later to expand, and *Notable British Trials* followed, with editors being selected for their legal knowledge as much as for their ability to create a compelling narrative.

In a number of the murder cases he wrote about, there was the sensational element of unsolved crime, or of miscarriage of justice. In the story of John Merrett, who was charged with matricide, we have one of the most notorious cases of police mishaps and inadequacies in the investigation, and the particularly Scottish verdict of 'not proven' was the result. Roughead was himself in court at the trial of Oscar Slater, and his opinion was that the real killer Dr Charteris (who was also suspected by Conan Doyle) had an accomplice who hid in the building where the victim was. It has since become clear that Slater's fate when sentenced was a miscarriage of justice.

Roughead's career explains exactly what the context was for the higher crime fact genre in the late Victorian and Edwardian years. In fact, he and Conan Doyle came together in a strong mutual interest – the Oscar Slater case. Roughead, who had edited *The Trial of Oscar Slater,* wrote of Conan Doyle at the time, 'That paladin of lost causes found in the dubious circumstances of the case matter after his own heart.'

The first members of the Crimes Club discussed and debated in that intellectual climate, explained by Roughead's life and work. The newspapers presented exhaustive accounts of trials, and the finer points of criminal law were injected into the more literate and informed journalism, just as Roughead did in his attendance at the trials of the highest criminal court in Scotland. The setting was perfect for such dinner table conversation, and for amateur interest to mix with the opinions of those who worked within the criminal justice system.

From this look at Roughead, we can see why a word is needed to explain the kind of activity was at the centre of the club's interests: criminal is too restrictive an adjective, not conveying the writing and discussion that took place around the case itself. In other words, the club members went deep and wide, looking into all possible connections, and more importantly, they never forgot the potential for crime stories as a branch of literature, something open to speculation and fanciful interpretation, which is where they markedly differ from the police's frame of mind. If we need a presiding genius, someone exemplifying the nature of such a club, then Roughead is our man.

The club has become a group whose members today are sworn to secrecy, but it was not always so. In an article in *The London Magazine* in 1923, Arthur Lambton was happy to write about the club's activities, and in the first three issues of *The Field* for 1932, the members' activities were explained, with the story of the club recounted from its origins. It is a bizarre reflection on the current attitudes compared with the sociable clubbishness of the Edwardian period, when such discussion was free of the great lumber of literature produced by academic specialists such as we have today. Any new Crimes Club, formed among enthusiasts now, would have to accept that they were to be seriously limited in their thinking and discussions by a lack of solid scientific knowledge of forensics in their ranks. As an insight into what the Savile Club (founded in 1868) describes today as its sodalitas (a word that, in Latin usage, could mean companionship, but also secret society), it is worth noting that when Superintendent William Melville of the Yard retired in 1904, a movement for a national testimonial to him was signed by such luminaries as judges and aristocrats, but also by Conan Doyle, Arthur Pearson, and George Sims, Crimes Club members.

The following chapters tell the stories of some of the club members, and their activities and investigations with regard to the world of crime and law. Some actively pursued the course of amateur sleuthing, others simply wrote or studied famous cases. Some promoted the cause of the criminous, as the great crime writer William Roughead was to call this kind of interest. In fact Roughead, a Writer to the Signet (a lawyer in the Scottish system), began his writing in court reporting at this time. In many ways, his career exemplifies the kind of person that the Crimes Club attracted.

The Edwardian years are surely prominent as being one of the great ages of clubmen and diners, perhaps to compare with the Regency and Johnson's literary London. Dining clubs were everywhere, and a man could find himself filling up his diary with dinner dates; some for sporting types, some for professional talks, and some for passionate hobbies. Conan Doyle was, by the 1890s, seen everywhere as a *bon viveur* and conversationalist. After all, he had been a ship's doctor, and seen large stretches of wilderness, and so had tales to tell. By 1903, when the friends met at the Great Central Hotel, he was also not only the famous creator of Sherlock Holmes, he was widely published in all kinds of journals and popular magazines. He was destined to be torn between his tales of detection and his ambitions to have a high status as a serious historical novelist. He had also tried his hand at adventure yarns and supernatural stories. In the midst of this seeming confusion as to his identity as a writer, there was a storyteller; a man who could instinctively tell and shape a compelling tale. At his many dinners, the talk over tobacco and brandy would always have a narrative turn when he took the floor.

In his Father Brown story *The Queer Feet,* G. K. Chesteron has fun with the idea of the clubs and clubmen. He writes, 'The club of the Twelve True Fishermen would not have consented to dine anywhere but in such a place, for it insisted on a luxurious privacy; and would have been quite upset by the mere thought that any other club was dining in the same building.' The Edwardians and late Victorians relished the thought of a club of select, professional men; peers in some particular field of work or play. After all, it was an age of magnificent and ubiquitous sociability. A perusal of the popular magazines of the day reveals dozens of clubs and societies, performances, parades, and entertainments. It was the age of militaristic togetherness, with expressions of this bonding ranging from rifle clubs to cyclists, and from thespians to ballad poets.

Yet the Crimes Club wanted to be special and exclusive. From the start, the idea was not to have members who were preeminent in the areas of expertise clustered around criminal law, but also with a wider span of interests. It was rather to have gentlemen enthusiasts, but that changed, and it became professionalised and rather serious. There was room for the amateur, but he would have to have a CV that would impress in some province of knowledge relevant to crime and law.

We know from Conan Doyle's passionate interest in all things related to solutions, remedies, and inventions that he was totally intrigued by the art of concocting practical solutions, as in his advocacy of a bullet-proof uniform during the Great War; a concept he progressed so far as to have a prototype made by a man called Herbert Frood, who had a small business in Chapel-en-le-Frith in Derbyshire. The War Office would have nothing to do with it, but the fact is that Conan Doyle did more than simply theorise and wonder; he had his ideas transmuted into action and achievement. His attitude was just the same when it came to such topics as injustice and police investigation.

The first meeting of the club at the Great Central Hotel was, although there was no intention in this respect, something symbolic of modernity, as the spirit of the age moved into some technical innovations and a new understanding of the nature of crime. There had been a struggle between various vested interests, and the hotel that finally opened on 1 July 1899 was integral to the station, owing its arrival to the Manchester, Sheffield, and Lincolnshire Railway. Therefore, Marylebone became the place where the first electrically powered platform trucks were used; surely a pointer towards that energetic spirit of enterprise that the Edwardian men of affairs aspired to, and this was no less present among the men of letters than in the men of business. Today, we need to see Conan Doyle as a typical man of that time, the same man who invented the bullet-proof clothes, and who wrote to *The Times* to suggest, 'Could a rain of bullets be dropped vertically over the enemy's position, your chance shot has the whole surface of his body to strike.' That same attitude in him was applied to actual criminal cases, and of course, to stories – whether invented or extended from a factual basis.

There was a precedent to the club, and it still exists today, alongside the modern version of the Crimes Club. This is the Medico-Legal Society, founded in 1901 by R. Henslowe Wellington. But there is a strong contrast between the two, and the professed aim of the Medico-Legal Society was (and is), 'The promotion of medico-legal knowledge in all its aspects. This object shall be attained by holding meetings at which papers shall be read and discussed.' Yet there was still a place for the literary man in the ranks of the earlier group, as their rules stated in the early years: 'The Society shall consist of qualified members of the legal and the medical professions, and of such other persons as may be interested in medico-legal work.' By the 1930s, Sir Bernard Spilsbury, the great forensics expert, was president, and he had been elected a member as early as 1908. Yet he was also a member of the Crimes Club. What really sets the two groups apart is that, whereas the Medico-Legal publications included, 'incapacity for work within the meaning of the National Health Insurance Act', the Crimes Club would only have been interested in bloody murder and ongoing mysteries of the law and crime detection.

My story here is of the first members, not the society that the club later became. Who were these men who gathered at the first few venues, and who sat in the dining room of the Great Central Hotel in 1904? Apart from writers Conan Doyle, A. E. W. Mason, Max Pemberton, George R. Sims, and William Le Queux, the others were journalists, medical professionals, an actor, a literary scholar, two aristocrats, and a press baron. They were all intrigued by the criminous, and that included something else, apart from the template of the criminal mystery and its investigation: the fascination with every facet of the criminal justice system, and with its human element. This may best be illustrated with reference to a now forgotten character who was on the fringe of the *aficionados* of crime in the 1890s: a Manchester-born sports writer called Robert P. Watson. In his autobiography, he gives accounts of cases in court, but he also described and sometimes visited prisons, and met officers, offenders, and even the hangmen. Watson gives an account of the incident that created the amateur criminologist he became:

> One incident I can well remember. Jeffreys was hanged outside Newgate for killing his son by hanging him in a cellar down the Seven Dials. When Jeffreys walked on the scaffold and reached the drop he faced St Sepulchre's Church. Calcraft [the hangman] hurriedly and very forcibly turned him round with his back to the church [...] Calcraft was compelled to walk several yards along the scaffold and return the same way. All this time the wretched person remained in full view of a densely packed crowd.

This kind of proximity to the law and to crime was something all the members had in common, although in the case of one or two of them, it was civil law rather than criminal. For some, it was their professional work (as in Oddie the coroner, or Crosse the police surgeon), and for others it was the eternal fascination of human transgression. The result was a burning intellectual passion for investigation and analysis – in fact, for everything Conan Doyle had created in the mighty Sherlock Holmes. After all, if we take a wider view of all this, surely it becomes evident that in a very large proportion of the classics of world literature, crime and law occupy a very prominent position. The Crimes Club members wrote popular genre narratives, and they saw the relation between what they created, with its stress on sensation and high drama, and the popular reporting of murder cases. In fact, as the club sat for their dinner in the evening of 17 July 1904, a man had been hanged just four days before: Samuel Rowledge, a man who had killed a woman, and had intended to kill himself also, but failed to die. The fact that he had not died meant that he would hang, as he was not deemed to be suffering from temporary insanity (which would have saved his neck). That paradox would have intrigued the members, and kept them in conversation through an entire, very lavish dinner.

What this tells us is that the first Crimes Club was arguably the first time that the criminous impulse that now drives our hugely successful crime fiction was recognised and absorbed into social discussion for the first time as a legitimate, rather dignified activity, whereas in the recent past, just a few decades before the club met, doubt had been cast on the whole nature and value of true crime, when such literature had been seen as partly to blame for the all too frequent horrible murders in Victoria's fast-growing society. The nature and activities of the criminous investigation was partly a branch of literature, before the term true crime came to be used. It was also partly a word used to explain some thinking and writing on the margins of the new science of criminology.

If we imagine criminology as a great house, then some of the most prominent rooms were occupied by the few Scotland Yard men, such as the fingerprint office, and they were the first specialists. But in other rooms, filled with cigar smoke rather than chemical effusions, there were lawyers, historians, novelists, and various literary types on the fringe, with a curiosity about prison cells and police courts.

Into that house came the Crimes Club, making their own space comfortable, and keeping the door firmly shut.

I

Arthur Lambton:
The Fight for Legitimacy

At the Eton and Harrow cricket match at Lord's in July 1935, Arthur Lambton fell down the steps leading down from the members' pavilion. He fractured his knee-cap and was taken to a nearby nursing home. That might have seemed a situation with no anxiety attached as to the man's health, but he developed a pulmonary embolism, and on 2 August, he died. Ironically, his close friend and fellow Crimes Club member Ingleby Oddie was the coroner at the inquest, and he pointed out that the great actor Sir Herbert Beerbohm Tree had died in exactly the same way. Oddie added, 'It is a sad experience for me to have to hold an inquest on a friend whom I have known for thirty-seven years. It is very sad that he should have died in this manner. It is sheer bad luck.' Of course, he returned a verdict of accidental death.

Lambton was sixty-five years old, and the obituaries in the papers noted that he had been collector of taxes for the City of London, and that he was known as 'an author and journalist'. *The Times* gave a neat summary of his varied and exciting life. On his literary achievement, the obituary reported that 'Mr Oddie and Mr Lambton were founders of the Crimes Club', and that Lambton had translated Sheridan's *School for Scandal* into Italian, and also Maupassant's *Bel Ami* into English. His novel *The Splendid Summer* was given a special mention. His other life, away from books and writing, included work for the Special Branch, involved in dealing with spies under the new MI5 led by Vernon Kell, where he worked in the spy department, and then later in censorship and alien supervision.

There was no mention of what had been a sensational story ten years earlier: his revelation, as one periodical put it, that 'the cousin of the Earl of Durham tells of wild parties [...] and reveals that his father, who was noted as a fashionable bachelor in the West End of London, kept his family secret in the suburbs'. In fact, that piece of autobiography had led Lambton to achieve arguably his greatest legal feat – a major contribution towards the creation of the Legitimacy Act of 1926, which established the principle that English children are legitimised by the marriage of their parents at any time.

Arthur's father was General Arthur Lambton, and he had spent a great deal of money – perhaps £150,000 – on his affair with the actress Ada Wilson. Arthur Lambton had no inheritance because of his father's unmarried state; General Lambton had not married because his very wealthy mother had said that she would disinherit him if he married anyone outside the peerage. So began Arthur's campaign to change the law. After the 1926 Act, all kinds of issues were thrown up in a range of courts across the land. Instead of the kind of situation faced by 3rd Lord Sackville for instance, who was challenged for his inheritance by a Mr Henri Jean Baptiste Sackville-West, who claimed to be the eldest son of the 2nd Lord Sackville by a Spanish dancer called Pepita, in which marriage had been claimed, but not actually officially obtained, the situation thanks to Lambton was much clearer. Evidence of marriage was all that was needed, and that marriage could happen at any time.

The work for the Legitimacy Act typifies the kind of man Lambton was with regard to the law. Decades after the founding of the club, he was known to readers of crime fiction, as his place in the adverts for the Crime Book Society, founded in 1928, shows. He is described as 'the ardent criminologist and founder of the famous Crimes Club'. He was there at the Carlton Club in 1903 when he was made honorary secretary, and he was still in that capacity at his death.

His work with Special Branch was at a time when spy hunting was just becoming an essential part of detective work. What was being learned in the dark and secret world of Bolshevism and Anarchism was also open to a revisionary inspection. Joseph Conrad's novel *The Secret Agent* (1907) had dealt with the undercover world of terrorism, and the villain Verloc operates his nefarious business from the cover of a London shop. The novel instructed readers on the new phenomenon; the spy who was so mundane and seedy that he was capable of slipping unobtrusively into the everyday affairs of life – he could be the man in the doctor's waiting room, or the man sitting opposite you on the omnibus. The character Vladimir looks at Verloc and thinks, 'This was then the famous and trusty secret agent, so secret that he was never designated otherwise but by the symbol of a triangle in the late baron Stott-Wartenheim's official, semi-official and confidential correspondence.'

Vernon Kell was leading the new MI5 outfit, and a significant step forward in his work came after he learned of something that had happened in 1907. A detective called Quinn told Kell about a German naval officer of senior rank who had gone for a haircut in a German barber shop in London. Quinn was sure that the barber was a spy, a certain Karl Ernst. To take this up as Kell wanted to do would entail looking at Ernst's mail, and for that, a go-ahead was needed from the Postmaster General. It was just the beginning of a new departure for British espionage. What happened was that a cache of letters was collected, signed by Fraulein Reimers from Potsdam. The correspondent turned out to be a major figure in German intelligence called Steinauer, known to the British Foreign Section. This mail interception was extended across the land and it brought incredible results. Then a German officer called Helm, who had been living with an English girl in Portsmouth, was taken while in the process of drawing fortifications. Helm was with Hannah Wodehouse, who had had an affair with a friend of his previously, but she became suspicious of him and told the local army at the Royal Marine barracks. Surprisingly, the officer did not act, but two other officers saw Helm sketching. Helm was arrested, and Kell's counter-espionage bureau was told of this. In the climate of the intervention of the mail of suspected aliens and others, Lambton found part of his police work. He was involved in censorship, which largely meant the important labour of snooping and checking mail. Kell had succeeded largely through this method of tracking suspects.

Lambton, born in 1869, began work with the bureau coded as MO5 g. in 1914. It had three sub-divisions dealing with aliens, and in 1915, Lambton was in action with the military control of passengers, particularly at ports. This is why he worked in at least three different locations in England. Then from 1915, he was part of the staff dealing with counter espionage.

When Lambton joined the Conan Doyle clubmen, he had tales to tell of detective work in the context of anarchists and undercover agents; a world that Conan Doyle did not know, but which was to figure in his writing. Lambton would have rare knowledge of the works of German agents in England in the first phase of the Great War. In much the same way as Charles Dickens had met and chatted with the Yard sleuths in the 1850s to learn how they worked and how crime was changing, so Conan Doyle talked with Lambton, who would know the world of the police. At that first dinner in 1904, when the Crimes Club proper met, the creator of Sherlock Holmes would have had Atlay, Irving, and Collins for the more scholarly and meticulous analysis of crime tales, and Lambton for policing matters. In fact, in Lambton's book *Echoes of Causes Celebres*, he recalls that one case directly influenced Conan Doyle's work. This concerns the murder of a police constable.

In December 1882, PC Cole was walking his beat at Dalston in the East End when he saw a man climbing the wall of the Dalston chapel. He chased the man and they fought, and in that scrap, Cole was shot and fatally wounded. This all happened in the fog, and so the man soon escaped into the dark obscurity of the night. Yet the fight was seen by a passer-by, and she called for help. But it was too late for PC Cole. However, there were objects left at the scene by the killer: two chisels and a wooden wedge, and the man had also left his wide-awake hat – a very distinctive type worn by Methodist ministers.

What happened next was a piece of excellent police work, after a period in which no progress was made. Detective Inspector Glass of the Yard was called in – the top man for the job – and he looked very closely at a chisel and saw the word 'rock'on it. A shopkeeper recognized the chisel, and she told Glass and his sergeant Cuff that their tools were etched with the names of the craftsmen, and that this one had been owned by a man called Orrock. One might have thought that his arrest was just a formality after that, but although he was traced to Coldbath Fields Prison where he was doing a term for a more recent crime, the evidence was not strong enough.

Sergeant Cuff (more than a Watson, one might think, in his skill and instincts) talked to more contacts, and his leads took Glass and himself to the Tottenham marshes; apparently, men tended to use a specific tree for target practice with their revolvers. Cuff dug out a bullet that matched the caliber of the gun that killed PC Cole. Almost two years after the murder, in September 1884, Orrock was convicted of the murder, and he stood in court as the widow of the officer screamed out 'brute, brute!' to him. He was on the gallows soon after, and dispatched to the next world.

Lambton, in his memoirs, explained the influence on his friend Conan Doyle, referring to *A Study in Scarlet*:

> The reader will remember the triumphant manner in which Lestrade came to Sherlock Holmes and said that the writing in blood on the wall which said 'rache' were the first five letters of the woman's name 'Rachel'. The reader will also remember the professional detective's discomfiture when Holmes informed him pityingly that there was no letter missing in 'Rache' and that it was the German for 'revenge'. In view of this digression will it occasion much surprise, will the reader have already guessed, that this incident was suggested to Doyle by the word 'rock' on the chisel discovered by the dead body of Police Constable Cole?

This was the man who had sat with his friends Oddie and Irving planning what was to become the Crimes Club. In fact, the germ of the club goes back to the period when Lambton was in Naples after leaving Cambridge. There he met Oddie, and in his autobiography Lambton explains, referring to a meeting with Oddie:

> It was during our walk on the Corso that our mutual love of criminology came to light. He suggested we form a small coterie of crime experts and dine together periodically, and asked me to put it into effect. It was not until over ten years later that I gave a lunch at the Carlton Hotel which was the foetus of the Crimes Club.

He added that the casual conversation with Oddie had led to 'what people in London today [1910] call the most interesting dining club in London'.

The 1890s was an age of absolutely fervent and rabid club making. In society, there were clubs to cater for afternoon tea events, for professional dinners, for military men, for ladies who lunched, for amateur theatricals, and of course, for anyone with a special interest. There was a Ballad Club that met in Glasgow, and a report on this in the *Daily Graphic* gives us a clue to the significance of these clubs:

> It was marked throughout [...] by scholarly weight and literary finish, but the passage that appears to have attracted most attention [...] was the formal acknowledgement that 'three new professions' – education, science, and journalism – have sprung up in competition with the older professions of divinity, law, and medicine.

That explains one of the profound reasons for this clubbable society of professional men. Conan Doyle was a medical doctor of course, so he was well defined as being of the established professions, but he also joined the other newcomers, the authors, in his attendance at clubs.

The new literary clubs welcomed men from all the other acceptable professions because their friendships confirmed that the new arrivals in society were peers of the old brigade who already sat in their comfortable leather chairs in clubs along Piccadilly and St James', but the younger men in the older professions were wanting more active, intellectual, and challenging company.

Lambton and men like him also started their clubs for more mundane reasons of course, such as simple vanity. Men who relish the sight of their names on the spine of a book, with the also welcome ego-trip of an appearance (or even a speech) at a formal dinner with other celebrities. There were also aristocrats amongst the cheery, alcoholic atmospheres of men being chums together. In the Crimes Club, Lord Albert Edward Godolphin Osborne was at the 1904 dinner.

Yet for Lambton and the men who met in 1903, it is clear that in creating a Crimes Club, they had their finger on the pulse of current media excitement and interest. As well as the arrival of fingerprinting, the talk about such things as borstals, and the use of witnesses in murder trials or speculation on courts of appeal, there was the booming market for tales of male adventure, boosted by the Empire – its past triumphs and its present problems. When the first members gathered together to talk criminality and legal details, the Anglo-Boer War had been humiliating in its desperate Pyrrhic victory. Yet in contrast, Kitchener at Omdurman had shown the true mettle of the British against the tribal hordes, and had made military heroes for the writers and poets of the time.

As for Conan Doyle when he joined the coterie in 1904, it was as the writer who had ridden the crest of a wave in his new Holmes stories, after being offered a huge sum of money in 1903 to bring Holmes back from the dead. In October 1903, his story 'The Adventure of the Empty House' had been printed in *The Strand*. Conan Doyle's famous scrapbooks of reviews testified to a host of favourable responses after the later collection *The Return of Sherlock Holmes*, which was in print shortly before the first club dinner at which Conan Doyle was present.

The creator of Sherlock Holmes absolutely loved attending dinners and being in a club of like-minded souls, and Arthur Lambton was just that kind of friend. John Dickson Carr, in *The life of Sir Arthur Conan Doyle*, points out that at the large dinners with fellow writers long before the Crimes Club, the writers found in Conan Doyle 'an ideal companion', and that, 'When Conan Doyle laughed, it was with no ultra-refined mirth; he laughed infectiously and people at the other end of the table joined in without knowing why.'

There was always another, second level and little-known element in Lambton's life, hinted at, but not fully known. For instance in 1896, when he was twenty-seven, it was reported in the press that he was sent to Australia 'for the benefit of his health', while his father, the general, and his mother, left for Hackness. It was expected that Lambton would stay in Australia for a year. By the turn of the century, he was clearly an accomplished and cultured gentleman, enjoying the delights of London's cultural scene. He was a member of the Windham and Reform clubs, and also of the MCC. He took a deep interest in sport, and in horse racing he had a family pedigree, being related to the famous trainer George Lambton. Clearly, he was at home in talk about the Derby, as well as in forensic investigation or points of law. The first rule of Windham's provides a perfect explanation of why clubs were formed: 'To secure a convenient and agreeable place of meeting for a society of gentlemen, all connected with each other by a common bond of literary or personal acquaintance.'

But in spite of his other endeavours in espionage and in criminology, Lambton's notable achievement was in the campaign for the reform of the legitimacy laws. In his autobiography, he wrote with a tremendous sense of the drama of his situation when his father left him with nothing, and also when he received nothing from his grandmother's death and all the money went to Lambton's uncle. Lambton senior was a famous officer, a man who had taken part in several of the major campaigns of the Crimean War, and later in the 1882 Egyptian war. He had kept his marriage a secret, as it would have deprived him of his inheritance from his mother, so in effect, his son Arthur was illegitimate, while the military hero lived like a bachelor in the wealthy circles of London.

This kind of arrangement was perhaps more common than we realise. An anonymous piece of doggerel from the 1920s expresses something of the strength of feeling generated in this context:

> I wish I was a fascinating bitch,
> I'd never be poor; I'd always be rich.
> I'd sleep all day and I'd work all night,
> I'd always do wrong and always be right.
> And once a month I'd take a rest,
> To make all my customers wild;
> Oh, I wish I was a fascinating bitch
> And not an illegitimate child.

When Lambton went to visit the family lawyer, a meeting he calls 'the awful Thursday, March 12 1908', he reported the lawyer's words, 'I fear I've not very good news for you, we've gone into the whole thing, and it will be impossible for your mother to keep up her former position [...] and of course, she cannot afford to do anything for any of you.' Lambton then asked, 'Has no provision been made for any of us three?' The answer was, 'None. He has left all three of you to starve.'

Lambton told the lawyer that 'there was only one way out' of the situation, meaning his suicide. But gradually, having nothing and deciding to stay alive and make something of himself, he began writing, and succeeded very well. Then began what he calls 'the attack' – his work to reform the law. Others were working in the same cause, such as the barrister Ernest Bowen-

Rowlands, who noted that back in Roman law, the Emperor Constantine had legitimised children who had been born out of wedlock when there was a later marriage of the parents. That was Arthur Lambton's situation; his father had waited until his mother's death before marrying, but Lambton had remained illegitimate. Lambton worked to have a debate on the matter in parliament, and finally, as he wrote in his autobiography, 'The Bill may become law today, tomorrow, or the day after [...] nothing can stop it becoming law [...] but I want the reader to imagine my exultation when I read that the Bill was included in the King's Speech.'

The Act was passed in 1926, with the revolutionary paragraph printed first in the text:

> Subject to the provisions of this section, where the parents of an illegitimate person marry or have married one another, whether before or after the commencement of this Act, the marriage shall, if the father of the illegitimate person was or is at the date of the marriage domiciled in England or Wales, render that person, if living, legitimate from the commencement of this Act, or from the date of the marriage, whichever last happens.

Before this, the only key legislation on illegitimacy had been the 1858 Act, which was only concerned with the possibility of a legitimate heir being able to form a petition for recognition. Legitimation by the subsequent marriage of parents (which would have given Arthur Lambton his inheritance) was also the case under the Canon law, but not in any statute of the realm. In fact, in 1926 when England finally passed this Legitimacy Act, all the other countries of Europe had followed the ruling of the Canon and Roman law on the matter.

As far as Arthur Lambton was concerned, it is difficult to imagine today the depths of suffering and deprivation that this situation imposed on the aristocracy, as there is no doubt that the Lambton family have a very noble pedigree. Lambton's autobiography begins with the words, 'Most of the denizens of the Chamber of Horrors killed the body. I am going to show that my father and his brothers killed the souls.'

2

ARTHUR CONAN DOYLE:
GOOD FELLOWSHIP AND SLEUTHING

In an age in which authors of all kinds emerged as personalities and rushed to join a variety of clubs and societies, Arthur Conan Doyle stands out as one of the most active. In the three years before the Crimes Club met, he had become chairman of the Authors' Club, and as the recently knighted Sir Arthur, he entertained guests in that capacity in July 1902. He gave a speech, and his words on that occasion tell us exactly why he was such a gregarious character: *The Times* reported:

> Sir Arthur Conan Doyle said that he had always said and felt that he would rather win the approbation of his fellow writing men than of any other men in the world, because they had common feelings, common aspirations, knew each other, and appreciated each other's point of view.

In 1900, he had been one of the founders of the Boz Club, which met at the Athenaeum, being a group of men who had known Dickens personally, with the addition of other notable enthusiasts for the work of the great novelist. The members' debates were printed in a publication called *The Boz Club Papers*.

This love of being a personality, admired and welcomed among peers, and of course his readers, also expressed itself in the new breed of literary journals, and he was fond of joining in the bubbly new brand of humour in *The Idler*, edited by his friend Jerome K. Jerome. Conan Doyle even took part in an interview printed in that journal that was in effect a pastiche, a simple *jeu'd'esprit*, which was in fact not an interview at all, but a spoof of the serious literary interview. *The Idler* even had its own paper equivalent of the literary club discussion, which it called The Idlers' Club, and a typical subject, discussed in 1893, was, 'Is love a practical reality or a pleasing fiction?' One of the Crimes Club members, G. R. Sims, was a regular participant. The fact that *The Idler* also carried a series of Conan Doyle spoof stories by Robert Barr, called 'Detective Stories Gone Wrong – the Adventures of Sherlaw Kombs', written by 'Luke Sharp', tells us just how much Conan Doyle had, by the time that *A Study in Scarlet* and the first two collections of Holmes stories had appeared, arrived on the literary scene. He relished that arrival, revelling in the opportunities it opened up in terms of the author as celebrity.

We are accustomed to the nature of creative people of all kinds today becoming media celebrities, but in the 1890s, the average author was hardly celebrity potential. Dickens was as example of how a novelist could become world famous, but for most, the typical writer was someone like George Gissing; a man with a massive output, slaving away in what he called 'New Grub Street' for little money and even less recognition.

Being already a seasoned clubman, Conan Doyle was a member of Our Society, as Lambton and Ingleby Oddie first called the Crimes Club, from the start at the Carlton Club occasion, when it was still very much just one more dinner date in a busy social calendar for its gentlemen diners and personalities. This last word – personalities – is an important one, for the spirit of the age, with the 1890s and early years of the twentieth century in mind, was one of sheer exuberance and intellectual fun. Time and again, records of those years testify to the enthusiasm for society, for bonhomie in the writers and journalists of the time. Most of all, for Conan Doyle, a dinner was a chance to tell tales and listen to them, to learn about the more obscure areas of crime investigation and to keep up to date with new ideas. Hence, his first colleagues in the club were a mix of scholarly types and excellent speakers. Their interests covered both the more sensational elements of crime writing and the analytical criminal approaches being made by those who knew the law, as well as appreciating the true crime aspects of a good human story.

His biography repeatedly brings up countless club activities, even including some he merely dipped into, if for nothing else, then for male company and fellow writers' talk. Such an instance was his meeting with the Omar Khayyam Club in 1895, to which George Gissing belonged. As Gissing's biographer Paul Delany explains, 'The club followed Fitzgerald's Rubaiyat in its devotion to wine and philosophising; it differed in being for men only, with no pleasure-girls to fill the gap.' Members included Thomas Hardy and Edmund Gosse, as well as Conan Doyle. On one occasion, E. W. Hornung, creator of 'Raffles' and Conan Doyle's brother-in-law, reported on a meeting with Gissing at which Conan Doyle was present, noting that Gissing 'has charm and sympathy, humour too, and a louder laugh than

Oscar's'. This is an interesting sidelight on why these writers relished their clubs and dinners. It implies that the focus of such meetings was the art of conversation, as a projection of personality, and as occasions for polite listening and sharing of experience.

In 1903, when Conan Doyle sat down with his literary friends, he was not only established as an author. He was also a war correspondent, home from the Boer War the year before, and well known as a contributor to a range of journals on any manner of socially topical subjects. He was also a correspondent to *The Times*, and was always keen to offer solutions to any issue in hot debate. Some writers on his life have claimed that he was one of the most famous men in the world by this date. The Sherlock Holmes stories in *The Strand* had played a part in that fame of course, and just a few months before the informal dinner of Our Society, he had received an offer from America for $5,000 per story for six new Holmes tales, and that sum was merely for the American rights; there were the British ones to add as well. He agreed, writing to his agent simply, 'Very well. A. C. D.' As he sat in the dining room of the Carlton, he was in the throes of creativity, at work on what was to be the renaissance of Holmes, a resurrection surely like no other in popular literature, and also on producing a stage version of his novel *Brigadier Gerard*, which was to be offered to Beerbohm Tree. The script had been completed by February, and in the early summer of 1903, he was arguably in the aftermath of so much energetic and concentrated writing that he was more than ready for some socialising. In fact, he attended a gala evening at the Union Jack Club in February.

Fundamentally though, it has to be asked: why did he feel the need to join the clubs of the establishment, and indeed take part in the formation of new ones? Some writers on Conan Doyle have explained this as his yearning, considering his Irish roots and his Catholicism, to be accepted within the patriotic circles of the established literary elite. That would explain some of the elements in his clubbable nature and his participation in many patriotic and imperial organisations, backing the ideology of the middle ground Britisher, even to the extent of giving financial support and investment in some such enterprises. However, there is no doubt that he gained profound delight in club brotherhood and in enjoying society. We are concerned here with his life between 1900 and 1910, and those years contained the death of his wife Louise to counteract his great literary triumphs. Also within that time there was his involvement in reporting on the Boer War, and other, less well-known aspects, such as his agent's purloining the immense sum of £9,000.

The place one member called the foetus of the Crimes Club was the Carlton Club, which had been founded by the Duke of Wellington in 1832, and had a very high status by the time the criminologists' meeting took place. But there were new clubs being formed all the time in the years between *c.* 1890 and 1910. In fact, within a month of the Carlton Club initial discussion about the Crimes Club, the Pepys Club was created. In 1909, the City Pickwick Club appeared. A gregarious literary man could attend a dinner almost every night at a different club if he had the cash and the energy – and of course, the right connections. But the Crimes Club was different.

When a little more time passed and Conan Doyle could perhaps unwind more easily and enjoy his clubbing, he must have seen the Crimes Club as something more than the usual social gathering. For him, it was a chance to air views on unsolved crimes, listen to theories of cases and criminals, and share the interesting perspectives of other men who approached crime stories from perspectives very different from his own. At the basis of this was the status of forensics. Back in his first Holmes story *A Study in Scarlet*, he had used the characterisation of Sherlock to explain what was, in effect, a new science: the study of crime. This was, *c.* 1880s, something lacking a definition, and Conan Doyle explained why in his story, when Stamford says of Holmes the chemistry student, 'I have no idea what he intends to go in for. I believe he is well up in anatomy, and he is a first-class chemist, but as far as I know he has never taken out any systematic medical classes.' Doyle himself was, as Sherlock is called in the same story, 'a walking calendar of crime'.

Peter Costello, in his book *Conan Doyle, Detective* (1991), has shown that Conan Doyle had looked into much earlier crime, particularly some sensational murders from the 1860s, and knew a great deal about several Scottish and other regional cases. He was well aware of the current state of forensic study when he first contemplated the creation of Sherlock and Watson. We appear to have no certain knowledge of whether or not he knew William Guy's book *Principles of Forensic Medicine*, which had appeared back in 1844, but he would have known about some notable failures in the field, as in the case of Dr Smethurst in 1859.

In that year, Isabella Banks and Smethurst were married at Battersea Church. Although this was bigamous, the first wife did not act. The barrister writing about the case in 1882 noted that, 'Oddly enough, no surprise was expressed by the doctor's wife, and her position in the affair is very difficult to be understood.' The new married couple moved to a new address in the London suburbs, and from that point, as was known afterwards, Isabella began to be ill. As she was rich, she was seen by a celebrated doctor with a good reputation, called Julius, and he confirmed that she was not pregnant, but that there was a problem with her digestion. He was worried, and called in some more advice. The sick woman's sister came, and the poor Isabella's condition deteriorated. A second medical expert was called for and he said directly, 'That lady is being poisoned.'

Arsenic was found in Isabella's vomit, and by this time there were three doctors involved, the last being Dr Taylor, who was very well known at that time. Together, they agreed that the law must be contacted, and they asked for a warrant for Smethurst's arrest. Amazingly, at the magistrate's court, Smethurst spoke about the possible fatal effects of his being away from his wife when she was in such desperate circumstances. There was apparently a disastrous level of naivety and amateurism at that court, and he was released. But Isabella Banks (she was not Mrs Smethurst by law) died a few days later, on 3 May. There was a post mortem examination, and not only was arsenic found in her body, but also antimony. The latter would be in the form of tartar emetic. If a large dose had been administered by Smethurst, along with the arsenic, then poor Isabella would have had a terrible and agonising period of dying, as antimony causes severe burning in the throat, and constant vomiting and diarrhoea; her limbs would have taken on a blueish tinge.

The landlady in the lodging house where the poor woman was dying stated that Smethurst was the only person taking care of the patient, as he would not pay a nurse, and she told the press that 'no portions of the food sent up to the room ever returned'. Smethurst had actually taken out insurance on Isabella.

The trial was before Lord Chief Baron Pollock, but before we recall the nature of the court events, we must return to the forensics, such as they were at the time. Dr Taylor, who was the last medical man to be called in to see the patient, was famous and admired for his post mortem work, but the barrister Ballantyne was convinced that Smethurst had set up the celebrated doctor to fail. After Smethurst was released from the magistrate's court, he found a way to get into his own rooms, and set a trap that would cancel out Taylor's attempts to prove the act of arsenic poisoning: he left a bottle of colourless liquid, along with other materials and instruments that a medical man would have. When Taylor later examined all this, his attention was drawn to the liquid of course, and he would have tested it using the reinsch test; the standard test for detecting the presence of arsenic.

At the post mortem, there was the undoubted fact that there was arsenic present in the body, but Taylor had to show that it had been given from the equipment in Smethurst's room. The test involved pouring a mixture of the tested liquid and hydrochloric acid onto some copper gauze, which would then attach itself to the liquid if there was arsenic present. But the gauze dissolved. Finally after several attempts, some attachment took place, and so the doctor told the court that there was arsenic detected in Smethurst's liquid. However, then scientists for the defence reported on the bottle and its contents, and stated with confidence that it was chlorate of potash. It was then shown that the only arsenic Taylor had found was in his own gauze – traces being there from the first two experiments.

The result was that there was no credence given to the scientific evidence of the prosecution. In 1859, arsenic was being used by women for cosmetic purposes, and of course, there could have been antimony from tartar emetic used as a treatment – an effort to make the poor woman vomit out the arsenic.

Conan Doyle had a particular interest in several murder cases from the middle years of Victoria's reign, and the Smethurst case typifies the limits of forensic medicine; not in itself, but in its regulation, usage, and control. In other words, it was not assimilated fully into the workings of the criminal justice process, even by the turn of the nineteenth century when the Club met, but it had been included in medical education for a long time. In 1844, Willaim Guy wrote that forensics was included in medical schools and that its principles were applied in courts of law. But that was far from the truth. However by 1900, it had arrived to such an extent that the club members could use the kind of knowledge Conan Doyle had given to his great detective as something integral to their theories of crimes. Specialists working outside of Scotland Yard were pushing the boundaries of the science by the Edwardian years, so that Conan Doyle's explanation of Sherlock Holmes and his monograph on varieties of tobacco ash may have had a boys' own fanciful quality to it at the time, but as various writers have commented, the best forensic brains of the time were not within the ranks of the police. Hence, people such as Bernard Spilsbury were called in until the later developments of an official forensic outfit and the creation of the Police College.

Another factor in understanding Conan Doyle the clubman is that even from his schooldays, he had been inured to debate and creative argument. He was a pupil at Stonyhurst, bastion of English Roman Catholic education, between 1868 and 1875, and part of the curriculum he experienced was the *concertatio*. Bearing in mind that this may be translated as 'wrangling', as well as the more civilised 'disputation', it suggests that the club members enjoyed some forceful expressions of differences in opinion over a topic.

All these factors hint at the appeal of such a club for Conan Doyle. The important point is that this was very different from the other clubs listed above. After all, it was formed for the free-ranging discussion of all subjects included in criminous literature, so the talk would have ranged between literature and criminal history, the biographies of people from judges to detectives, and from villains to victims. The club offered Conan Doyle the chance to try out theories, and it has to be recalled that he was an amateur detective himself, leaving aside his fictional creation and his conversation on other cases of detection.

After more than a decade of fiction, he became a true crime author too, writing a series of pieces on crimes from c. 1860 in *The Strand* magazine in 1901. But then, as the club became more of a group at least partly interested in the actual investigation of crimes and mysteries, he began to play a prominent role in several high profile cases. In his autobiography, he notes that one of these, the Edalji case, preoccupied him in the period shortly after the death of his wife.

George Edalji was a law student, the son of the vicar of Great Wyrley in Staffordshire. The family were Parsee, an Indian ethnic group whose view of life follows that of Zoroastro, originally an Iranian in the early Medieval period. The racial factor is important for the case, because in the first phase of this case, the family were subjected to xenophobic hatred and torment. Yet this was nothing compared to the consequences of an outbreak of horse-maiming in the area, because George was suspected, blamed, and arrested for the crimes.

There had been a series of anonymous letters that George was linked to. His trial and conviction at Stafford followed on, with a sentence of seven years of penal servitude. Conan Doyle read the reports and saw the enormity of this. He wrote, 'It was late in 1906 that I chanced to pick up an obscure paper called *The Umpire,* and caught a statement of the case [...] as I read, the unmistakeable accent of truth forced itself on my attention and I realised that I was in the presence of an appalling tragedy.'

From today's viewpoint, George Edalji's trial reads like an example of the local police being so determined to prove the guilt of their subject that they shifted the alleged circumstances of offences to suit their prosecution rationale. Conan Doyle saw all this, and he also saw what any perceptive investigator or defence counsel would have seized on immediately: that Edalji had very poor eyesight, and in order to have perpetrated these horrendous mutilations, he would have had to deal with, as Conan Doyle put it, 'the full breadth of the London and North Western Railway, an expanse of rails, wires, and other obstacles and hedges to be forced on either side'. As a result of Conan Doyle's articles, a committee was created to enquire into the case, and eventually Conan Doyle's work brought to light a man who was the author of the letters, and who, as Conan Doyle put it, 'belonged in an asylum'.

The committee were not convinced by new arguments and evidence, but again, Conan Doyle determined to have the man released. What had to be proved was that a certain Peter Hudson was the main author of the abusive letters, and Conan Doyle (with his allies) did what was necessary: they called in Europe's acknowledged expert on handwriting, Dr Lindsay Johnson, who showed that Hudson, not Edalji, was the culprit. Edalji was released after three years in prison.

Conan Doyle's work on behalf of Oscar Slater has arguably received most prominence, perhaps because it is related to one of the most sensational elements of detective work and investigation: mistaken identity. On 21 December 1908, Marion Gilchrist and her servant Helen Lambie were at the former's home in Glasgow. Helen went out, locking the door behind her, because her mistress kept a great deal of valuable jewellery in her house and was always afraid of robbery. The people below heard a thump during the period in which Miss Gilchrist was alone. One of these, Mr Adams, ran up to investigate, but could only stand at the door, and from that place he heard chopping noises from inside.

Helen then returned, and Adams spoke with her about the noise, and the servant thought the source of the sounds would be the pulleys of the clothes-lines in the kitchen. But as they entered, they saw a man, and he walked past them. Inside, Miss Gilchrist had been battered to death, with a rug thrown over her body. A diamond brooch was missing, and a pawn ticket for such an item led the police to a certain Oscar Slater. Slater left with a woman to board the *Lusitania* in Liverpool. What happened next was to lead to the heart of the case: a young girl called Mary Barroman had been passing the house on that night of the murder, and she claimed in court that she saw Oscar Slater, or someone very like him. This was strange, because both Helen and Mr Adams, who had seen the man leave the house, gave descriptions that did not tally with Mary's. But Helen Lmabie changed her mind. The law caught up with Oscar Slater in New York, and in court there, Helen and Mary testified against him.

The man in the house, so Conan Doyle saw, had gone to open a box full of papers, and had passed by the jewellery. So logically, the man (and the killer) was perhaps there for something other than robbery. What was the mystery then?

Conan Doyle developed the theory that a man called Dr Francis Charteris, with an accomplice, had gone to the Gilchrist house that night to look at legal papers, most likely those relating to his potential inheritance, as he was accepted as being an 'unofficial' nephew of Miss Gilchrist. Conan Doyle, and others with this view, considered that Charteris went with someone else, and that the murder was done then, and that Helen, who thought she knew the man she saw leaving the house, would indeed have known Charteris.

Was this scenario the truth, or was it a robbery gone wrong? Opinions still differ. But some uphold the argument that Dr Charteris had nothing to do with the crime. As Peter Costello wrote in *Conan Doyle: Detective*, it comes down to two lines of thought – the doctor or the assumed burglar. The jury is still out.

As for Slater, he remained in prison for eighteen years, and received £6,000 compensation when he was finally released. Fundamental to the investigation was the fact that Slater's brooch had been pawned three weeks before the Gilchrist murder. The repercussions were highly significant.

These cases give us a glimpse of Conan Doyle as an active investigator, and his adventures in detective work gave him ample material for dinner topics when he met the club members for their discussions. Of all the investigations he was involved in, perhaps the one in which he was closest to Holmes was the case of the Irish crown jewels.

On the morning of Saturday 6 July 1907, a cleaning lady called Mary Farrell, working at Dublin Castle, was going about her duties, and had reached the library when she noticed that the door was unlocked. She had found the same situation three days before, but no action had been taken by Sir Arthur Vicars when it was reported. Vicars was the Ulster King of Arms, and he was responsible not merely for the security of the library and rooms, but for something far more important – the Insignia of the most illustrious order of St Patrick, otherwise known as the Irish crown jewels.

These were in a safe in the library, because when the safe had been taken to the castle from a bank vault in order to be kept at the Office of Arms, it was found that the safe was too large to be taken in, so it was placed in the library of the Bedford Tower. Not only was it a solid safe, it was also positioned so that soldiers and police officers would always be in close proximity, therefore it must have seemed a safe place to store such valuables. How wrong could the men responsible have been, for after the cleaner made the second report on 6 July, William Stivey, who was an assistant to Vicars, went to the safe, and found that it was unlocked and that the jewels had gone.

The jewels were the insignia of a group formed by George III in 1783 as an Irish form of the famous Scottish Order of the Thistle. The jewels had been made in London by a company called Rundell & Bridge, and the glory of the collection comprised two items: a star and a badge of the Order of St Patrick. The statutes and rules of the order had only been revised two years previously, and the Office of Arms had been moved to the castle in that year. There was a whole panoply of officers and honorary members entrusted with the safety of the jewels, including the Dublin Herald Frank Shackleton, who was the brother of the famous explorer. He became a suspect, for clearly the valuables had been stolen by someone with access to a key, and he lodged with Vicars at his home in Clonskeagh Road.

The main pieces of the collection were incredibly valuable. The star and badge had in them rubies, emeralds, and Brazilian diamonds, and they were meant to be worn by the Lord Lieutenant of Ireland (in fact, a Viceroy) on ceremonial occasions. Estimates of their value today are around the figure of over £1 million. In 1907, they were valued at £40,000.

Sir Arthur Vicars was born in Leamington in 1864, the son of Sir Arthur Edward Vicars, Colonel in the 61st Regiment. He had been educated at Magdalen College, Oxford, and then in 1893 he was appointed as Ulster King of Arms. *The Times* wrote of him on his death, 'He was thoroughly versed in the sciences of heraldry and genealogy [...] He was a Fellow of the Royal Society of Antiquaries and a trustee of the National Library of Ireland.' Vicars had actually been the man who founded the Heraldic Museum at the Office of Arms. But all this counted for nothing after the disgrace and scandal of this daring and outrageous theft.

Vicars had in his possession the only two keys to the safe. One of the first lines of thought was that Shackleton had used or copied one of these. They had not actually been seen since 11 June, when Vicars had proudly shown them to a visitor, the librarian of the Duke of Northumberland. It was rare for anyone to open the safe but Vicars himself, and so for him to ask William Stivey to open it, and to give him a key, on the day the theft was discovered, was a notable fact when the investigation began. Vicars believed that he and been drugged and the keys taken, and he looked very much like the victim in the affair, as Conan Doyle saw and believed.

The police suspected Shackleton, but on slender information, including the detail that a few days before the theft he had been heard to remark that one day the jewels might well be stolen. He was also in debt, and so had a motive. Conan Doyle came to believe that Vicars was indeed a scapegoat.

It was a major scandal: the status of the Office of Arms was of the highest order. They had been established in 1552, and they administered the protocol and precedence at Dublin Castle. Vicars, as Ulster Kings of Arms, was the Chief Herald of Ireland, Knight Attendant, and registrar of the Order. In the records, he was defined as 'the first and only permanent officer of the Lord Lieutenant's household'. A painting of Sir Arthur Vicars in his ceremonial dress is at the castle, showing him in Elizabethan court garb with doublet and ruff, and with the harp of Ireland prominent on the lower left side of his garments.

The police went into action. They issued a poster offering £1,000 reward for information leading to the retrieval of the jewels. They are described there as having '150 white, pure diamonds issuing from the centre', and the badge was 'set in silver, with a shamrock of emeralds on a ruby cross surrounded by a sky blue enamelled circle' – with their motto, *Quis superabit* (who shall separate it). The whole was 'surrounded by a circle of large single Brazilian stones, surmounted by a crowned harp in diamonds'.

There was to be a royal visit just four days after this discovery, and that had of course been planned. There was to have been an investiture of a knight in St Patrick's Hall in the events of that visit, and of course, that was something that caused a furore in London. King Edward VII demanded that Vicars be sacked. There was a smear campaign against him, including accounts of orgies he was supposedly involve in, and the allegation that he was homosexual, which was then a criminal activity of course, with Oscar Wilde's trial fresh in the public memory.

When it came to the establishment of a Viceregal Commission of Inquiry, after a period when there had been no success in the hunt for the villains, Vicars kept out of it. The commission met in January 1908, and heard evidence from Shackleton. The due process of enquiry took place, and in the end Vicars was totally at fault. It vindicated Shackleton and, made it clear that Vicars was a disgrace to the office. The commission was appointed by the Irish government, and included Chester Jones, a London police magistrate and the Chief Commissioner of the Dublin Metropolitan Police. At the time, it was reported by the chairman that:

> Sir Arthur Vicars had definitely declined to come forward to facilitate the commission in any way. He recognised that the commission had no power to control or to compel Sir Arthur Vicars to give evidence. The government considered that the enquiry should go forward.

Vicars was dismissed and went to live in County Kerry, where on 14 April 1921, a party of IRA men shot him dead. *The Times* reported on his death that he had faced a mob of gunmen a year earlier, and had stood firm when they demanded the key to his strong room. On that occasion they had left, but the second attack was more desperate and determined. He was taken from his bed in his dressing gown and murdered outside his house. A label was placed around his neck with the words, 'Spy, Informers beware. IRA never forgets.' His house was then set on fire.

One theory about this mystery is that Shackleton and a rogue called Captain Gorges were responsible, but this is only a conjecture put forward in an article in *The Gaelic American* by Bulmer Hobson of the IRB. Hobson wrote that he had information to suggest that in one of many drunken parties, Shackleton had taken a key from Vicars as he slept, then the jewels were stolen, and that both Shackleton and Gorges had huge debts that led them to that desperate measure. Hobson also claimed that Shackleton had been energetically grilled by officers of the Dublin Metropolitan Police, but there had been no conclusive evidence, and that the authorities were content to know that Shackleton had left the country and was out of their hair.

Another suspect is one Francis Goldney, who was discovered (after his death) to have robbed antiquities from a range of places, including from the city of Canterbury and from the possessions of the Duke of Bedford. Goldney had been made Athlone Pursuivant (second in order of precedence to the Ulster King of Arms) in February 1907, and according the historian Sean Murphy, 'grounds for suspicion certainly exist [...] but no hard evidence has been found to connect him with the theft of the Irish crown jewels, nor do contemporaries appear to have suggested that he might have been involved.'

Vicars was shot dead, and Shackleton's later life confirmed certain opinions of him. In 1913, he was convicted of fraud, and on release, he died in Chichester in 1941. He is on record for saying while in gaol that he knew more about the theft than he had previously said, but nothing came of that. The case remains a mystery. But there is one fascinating coda to the tale: in 1976, some papers from William Cosgrave's estate were read, and there was the statement in a government file of 1926 that read, 'the castle jewels are for sale and they can be got for £2,000 or £3,000.' There have also been rumours that the jewels are stashed away at Three Rock in the Dublin Mountains. Writer and Dublin historian Frank Hopkins even suggests that some tales insist that the jewels are beneath the ruins of the Vicars' house in Kerry.

The story has the hallmarks of a Holmes casebook narrative: international, concerning people of high status in need of a detective, and major consequences for all if a solution is not found.

The Arthur Conan Doyle who went along to his club dinners with such adventures to tell must have stood out as a man of action amongst theorisers – with one exception, the learned Professor Collins, whom we shall look at next. Perhaps even without realising it, he had achieved what G. K. Chesteron spotted very early on in the Holmes detections: that criminal catching had raised language to a kind of 'romance'. Chesteron wrote, 'We may dream perhaps that it might be possible to have a higher romance of London, that men's souls have stranger adventures than their bodies,' and that Conan Doyle had achieved a poetry of London – a city with 'a chaos of unconscious forces'. The detection of real crime was enhanced with the same sense of the poetic as fiction. This was, in a word, the business of the club – its criminous material.

3
JOHN CHURTON COLLINS INVESTIGATES

On October 12 1908, the Classical Association held its annual business meeting. It was announced that Professor John Churton Collins was scheduled to read a paper on 'Greek as a Factor in Popular Education', but instead, Collins' death was announced. A few weeks before, his body had been found in a ditch near Lowestoft, and the inquest returned a verdict of accidental death. His son wrote in his memoir of the scholar that his 'lonely and premature death remains, and always will remain, terrible to those who miss him sorely'. He was accustomed to the lecture hall and the deadlines of his literary productions: a week's work in 1897 included a review of a new work on Virgil, a lecture on Tennyson in Richmond, two lectures at Wimbledon on Elizabeth I, and a lecture at Hayward's Heath on *The Iliad*.

Collins represents that bookman of the late Victorian years who expressed opinions on a broad range of topics, from a solid base of wide reading, firm opinions, and a sound university education. He graduated from Balliol in 1872, and began a career of busy and committed discourse on books of all kinds. In his life, there was always an essay to be written, a book to review, and a lecture to give. But he also excelled in the *conversazione* and the club. After his busy week of lectures listed above, he attended a dinner party with Sidney Lee and other literary men. He came to maturity in the 1890s when periodicals such as *The Idler*, edited by Robert Barr and Jerome K. Jerome, catered for the growing readership of literary opinion. There was a hunger for debate, informed discussion, and educated reviews. Autodidacts (such as Leonard Bast in *Howard's End*) found that this climate of opinion and reverence for books suited their temperament, and Churton Collins became well respected – a professor who had the common touch, and he shone in the world of university extension lectures.

He was born in 1848 at Bourton-on-the-Water in Gloucestershire. His father died when he was very young, and an uncle became something of a guardian. Collins went to King Edwards School, Birmingham, and then to Oxford, at Balliol, where he had such luminaries as Herbert Asquith, Canon Rawnsley, and Andrew Lang as his fellow students. Without any special academic distinction, he set his mind on London, and earned his livelihood by working as a tutor. He then submitted work to *The Globe*, writing on a range of literary subjects. Gradually, he made a name for himself, and made contacts, most notably the poet Algernon Swinburne, who he came to know very well.

Collins then worked tremendously hard, writing for a number of journals, and went to almost all of Swinburne's readings and soirees for his literary friends. When his interest in crime developed, he published a few pieces, particularly for the *Nineteenth Century*. Among very academic and literary friends, he defended his interest in what was then merely popular narrative, not much above the penny dreadfuls in the minds of university men. But on one memorable occasion, at a dinner given by Francis Coutts at White's Club, a guest lamented the current state of literature, saying, 'Look for yourselves. Who are the men at the top of the tree? Men like Conan Doyle.'

Collins' son recalls that his father responded with, 'And why not? I am indebted to Sherlock Holmes for some of the most delightful hours of my life, and *The White Company* is a classic.'

Collins was renowned also for his phenomenal memory. When his friend Arthur Lambton was with him in Worthing at a literary gathering, Lambton called him 'my brother in crime', and explained that when a guest asked Lambton what his favourite poem was, he said it was Whyte-Melville's *Ave Caesar! Moritori te salutant!* Collins immediately recited the whole poem from memory. Another friend of Collins recalled, 'The Professor was at his best when he was illustrating and expounding the writers whom he loved [...] he reeled off long quotations with marvellous verbal accuracy.' It has to be said that such a skill is of course an excellent attribute for a criminologist to possess.

Yet this was not all: the law and crime seemed to dog him all his life. In 1888, he was at a house on Torrington Square when thieves broke in and he had property stolen: two pistols and an overcoat. The pistols perhaps hint at another dimension to the man. Then in 1899, he was in court in the libel case of Yeatman v Harris, after reviewing a work on Shakespeare by John Pym Yeatman for Harris' *Saturday Review*. In the dock, Collins was accused of having a 'clique of barristers behind him', and questions were asked as to his qualifications for reviewing such a work. He sensibly admitted that he was not able to read and understand some of the sources used, but 'he had sufficient learning to criticise the book', as the press reported on the events at the court of Queen's Bench.

It should come as no surprise then, that Collins was a member of the Crimes Club. He had developed an interest in contemporary crime before he mixed with Sir Arthur Conan Doyle and other leading lights of that society. Collins had always been at home with intellectual debate, being a natural participant in senior common room theorizing. His skills in literary analysis were smoothly transferred to criminological discussion among his new friends in the Conan Doyle circle, and he soon gained respect for his phenomenal feats of memory and his Holmesian ability to apply logic.

For Collins, the attraction of criminal mysteries was perhaps akin to that of interpreting texts and ascertaining the intentions of authors at a time when books were written and lectures given in the manner of the 'life and work' tradition, as if literary intentions were plainly explicable. At a deeper level, the interest in criminology, in its amateur version as it existed then, was also concerned with human motivation and the darker side of human nature. He was always open to communal and open discussion on every aspect of humanity. In 1904, he was one of the founding members of the Ethological Society, whose aims were to study human nature, as *The Times* reported, 'Not through any one department of science, but taking from all the different branches the most practical and useful to arrive at a knowledge of the intellect and character of man.'

He not only read the journals and the law reports, but was active in the search for William Roughead's criminous. Collins delighted in meeting and interviewing criminals when he had the chance, and his curiosity led him into correspondence with them at times.

In 1897 for instance, he went to meet the infamous Tichborne Claimant. This was the case involving an impostor called Arthur Orton. The heir to the Tichborne estate was shipwrecked and drowned in 1854, but in 1865, a butcher from Wagga Wagga in Australia started to claim the title and behave as if he was in fact the proper heir. He was eventually tried for perjury, and the famous judge Henry Hawkins, Lord Brampton, prosecuted for the Crown. Orton was sentenced to fourteen years hard labour, and after release from Dartmoor in 1884, he survived until 1888. At this time, Collins knew him. The perjury trial had lasted for 188 days, and Judge Hawkins wrote in his memoirs, 'I did what I could to shorten the proceedings. My opening speech was confined to six days, as compared with twenty-eight on the other side.'

In his notes after meeting the Claimant, he wrote, 'His voice was soft with a curious mixture of accent, partly cultivated and that a little overdone, and partly vulgar.' Collins had a correspondence with the Claimant, and this traces the decline of the impostor. He wrote to Collins in one of his last letters:

My illness prevents me going out. On Thursday my wife gave a music lesson and earned a shilling, and that is all we have to live on [...] If you could only spare a shilling or two for our immediate wants, I should be very grateful. Having no means of getting a stamp my wife has kindly consented to walk down with this in the hopes of finding you at home.

Four months later, the Claimant was dead.

Of course, the case of Jack the Ripper absorbed his interest too, and in April 1905, he went with members of the Crimes Club to all the scenes and sites of the murders. He listened with attention and fascination to the account given by Dr Gordon Browne of the post mortems done on the Ripper victims.

But if we look for the origin of Collins' interest in true crime, the case in question is the Ireland's Eye mystery of 1852. Collins' son wrote that his father had always been interested in the study of crime and criminals, but that in 1891, he bought a publication on the trial of William Burke Kirwan, the man convicted for the murder of his wife in that 1852 case. So intrigued was he by the case that he suggested to Mary Braddon that she used the story as material for a novel. She replied that Collins should write the story: 'Your own pen, I am convinced – as a logician and profound thinker – would be much more effective in rehabilitating this unhappy man.'

The fact is that Collins did indeed try very hard to gather more information about the mysterious death of Kirwan's wife Maria. William Kirwan had been married to Maria for twelve years in 1852, when they set foot on Ireland's Eye for the day. But he had also had his mistress Mary Kenny in the village of Sandymount, just a little way south of Dublin. It appears that the two women knew that they had to share their man almost from the beginning of William and Maria's marriage in 1840. By the end of that day, Maria was found dead in suspicious circumstances, and Kirwan was destined to be charged and convicted of her murder.

William lived by his trade: when he was not earning from art directly, he was an anatomical draughtsman. He lived in Merrion Square, close to the centre of Dublin, just a few streets from the Dail, the parliament house, where he lived among medical men, who were always in need of such skills. The example of George Stubbs, the famous painter of horses who studied anatomy in depth, shows this: his friend Dr Atkinson at York, found him work in drawing for anatomical studies. Artists had traditionally been assistants to surgeons, as was the case with the great surgeon John Hunter, who had an artist called Bell as an assistant; Hunter had issued a ten year contract with Bell, for him to draw the contents of the surgeon's special collection of medical items. He even paid Bell to write a catalogue of specimens a little later. An anatomical draughtsman was paradoxically a talented dogsbody in some places: though he had exceptional skill, he was not seen as a 'proper' painter.

It is not hard to imagine this artist, a man trying to keep his business alive in one of the smarter areas of the city while spending time with Mary as well as with Maria. What emerges is a double life – something common in the middle class Victorian world, in which a mistress was often a family acquisition little different from a horse or a servant. Here was a man struggling to keep his head above water; an ironic metaphor, given his destiny. He was clearly increasingly desperate once his family with Mary grew apace: by 1852, he had seven children by her.

Money did not flow freely, and aspirations were high. William had married into a little money, and certainly had a status above the norm. But when Maria's body was brought in from the island, gossip was about insurance money. Yet the topic was never raised by the prosecution. For many, it was a working class crime – insuring the lives of relatives who would die mysteriously. Just six years after this death, a case in Liverpool was found to be a systematic poisoning of a whole family for insurance profits.

We have a man living with a front of the respectability of Merrion Square, yet with a family tucked away just down the road. He is man in need of finance, a man with a false face shown to the world. His landlord in Sandymount was a Mr Bridgeford, who said in court:

> Mr Kirwan lived in one of the four houses in Spafield of which I am the landlord. He resided there for about four years. I saw a woman there whom I always supposed to be his wife. I saw children in the house. I have notes from the woman and I think she signed herself Theresa.

This was Mary Kenny – her full name being Theresa Mary Frances Kelly. The Kirwans were not so badly off that they could not afford a servant: Catherine Byrne lived in the house as a maid, and she told the court that there were seven children, and that Kirwan was often there for long periods in the day, and often he stayed the night.

William Kirwan then, was a man with one foot in respectable and bohemian Dublin, a man to find being sociable at parties or alone in the early hours being melancholic; the other foot was in the dangerous underworld of crime and fear along the bay by the South Wall. Was he a man who longed for the thrill, the challenge, the pump of adrenaline?

One writer in 1853 gave us a picture of William: 'Mr Kirwan is a little above forty, a native of Mayo [...] He is tall and well-looking, strongly built, and the expression of his countenance, firmness, corresponds with his strong limbs, broad chest and duly-proportioned body.' The writer knew him, and commented that he was admired as an anatomical artist, 'from which he realised a handsome income'. Yet he would have had to be vastly wealthy to support so many people, along with two households' rent.

An artist who was reasonably well off then, but had an obstacle to further success that he had to remove? It makes no sense; he and Maria had taken a lodging for the summer at Howth, and they often went out to Ireland's Eye. He had no reason to kill her. That was lost in the supposition and legal bungling. Collins wanted to know more, and in 1891, after reading an account of the case, he wrote to some of the best legal minds in Ireland. It was forty years after the case, but one man, Walter Boyd, had some strong opinions. By 1885, he had risen to be a judge, and had been admitted to the bar in 1856 while the Kirwan case was fresh in the minds of Dubliners. He was a QC by the Hilary term in 1877, and had learned his trade on the north-east circuit. In retirement, Boyd found himself the recipient of questions from Collins, and their correspondence, though it offers nothing conclusive about Kirwan's guilt or otherwise, says a lot about Collins.

John Gross, in his *The Rise and Fall of the Man of Letters,* opines that Collins, after the Merton Professorship of English language and literature had been established at Oxford in 1885, was passed over, and was not happy about it. Gross writes that Collins was 'a hustler, a trouble-maker', and he had a bad name, being seen as 'a kind of intellectual cabaret turn'. That exuberant, expressive, and provocative side of him was exactly what would have made him a successful barrister in some ways; now here was a literary man in search of a new thesis, solving a criminal mystery rather than a question of literary authorship, or the trickier bits of the Linear B text in the Anglo-Saxon studies that his beloved Oxford would have appreciated.

Collins's letters to Boyd, and also to the former prison surgeon who had known Kirwan, brought out some stunning statements, such as, 'Kirwan refused to produce evidence for the defence as he said he could not be convicted,' and Boyd's assertion that he had no doubt about 'the religious element, having had much to say to the hostility displayed toward Kirwan, but I think it would be publicly undesirable to mention the fact'. Kirwan had been sentenced to hang and was later reprieved, and Boyd wrote to Collins to say that he was 'greatly struck at the time of the reprieve by a remark by Kirwan when I visited him in prison. He said, "If they believe me to be guilty why don't they hang me?" I thought a guilty man would not have said so, as he would have been only too glad to escape with his life'.

Collins' other major interest, equal to that of Ireland's Eye, was the Merstham Tunnel Mystery. This was in 1905, and it was focused on the discovery of Mary Money's body in Merstham Tunnel. All signs at the scene suggested that the woman had been thrown out of the window of a moving train, after being gagged with a scarf. Collins set to work, stepping easily into his role of detective. His report was published, but he spoke about the case to the club. Arthur Lambton told Collins' son that his father was, 'The mainstay [...] the life and soul of the meetings [...] his desperate earnestness found full scope.' The members must have been enthralled by Collins' account of the mystery. Was Miss Money's death one of murder, suicide, or accident? The gag in her mouth was a strip of veiling. So was it a gag or was it there from some other cause? It seems highly likely that she met a man in the carriage, and it was ascertained that she had eaten a meal a few hours before her death. Collins set to work.

He expressed his confidence in sorting out the mystery with some combative words: 'No-one who has carefully reviewed the evidence in the present case could doubt that if it is properly sifted and weighed it would be found to furnish clues, any one of which might lead to important clues.' Collins was very much of the school who saw the police as being of the Lestrade type. His study of the mystery, published in *The National Review* in 1905, made it clear that the police investigation had 'taken an entirely false direction'.

Collins was convinced that Mary Money was pushed backwards out of the train, noting that 'she would scarcely have been able to throw herself backwards'. A key finding was that the man working in the signal box at Purley Oaks, who had had a clear view of a struggle taking place between a man and a woman in the right carriage – one relating to another passenger's sighting of Mary getting on the train – had been undervalued in the first investigation. Collins theorised that the point on the journey at Purley Oaks would be exactly where an attacker would choose to make his move, and this confirmed his view that Mary met a man she knew, but that he had attempted a sexual assault on her. The train was moving at only 30 mph when the struggle was seen.

The theory was that Mary had met a man she knew at Victoria, had a meal with him, and then travelled with him. She was attacked 19 minutes into the journey. A guard gave a description of the man most likely to have been the killer. He had 'a long face and thin chin', and was around 5 feet 8 inches tall. The witness added, 'It occurred to me that they were not first-class passengers and that they had taken tickets for a certain purpose.'

Mary Money's past relationships were also the subject of scrutiny. Collins gave a thorough account of one Arthur Bridger, the manager of the dairy where Mary worked. The conclusion was that he was 'a model husband', despite the statement by Mary's brother George that Bridger had gone on a train journey with Mary in the past, and also taken her to the theatre. The Bridgers were grilled, and the outcome was that, for some reason, George Money had been lying.

Then there was the question of police work and forensics. Collins was particularly incensed at this. A constable at the scene had interfered with the body by taking out the material from Mary's mouth. Then, no doctor was called to the scene until 3 p.m. the day following – so the surgeon arrived 16 hours after the discovery of her body.

Collins concluded that it was inconceivable that 'Miss Money's murderer could have been any other than some man who was, and probably had long been, on intimate terms with her'. He had investigated what appeared to be an incompetent and piecemeal police operation, riddled with shortcomings and bunglings. It was exactly the kind of story that Conan Doyle would have relished at the Crimes Club meetings, and it is on record that Churton Collins was perhaps the most fervent and highly motivated amateur sleuth of the club.

He also wrote on another railway tunnel mystery: the case of Lillie Rochaid, whose mutilated body was found in the Crick Tunnel, near Rugby, in January 1906. She was the daughter of the Count Rochaud, and was on her way to Princethorpe Priory. She had telegrammed Father Hand at the Priory, telling him that she was going to be travelling on the Ostend Mail from London. Father Hand was the one who first identified the body.

At the inquest, held at Kilsby Station Hotel, evidence was given that the carriage door was found to be open at Rugby, and *The Times* report had this information:

> In reply to Father Hand who asked whether it was possible for someone who might have been travelling in the same carriage to leave it on the offside as the train was running into Rugby station, [staff] stated that it was possible, but that hardly anyone could do it without sustaining an accident. The medical evidence was to the effect that the injuries were quite consistent with the lady's having been run over by passing trains, and that there was nothing to suggest foul play.

At the inquest, police made it clear that nothing appeared to have been stolen from the lady, stating that there were jewellery and a purse with cash in it found on the body. There was one obvious motive ruled out. However it was still a mystery, and Collins loved that kind of situation. He was surely prompted to ask questions by the uproar in some areas of the press, in which statements such as this were made, calling for a detective force of a new kind:

> The Crick tunnel tragedy is one of a series of mysteries which emphasise in striking manner the necessity for the inauguration of a new body of official detectives [...] To deal adequately with this tragic mystery such as that at Crick or at Merstham requires a force of investigators who are not only armed with authority, but who have at their command the resources of special education.

In effect, some journalists called for existing detectives to deal with such domestic matters, rather than hunting spies or terrorists. The general tenor of the complaints was, 'What about the ordinary folk who's protecting them?'

The press also were quite aware of men such as Collins, with one feature noting, 'Meanwhile a little army of private persons, who can have no other object than the elucidation of truth, are using every effort to find out whether the young girl who lies dead has been the victim of a mysterious accident or of a terrible murder.'

Ever since the 1864 murder of Briggs by Muller on a train, there had been pressure for railway companies to improve the awareness of railway staff with regard to passengers' safety. The Merstham Tunnel affair had brought all that concern back to centre stage. An Act of 1868 had stated that the companies had to:

> Provide and maintain in good working order in every train worked by it [that] carries passengers, and travels more than twenty miles without stopping, such efficient means of communication between the passengers and the servants of the company in charge of the train as the board of trade may approve.

Clearly, such systems were not working, hence the concern about the various means of exit from the carriage at Rugby. Cases of assault, especially by men on young women, were fairly common. Collins saw the solution of the Crick affair as having exactly the same scenario as a case of 1892, in which a woman on the Midland railway had escaped from her compartment, and tried to rouse some help by hitting the next carriage window with her brolly. But she slipped from the footboard and was later found on the line. She was more fortunate than Lillie Rochaud, as she survived.

The key to understanding the case is that the train would have been all-corridor; these came into use on the Great Western locomotives in 1892, and although these were not installed everywhere until after 1918, the mail train going north that Lillie Rochaud took would have had that facility. The scenario was then, that we must assume she was attacked in the carriage, or at least felt so unsafe that she went out of the outside door, and so to a very dangerous situation. There would have been a door from the corridor into the carriage space, and then the exterior door. Attention was being given to comfort on trains – such as better heating, with gas being used from the 1880s – but not enough thought was given to protecting vulnerable passengers. There had been an acute awareness of the perils of rail travel from the first appearance of the railways, and in 1864, *The Lancet* published a feature arguing that 'an uneasiness, amounting to fear, pervades the generality of travellers by rail'.

The crime investigator in Collins came to realise that there was much potential for his lines of thought in railway incidents. It was an age of spectacularly horrendous rail disasters, but what was less well observed and acted upon was the alarming occurrence of attacks on women at the *fin de siècle*, and in the early years of the new century.

There was one case however, described by Max Pemberton, in which Collins theorised and then dropped. Pemberton wrote:

> For all his cleverness however, Collins once came a terrible crash when he investigated a strange murder in a building by the Westbourne Grove, Bayswater. A young man had lived alone in the flat, where he did, or was supposed to do, artistic work. His leisure hours he spent with his people, a most worthy couple. One day the young artist had been found brutally murdered in his studio and everybody said 'burglars'. So strongly did Collins hold to that opinion that he wrote two columns in a great daily paper and showed exactly how the thieves must have entered and left the building.

Collins was completely wrong, because the 'Studio Murder' as it came to be called, involved a murder in a gay relationship. Pemberton, predictably added that it was a 'horrible affair' about which, 'the less said the better'.

In fact, the case that Collins was so wrong-headed about highlights what modern sociologists might call a sub-culture of the time, and a very sad story concerning the artist Archibald Wakley. Wakley, thirty-three, was found dead at his studio in Westbourne Grove on Thursday morning, 24 May. At the inquest on 6 June, no less a person than Melville Macnaghten, Assistant Commissioner at Scotland Yard, was present, and Inspector Stockley told the court that he had found the body only partly dressed and covered in bedclothes. The detective found no evidence of theft, and no furniture disturbed. He noticed that a portrait of a woman was on a chair, and had very recently been completed, as the back was not fully nailed.

A second search brought to the attention of the police a hammer that had been hidden on top of a bookcase, clearly secreted there. There was blood on this, and there had been an attempt to wipe it off. There was also blood in the lavatory, and at the inquest, Stockley said that he thought the artist had been attacked while standing in the lavatory.

All this contradicted Collins' theories, so despite his best intentions, he had the facts completely wrong. Other details began to open up a sad story of a homosexual encounter that had turned violent. A witness called Muskett said that he had found around forty pieces of paper at the studio, the corners of letters, torn off to keep addresses private. One address was 'Trooper J. T. Walker, D Squadron, RHG [Royal Horse Guards].' Social historians have discovered that central London parks were known haunts for soldier prostitutes at the time, particularly Hyde Park. Trooper Walker's address was written as 'Hyde Park'. Significantly, a number of pictures of soldiers were found at Walker's flat.

A bystander had seen Wakley walk home accompanied by a soldier, a man from the Horse Guards. John Thomas Walker, referred to in the batch of addresses, stood as witness, and he gave an account that was typical of such encounters at the time: 'His explanation of the paper being in the studio was that about four months ago he met Mr Wakley in Hyde Park. Mr Wakley offered him a cigarette and as they walked through the park, the deceased asked him if he had anything to do and invited him to his studio.' But on the night of the murder, Walker had an alibi, being out with other troopers at a bandstand, and then spending time with a young lady.

Walker added that 'something was proposed which was distasteful', and there was little more added at the inquest. Wakley had been bludgeoned with the hammer and killed 'by person or persons unknown'.

A few weeks later, reports began to embellish the tale, one report even stating that Wakley's body had been mutilated 'in the old Whitechapel Jack the Ripper style'. But one feature proclaimed boldly that 'the police claim to have their hands on the murderer. They describe him as a soldier of a vicious and neurotic temperament, one thoroughly capable of working himself into an ungovernable passion and battering Wakley into a shapeless mass'.

The case, at a time when of course the trial of Oscar Wilde was fresh in the public mind, highlighted the risks involved in the soliciting of male partners by homosexuals, in particular in the context of army barracks. The long periods of enforced celibacy in the military led to all kinds of problems with regard to outlets for sexual activity, and historians of the subject have pointed to the fact that there has been a reluctance to research the subject in the army, although equivalent work has been done on the problems in the ranks of the sailors in her Majesty's navy at that time. Hyde Park was the focus of many gay meetings and liaisons, the place even finding its way into poetry, as in Marc-Andre Raffalovich's 'Hyde Park, November' (written in 1985) with the lines:

> Pale love, sweet sufferer whose cold hands I chafe,
> To whom my show of courage courage lends
> How do they love whose love is always safe?
> Sure of the base approval of their friends?

The Wilde affair was not the only recent scandal involving gay sub-culture. In 1889, the Cleveland Street scandal was reported in the press, and one bold editor called Park named names in his paper, including some aristocrats. For that he was sentenced to two years hard labour: the publicity had implicated Prince Albert Victor, the son of the Prince of Wales.

Collins had innocently built a theory on a case in which, in effect, he was out of his depth. It seems incredible that he actually worked out a line of thought proving the killing to have been made in the process of a bungled burglary, but then, all detectives make theoretical mistakes at some point.

He was also fascinated by prison and prisoners. Not only did he meet and chat with the famous Tichborne Claimant Arthur Orton, but he also went to visit prisons, as in 1906, when he went to Parkhurst on the Isle of Wight with Sir Horatio Bryan Donkin, who was one of the national prison commissioners. Collins had become a friend of Donkin, and with his help, he could learn a great deal about the current debates on crime, in particular such matters as the question of insanity related to crime, and also of heredity. Donkin had strong views on these topics, and often wrote to the papers to make his voice heard. Donkin was a medical man with a deep interest in criminology. In 1901, he represented the prison commissioners at an enquiry in Holloway Prison, where he met with the visiting justices with regard to allegations of vermin infesting the cells.

In 1914, Donkin engaged in the debate on the force feeding of suffragettes. To his discredit, Donkin agreed that the methods of force feeding were normal. He wrote that, 'I assert that artificial feeding by the introduction of food into the stomach by either nasal or oesophageal tube is in common use in private and hospital medical practice.' He was not one to argue with, and in 1906, he took Collins into Parkhurst, where, as a prison commissioner, he was familiar with every aspect of prison life. Collins wrote in his diary:

> Next day visited the prison – saw it thoroughly – sat with him [Donkin] while he heard the convicts who had any complaints or requests to make: most interesting. Saw all over the grounds and in fact the whole thing [...] Visited the prison again – saw this time the Weak Minded.

He was on his way to visit Conan Doyle at Hindhead, and had made the most of the opportunity at the prison. In fact, in seeing the 'weak-minded', he was a witness to a current hot topic. There was much debate about the treatment of that category of prisoner, and Donkin was one of the loudest voices among the experts and professionals in that area of penology.

There is no doubt that Collins tended to make enemies. As a scholar and reviewer, his attacks and harsh critiques sometimes caused arguments in his fraternity of writers. One notable example was his contretemps with Edmund Gosse, the famous Victorian autobiographer and literary critic. In 1901, after the two friends had experienced a certain cooling of their affections after Collins's attack on the scholarly expertise of Gosse, the latter wrote in a letter, 'Please send the *Revue Critique* – something about Shirten Collars, I suppose.' He had turned bitter, and that was after Collins' article in *the Quarterly Review*, in which 'Shirten Collars' wrote, in the words of Gosse's biographer, 'With the ferocity of a scholar's contempt for off-hand inaccuracies, intensified by jealousy of a successful man of letters.' Collins' failure to have the professorship at Oxford certainly left him with a chip on his shoulder, and it cost him a friendship.

Collins' remarkable ability to make caustic comments in reviews also cost him his friendship with Swinburne. He criticised Swinburne in a review and it took years for them even to speak again. When Collins finally did meet his friend again, it was a cold affair: 'I had not seen him for fourteen years [...] he received me with rather stiff courtesy [...] I saying that this was one of the happiest days in my life, referring to meeting him again after the estrangement.' Collins did know how to make enemies, but in spite of the mystery of his death, we are too far away from any possibility of foul play, which would naturally be ironically very powerful for such a club member.

Churton Collins exemplifies the kind of involvement in what we now call true crime that the writers and critics of the late Victorian period had enjoyed; theories and opinions on current or recent 'horrible murders' reported in the penny dreadfuls was partly a development of what De Quincey had in mind in his richly ironical treatment of murder as a 'fine art' in his essay dealing with Williams of the Ratcliffe Highway murders, and other Georgian horrors. As explained in the introduction, the periodicals of the last two decades of the nineteenth century were eager to feed the public curiosity for such things as 'criminal types', or the work of the lawyers and the police. Literary men weighed in with their interest, and a niche for the more profound and informed discussion on matters of murder was established. The Crimes Club certainly took off and was transformed. Ingleby Oddie, a founding member, was disappointed when the chat and entertainment became a version of literary criminology.

4

SAMUEL INGLEBY ODDIE AND DR CRIPPEN

When Ingleby Oddie died in 1945, his obituarist in the British medical journal pointed out that Oddie had supervised at almost 30,000 inquests in his capacity of HM Coroner for the County of London, an office he held for almost twenty-eight years. He was a very remarkable man, who had switched careers from naval surgeon to barrister, and just two years before he joined Lambton and the others in the first informal club meeting, he had been in the top six candidates at the Bar Final, being called to the Middle Temple in 1901.

After some time in the chambers of Sir Richard Muir, Oddie chose to be a coroner rather than a barrister, taking up the post in 1912. But surely his greatest moment, in terms of how and why he is remembered, was his part in the infamous Dr Crippen trial of 1910.

Our entire view of the Crippen case has recently been revised after some DNA research showing that he did not kill his wife – the body in question at the time in the cellar of his home being male. A campaigner called Giovanni di Stefano is lobbying for Crippen to receive a posthumous pardon, but of course, there was a body in the cellar. The only dispute is about the identity of that corpse. The fact remains that a murder was committed in Hilldrop Crescent.

First, here is an outline of the Crippen case. Crippen, an American with interests in fringe medicine and dentistry, settled with his wife, musical artiste Belle Elmore, in North London in 1900. Their address has become one of the most notorious in the history of murder: 39, Hilldrop Crescent. They had a strange, unconventional life; Belle was a member of the music hall and variety fraternity, but had very little work. She took in paying guests to make ends meet. Crippen became very friendly with a secretary, Ethel Le Neve, and after spending time together with little thought for what people might think, it became obvious to many in their circle that Belle was not at home –

or anywhere else. Crippen concocted a fabrication that she had returned to America because her mother had died, and then later he broke the news that Belle herself was dead. But eventually, her worried friends, with plenty of cause for suspicion, went to tell the police about Belle's disappearance.

The man who took charge of the investigation was Walter Dew. He was from Northamptonshire, and was forty-seven at that time; he had been in the metropolitan Police for thirty years, and had been part of the group of detectives working on the Jack the Ripper case. When the Crippen case came along, he came to realise the importance of it, and how it would engage the public imagination. He sat and listened to the story told by John Nash and Lil Hawthorne, two of Belle's closest friends, and then he went, together with Sergeant Arthur Mitchell, to pay a call on Crippen.

Belle had indeed been murdered; Crippen had shot her and buried her under the floor of the cellar. The Crippens had a French servant, and she opened the door to Dew. It was to be a visit that would cause recriminations aimed at Dew later on. Ethel Le Neve was in the house; a point that was of utmost significance of course. Crippen was at work at his business address, and Dew insisted that Ethel went with them to that address. Dew's words when he came face to face with Crippen are loaded with irony to this day:

> I am Inspector Dew and this is Sergeant Mitchell, of Scotland Yard. Some of your wife's friends have been to us concerning the stories you have told them about her death, with which they are not satisfied. I have made exhaustive enquiries and I am not satisfied so I have come here to see you to ask if you care to offer any explanation.

Dew was a very experienced policeman. He was being careful; so cautious was he that he began to take a very long statement, and soon the two men were delving deeply into Crippen's life. It was then that truly unusual step was taken: that the detective and Crippen should have lunch together. As they sat in an Italian restaurant in Holborn, naturally Dew was studying his suspect. But Crippen ate heartily and appeared to be free from any nervous anxieties or defensive strategies in the conversation. All that encouraged Dew to take an open-minded view of matters.

It was late in the afternoon before attention switched to Ethel. Her story, told repeatedly after the terrible events of the murder and the aftermath, was that she was deceived by Crippen. Dew had come up against a criminal who was capable of misleading anyone, for he presented to the world an eccentric mix of professionalism and bluster. But when Crippen and Ethel were on the run, going to Holland, with the intention of travelling from there to America, Dew went with his sergeant back to Hilldrop Crescent and then the discovery of Belle's body was made. This time, the search was a thorough one; first they found a pistol in a cupboard and a sheet of paper with Belle's signature written on it.

After that it was only a matter of time before they reached the cellar, and on 13 July 1910 Dew picked up a poker, tested the bricks on the floor, and the end of the poker went between two bricks. Then it was a case of going down there. Dew wrote later, 'Presently a little thrill went through me [...] I then produced a spade from the garden and dug the clay that was immediately beneath the bricks. After digging down to a depth of about four spadefuls I came across what appeared to be human remains.' It was big business for the Yard. Assistant Commissioner Macnaghten came to the scene, and had the presence of mind to take cigars with him to help cope with the noxious fumes that Dew had said were emanating from the remains.

One remarkable aspect of this dig in the cellar was the way in which the scene of crime was not 'safe' in terms of forensic methodology. Disinfectant was used for instance, and therefore all kinds of substances were removed, which may well have been important later. Of course, the hunt for the fugitives was then in process.

In the annals of detection, the Crippen case is, of course, celebrated as being the first time that the telegraph was used to help capture a murderer. But the detective work was actually done by the commander of *The Montrose*, the ship that Crippen and Ethel were on. This was Henry Kendall, and he was very observant. Ethel was travelling in the clothes of a young man, and for most of the time that seems to have been effective. But Kendall had slight suspicions when he saw the clothes, and noted that her movements were not masculine. Finally, he saw Ethel squeezing Crippen's hand, and that was the detail that led to his certainty that he had the fugitives on his ship.

The wireless telegraph was then used, somewhat momentously; the submarine cable had been used sixteen years earlier to catch a murderer called Muller, who was also on board ship heading for America. Another killer, named Tawell, had been spotted on a train, and the telegraph was used to make sure that police were waiting for him as he alighted. But now the wireless telegraph was used, and a dramatic pursuit on a faster ship meant that Dew was waiting for Crippen when he docked.

The elements of the case are well-known, but the most interesting aspect of the arrest and the following events is the relationship between the media and the detectives involved. Dew made enemies, as he did not co-operate. He was, naturally, the subject of a media frenzy, and was offered large amounts of money for his story. So high profile was the case that, as the build-up to the trial proceeded, the Pinkerton agency were brought in, their task being to protect key witnesses who had to journey over the Atlantic to London. Criticisms of Dew's handling of the whole affair, right from the start, now began. Even the famous judge Sir Travers Humphreys joined in with the criticism, as in the fact that Belle's furs were still at Hilldrop Crescent – an oversight on Dew's part at the time of his first inspection there. The essence of that line of thought was the rhetorical question: what woman would go to America for a lengthy stay and not take her furs?

In 1903 and the year after, at the first club dinners, Oddie was still a barrister, and clearly relished the club meetings, noting that at one dinner, 'Professor Churton Collins produced in triumph the right-arm bones of John Williams, the famous murderer.' At that time, he defended his first murderer as well, in the first murder case tried at the new Central Criminal Court: an unemployed fitter who had stabbed a woman to death with lots of witnesses present. The defence failed, but the death sentence on the man was commuted to life imprisonment and there was no hanging.

But in the Crippen case, he really experienced a full scale, sensational murder trial. The result was that, as he was junior counsel, he had time to study every aspect, and from close quarters. He developed his own theory: that Crippen had arranged a dinner party, with a couple called Martinetti as guests. He had insisted on their coming, even though they said that Mr Martinetti was ill. The result was that the Crippens were seen to be happy together. She was to die that night, and the couple's testimony would have been useful. Oddie undoubtedly told the Crimes Club that he thought Crippen had used the hyoscine poison, and that one side effect was that the victim became uncontrollably hysterical and loud. He had therefore shot Bella in the head, and that accounted for the testimony of neighbours that they had heard a sound like a shot. Crippen then had three days alone in the house, plenty of time to cut up his wife's body and to dispose of most of it piece by piece, finally burying the last remains.

Oddie, being a qualified doctor, also opined that a certificate of death could have been obtained (before the need to shoot her!), as she had some heart disease, and that if the coroner had not been totally satisfied, a post mortem examination would not have found any hyoscine.

From Oddie, we have an insight into the Crimes Club meetings. They did more than discuss: they had an antiquarian taste, being fond of having members bring in exhibits and often ghoulish mementos. He wrote in his autobiography, 'It was always interesting to examine and handle exhibits from celebrated trials, to see photographs, and to learn what had become of famous persons who had been tried for murder but acquitted.' He mentions that at one meeting, one member brought a box of the pills used by serial killer Neil Cream, along with some letters sent from prison. Cream took delight in ingratiating himself into the company of woman around the public houses, and then giving them strychnine pills. Oddice notes that Cream gave these fatal doses and then took great pleasure in watching the following deaths, which were agonizingly painful of course.

At the meeting in which Churton Collins took the right-arm bones of John Williams, the infamous killer in the notorious Ratcliffe Highway murders of 1811, they all argued at length. Clearly, the members had a fascination with the artefacts and remains of famous cases, and the people involved. But they also had occasional field trips, and the most memorable was the tour of the Ripper murder sites. Oddie's account is the most detailed of the various memoirs of this event, in which Dr Gordon Brown, the City of London police surgeon who was a friend of Oddie's, led five club members, including Conan Doyle, through the streets of Whitechapel. Oddie, naturally developed a theory, which was a now commonly accepted one – that Jack the Ripper was a doctor who was what he called a 'lust murderer', whose insanity increased until it 'culminated in a wild orgy in Dorset Street and was followed by his own suicide in the Thames'.

However, one persistent line of thought about the Ripper began with the opinion of a club member. Arthur Diosy was one of the leading experts on the Far East around 1900, and also in the ranks of Our Society. He originated the notion that Jack was a practitioner of black magic, and he saw in the 'bright farthings and burnt matches' at the killing sites what was seen in some parts of the East as the *elixir vitae*. Diosy saw these items as forming the pentacle of flaming points by the victims' corpses. The scholar of eastern cultures even went to tell officers at Scotland Yard about his theories, but was not taken seriously.

There is no doubt that Oddie had stories to tell the club at their dinners concerning his experiences as a coroner. He took his office very seriously, and was often a correspondent to a range of publications on matters relating to the work of coroners. In 1936, when the Government had proposed closing the office of coroner to all except those who had been solicitors or barristers, he wrote to *The British Medical Journal* that, 'The great bulk of cases dealt with by coroners involve questions of a medical nature and very few call for any legal knowledge at all.' When he came to the club, he relished the opportunity of putting before the members issues and debates, mysteries, and open questions. Yet one of his mysteries which surely typifies a club topic for debate is the Chatfield mystery – something from Churton Collins that in fact does not appear in the biography of Collins published by his son.

Chatfield was an American who claimed that he had developed a method of retaining natural oil in wool. This would have been a technological revolution, and he won the backing of a number of industrialists and planned a to give a private demonstration at the Cumberland House, opposite Marble Arch. This was to provide evidence of his technique to any men of influence and power who were not entirely convinced by this apparently amazing achievement.

Chatfield had not taken any money except small sums for expenses, yet on the night agreed for the demonstration, he did not appear. He was never seen again, and his technological advance was therefore never known and used. Oddie reports that Collins' account of this ended with the report that a man called Hounsel, who had been Chatfield's secretary, had met the man who had been the butler at the planned Cumberland House event. This man stated that, on that evening, he had heard a conversation between two woolen manufacturers in which one had said that the thing would ruin them and the other replied, 'Yes, there is no doubt about that if it ever comes to anything, but it never shall.'

Oddie simply adds the fact, 'It never did'.

In the first few years of the club, Oddie had the story of the Brinkley murder to tell. This would have interested Conan Doyle and the *aficionados* of crime and transgression for two clear reasons: first, it involved a murderous and fraudulent scheme so implacably evil that it was revolting; second, that the killer was a bizarre, twisted fantasist with a dark side that we will never fully know.

Richard Brinkley was a fifty-three-year-old carpenter with a penchant for nefarious thought. He had the crass inventiveness of the worst, most depraved double-faced criminal. In early 1907, he located an aged German widow Maria Blume, and he cultivated a friendship with her, ingratiating himself to such an extent that he was working to become as close as anyone in her family. It was a cunning piece of fraud he had in mind in order to inherit her home and money. Mrs Blume's grand-daughter left early every day for work, so Brinkley had all day to insinuate himself into the affections of his victim.

He devised a crude piece of fraud, talking Mrs Blume into signing her name on a sheet of paper that she thought was a list of names signing up for a jaunt in the country. Of course, it was her will. He also duped two other acquaintances into signing, thus obtaining witnesses. Then, his only obstacle to her wealth was the fact that Mrs Blume still lived. Conveniently, she died just a few days after the will was signed. He lucked into his new property, and at the inquest for Mrs Blume, Oddie presided.

Oddie's court found a verdict of natural death. However in his memoirs, he notes that he felt the medical information stated was not convincing, but that he had to decide on expert witness testimony. Then Brinkley had a problem: Mrs Blume's daughter saw a solicitor and a caveat was put forward, meaning that the witnesses would be tested and the circumstances of the supposed will examined. That meant one move for the killer: to remove the witnesses. Oddie recounts the failed attempts to poison one Clifford Parker, whose suspicions about Brinkley saved his life. However in the process, two innocent bystanders, Richard and Elizabeth Beck, took some poisoned beer and died.

Evidence was found linking Brinkley to the poison. Inspector Walter Dew, who was prominent in the Crippen case, figured once again. He had seen Brinkley on the station at Chelsea on a date that tallied with other facts, mainly that a certain train from there would have got him to Croydon, where the Becks lived, at a time on which he could have been at the murder scene. He was arrested and charged, and as the case progressed, Mrs Blume's body was exhumed and the presence of prussic acid was found – the same poison that had killed the Becks.

There was a sick, depraved core at the heart of Brinkley's being. This was hinted at when, visiting Mrs Blume's daughter, he had offered marriage and, as Oddie notes, he was 'quite prepared to make love to her daughter now and then for a change'. Oddie adds that when Brinkley's possessions were examined, a black wig, hair dye, and cosmetics were found, which he said he used for 'private theatricals'. He had a distinctive black moustache with ringed ends, and Oddie comments that it lost its colour after his arrest and became grey.

Richard Brinkley was hanged at Wandsworth by Henry Pierrepoint on 13 August 1907. The one outstanding detail in the case for the prosecution had been one of such remarkable obtuseness that it defines the man. When arrested, he told the police officer, 'If anyone says I bought beer they have got to prove it.' There had been no mention anywhere of any poison being placed in a bottle of beer.

In the Crimes Club, Ingleby Oddie, original member and a man of great bonhomie and gentlemanly qualities, was a leading light, respected for his extraordinary knowledge of both medicine and criminal law. He knew Conan Doyle well, and attended séances with him as well as discussing famous crimes. His description of the great writer was that he had 'Robust common sense and shrewdness [...] and extraordinary mental acuity'. Yet strangely, as we try to understand him today, Conan Doyle was duped by sham spiritualists. Oddie wrote that he had a childlike faith in the 'ridiculous antics' of the trickery involved in some so-called communions with the dead in suburban parlours. But to be fair to Conan Doyle, Oddie does report conversations in which the rational, skeptical mind comes to the fore.

One friend wrote of him, 'He was a good friend and a most entertaining companion.' That sums up the heart of the Crimes Club, which, as Arthur Lambton relates, was Oddie's concept. As referred to earlier in chapter one, it was Oddie who suggested the 'coterie of crime experts' as he and Lambton walked in Naples, long before the first meal at the Carlton.

5

HENRY BRODRIBB IRVING AND REMARKABLE CRIMINALS

Harry Brodribb Irving impressed a lot of people. The author of *Zuleika Dobson* Max Beerbohm had a story to tell that shows this charisma: 'As Irving crossed the threshold, he said in a deep voice, "Ha!" He clapped a hand on Bancroft's shoulder, rather in the manner of a very eminent detective arresting a very important thief, then with a hand still on that shoulder, his gaze alighted on me.' There followed a powerful, impressive presence from a man who was supposed to become a lawyer, but he trod the stage like his father Henry Irving before him.

In the modern world of celebrities, and the frenzied pursuit of fame in the media, historians naturally look for stars from the past who would match up to today's media darlings. Undoubtedly, Sir Henry Irving is in this category, being adored by the Victorian public and highly respected by his peers. Yet in his personal and family life, there was almost always an element of passion, chaos, and stress. One result of this was that he had difficult relationships with his sons. Both Laurence and Harry felt drawn to the stage, but Sir Henry felt that it would be wise to let them progress on their own merit rather than step in and use his network of friends.

The result was that the two sons faced challenges, and possibly also their demons. In Laurence's case, one expression of his profoundly complex nature was the occasion when he was shot while staying at lodgings in Belfast. The story is that he was playing with a gun and accidentally shot himself, but there are doubts. Whatever the truth is deep down in Laurence's self, Harry's, in contrast, comes over to us now as a case of hard work and application to a bundle of interests and enthusiasms, one of which was true crime. His son wrote that when Harry Irving's first book *Studies of French Criminals* came out, it reflected a long-standing project: 'My father had been working on this grim project since, when he was at Oxford, Laurence had sent him *Causes Celebres*, a record of crime in France that was being issued in monthly parts.'

Here was a club member who was to add a dash of international reference to the talk at dinners. His son also notes that at a time when there was a particular crisis in the stage, and tastes in theatre-going were changing the economics of the business, his father took refuge in his criminous conversations, and he had other writer friends outside the club with whom he socialised:

> Harry returned to London and for a time sought reassurance in the company of convivial friends – men younger than himself such as Frederick Lonsdale, Eddie Knoblock, Reggie Eves, and E. V. Lucas [...] This brief resurgence would be the fond recollection of those who shared the Indian summer of his conviviality, remembering only his debonaire dignity, his penetrating analysis of human nature.

Henry, known as Harry, was the eldest son of Sir Henry Irving and Florence O'Callaghan. Born in 1870, he was to emulate his famous father in some ways, with regard to his stage career, but when he sat for his first meeting with the Crimes Club friends, he had been married for nine years to Dorothy Baird, well known for her part in the amazing success of George Du Maurier's play *Trilby*, and he was an Oxford graduate who was expected to become a lawyer rather than an actor. Yet he had appeared on stage in 1891, at the Garrick Theatre. Theatre was in his blood, but so was the study of the criminal mind.

Harry's son Laurence was to become a literary biographer, and so we know a great deal about Harry and his brother Laurence (also an actor). One of the most insightful memoirs regarding Harry Irving, the student of crime and law, comes from an obscure broadcast talk given by Max Beerbohm and recorded for posterity by Harry's son Laurence, in his book *The Successors*. Beerbohm wrote, 'What a terror to witnesses was lost by young Irving's abandonment of the law! Young Irving would have somewhat restored the fine old traditions, shining from even his stuffed gown, the eminence of Judge Jeffreys.'

Harry was a freshman at Merton College in 1890, and while there, he had made a special study of Judge Jeffreys, and had read a paper on the subject, to 'more than one essay society', according to Laurence. His rooms in Radcliffe Square must have been the testing ground for his later criminological disquisitions, and as his son notes, as far as the family were concerned, Harry was to practise at the bar when he 'went down' from university.

His famous father was also fascinated by criminals, and of course Sir Henry Irving was outstanding in acting the roles of great tragic characters from classic drama, and so Harry naturally had a profound interest in the higher and deeper levels of deviance, and the extremes of human emotion, expressed in the most unspeakable transgressions. The great actor shared his son's fascination with crime, and the importance of the subject in Harry's life must be at least partly owing to his father's enthusiasms.

At the time of the trail of Amelia Dyer, the murderous baby-farmer, in March 1896, Harry was in Blackburn, from where he wrote a letter that gives us an intriguing insight into the man who would sit to dinner with the club – a man fascinated by the gruesome objects of murder and the small biographical footnotes to criminal history. The hangman at the time of the Dyer trial was the Bolton man William Billington, and this letter concerns that somewhat mysterious celebrity:

> Yesterday I went to Bolton, a journey fraught with adventure [...] After lunch I hurried off to see Billington the hangman [...] we had our hairs cut by him, and well cut too. He had a sure and careful hand. He is rather a forbidding looking man and seems to relish putting criminals out of the way. He speaks of it with a gloating satisfaction, as though he were doing a very good thing in ridding the earth of such vermin. A man told me his great pleasure as a boy was killing vermin of the rat type. His father was in an asylum. The man really seems to have been born with a passion for execution [...] I have had my hair cut by him so I have not lived in vain.

In this we have the authentic voice of the intellectual who relishes the finer points of the law's most dramatic elements, an expression of William Roughead's criminous interests put into absolutely classic context. Harry even adds that there is a link to his own world too, reporting that Billington liked to go to the theatre, and that, if there was a play with some hanging in it, he was there every night.

In 1904, as Harry sat and talked crime and criminals with Conan Doyle and the others, fate had suffering in store for the young actor. The year after, his great father was to die while on tour in Bradford, his life ending in the foyer of the Midland Hotel after a performance of his adaptation of Lord Tennyson's *Becket*. Two years later, his brother Laurence and his wife Mabel perished in the sinking of *The Empress of Ireland* in the St Lawrence river, Canada, after a successful theatrical tour by their company.

Harry, in the years after these losses, was to become first a London actor-manager, even playing in some of the roles his father had become famous for. But as Mrs Aria, his late father's female friend, was to recall, 'books and books and books again absorbed most of his affections'.

His emergence as a crime writer did not come easily. Max Beerbohm, in a letter to his friend Reggie Turner, gives us a picture of Harry before his success:

> He has not allowed the grass to grow under his feet – seeing that he has played a part twice under the auspices of his father's old friend Mr John Hare, has read for the bar in Mr George Lewis's office and has written for *the Albemarle Review*, though I long to add that though his article, which dealt comprehensively with the question of crime, was not accepted by the editor.

He had his learning curve, as all writers do of course.

In the first five years or so of the club then, Harry Irving had been the good family man, but had split his life outside family life into the spheres of acting and criminology. Mrs Aria recalled the nature of Harry and his father's drives into the country, when they would share tales of 'ingenious murders', enjoying the bloody tales the most. Surely one of the most informative instances of his two worlds coming together is his playing Hamlet in 1904: at the same time that he attended the dinners and talked murder, he was playing the part of the young prince who killed Polonius and was tortured by the torment of revenge for the murder of his father. It is no accident that Harry's writings on criminal themes were based on a deep interest in the motivations people have when they take a life.

The acting and the criminal studies also came together in one of Harry's most successful roles: the part of Dubosco in *The Lyons Mail*. His father had also played the part, and the stage adaptation was by Charles Reade, the novelist who had been *in loco parentis* to the Terry sisters (Ellen Terry being the leading lady with Sir Henry at the Lyceum for many years). The story from France in 1796 is perfect for a Crimes Club topic: a famous miscarriage of justice in which the innocent man Lesurques is guillotined as the cries of the guilty man ring out on the way to the block.

Harry Irving's most striking contributions to true crime writing, and no doubt to the club discussions, was the stories he had based on French crime history, although he was very much interested in the life and career of the infamous killer and burglar Charles Peace, and in Irving's collection of tales called *A Book or Remarkable Criminals* (1918), he has an account of Peace among several French cases.

The criminal adventures of Charles Peace offer many aspects on themes that would have interested Conan Doyle and the others. He represented the classic profile of the master criminal – having some features that remind us of Moriarty himself. Harry had a deep fascination with the Yorkshire villain, seeing in him the kind of picaresque adventurer we find in the old Newgate tales of Jack Sheppard and Dick Turpin.

If nothing else, the Ripper reign of terror, and it mediation in the popular press, running alongside the incredible success of Sherlock Holmes, helped to intensify the mystique and appeal of the detective in the popular imagination. Detectives were parodied in literary journals and caricatured along with the uniformed men. But the writers did their part to heighten the interest. To take merely a few examples from the Ripper period: Dick Donovan in *The Strand* magazine, a detective superhero against arch-villains; Robert Barr, who invented Valmont the French detective; most celebrated of all, Wilkie Collins and his novel *The Moonstone* (1868). Of course, most fictional detectives were private investigators (like Holmes), and we must not overlook the importance of Inspector Lestrade in the Holmes stories. In *The Norwood Builder,* Holmes says in response to Lestrade's delivery of his theory:

> 'It strikes me, my good Lestrade, as being just a trifle too obvious,' said Holmes. 'You may not add imagination to your other great qualities; but if you could for one moment put yourself in the place of this young man, would you choose the very night after the will had been made to commit your crime?'

By the last decade of the nineteenth century, writers and journalists appeared to be wanting to denigrate the detective force and to celebrate the amateur, but at this point, it is worth recalling that there had been notable victories by the official detectives, and plenty of real-life action to rival the fictional sleuths, as in the story of Charles Peace, from a decade before the Ripper appeared. Peace was so famous that Conan Doyle references him in a Holmes story, referring to Peace – a violinist like the Baker Street genius – as a man respected and complimented for his musical skill. Richard Whittington-Egan has pointed out the strange paradox of Charles Peace: 'There exists [...] the extraordinary physical as well as psychological dichotomy between the blameless old gentleman with the frail, bowed shoulders and the crippled leg, and the mischievous little monkey of a creature.' This was just the thing to attract Conan Doyle: a Moriarty in his transmutations and switching identities.

In 1884, there was a proposal to appoint a director of public prosecutions to take some of the work from the belaboured treasury solicitor's office, and to back the police investigations into the proliferation of receivers of stolen goods across the country. This important step forward in establishing support mechanisms for detective work was, ironically, the outcome of the Charles Peace case. Peace, when finally captured, gave the police a list of such criminals across the land, and the centre of such illegal commerce – London – was investigated as a first step. This was arguably the one beneficial outcome of the staggeringly eventful life of an arch-villain whose name permeated popular culture almost as much as the Ripper, but who is perhaps most productively compared with the likes of Jack Shepherd and Dick Turpin in the previous century.

Peace was born Manchester in 1832. His father was an animal trainer. The events of his life are a mix of recorded fact and sheer urban myth; the product of eager journalists. But the fact remains that his story plays a significant part in the history of the detective. This is mainly because the hunt for the man who had multiple identities meant that detectives had to move from north to south, and from one local piece of police liaison to another. In addition, his crimes entailed a more refined and streamlined version of detection of identity than was normal.

He suffered an accident in a mill when he was young, and so Peace had an artificial piece made for his arm. He was also distinctive in many other ways, so that in theory, he would have been very easy to spot when a constable was in pursuit. But the story does not end there. Pearce was a master of disguise, and was skilled in the art of gurneying; he could manipulate his jaw to change the appearance of his face. His appearance was therefore most striking, as W. Teignmouth Shore described in the volume on Peace in the *Notable British Trials* series, quoting a police description:

> He is thin and slightly built, from fifty-five to sixty years of age, but appears much older; five feet four inches high, grey (nearly white) hair, beard and whiskers [...] He lacks one or more fingers on the left hand, walks with his legs rather wide apart, speaks somewhat peculiarly as though his tongue was too large for his mouth, and is a great boaster.

One would expect such a singular character to be observed anywhere, very easily, and apprehended when the police wanted him for enquiries. But he was always hard to find, shifting from one identity and lifestyle to another. He had exceptional artistic skills, including being a very talented violinist. He lived as a picture framer and carver, and he also managed to carry on his burglary while engaged part-time in these occupations. After being released from Chatham Gaol in 1872 however, his criminal career was to move from burglary and larceny to murder. Between 1872 and 1875, his career is obscured by slender details and much myth-making. He was already a popular figure in the Yorkshire press by the time he committed his first murder: the shooting of PC Cock in Manchester in 1876. Two brothers were arrested for that murder at Whalley Grange, and one was given the death sentence, although it was commuted.

With his first killing done, he moved to Sheffield, and there he began to harass the wife of a Mr Dyson who lived a few doors down from Peace and his family in Banner Cross. Mrs Dyson made the mistake of encouraging Peace's romantic interest in her, and the Dysons tried to evade Peace by moving house. Peace tended to appear and confront the woman, obviously engaging in a reign of fear. At one time he came to her and said, 'I'm here to annoy you, and I'll annoy you wherever you go.' Peace persisted in this shadowing of his victim, and one night, as Mrs Dyson came outside her house to the water closet, there was Peace. When she screamed, Mr Dyson ran out, and Peace shot him twice.

It is after that second murder that Peace's career starts to have an effect on the detective branch. He moved to London and stepped into a new identity as John Ward, a gentleman of leisure and burglar by night. His distinctive mode of work was to go to the venue designated for the theft in his pony trap, and he always had his tools in his violin case. He very nearly committed murder number three in Blackheath, when he shot another police officer. He was caught, and was in custody simply as John Ward until he was too bold and took the risk of writing to a colleague, so making his identity ruse open to police knowledge after they talked to the man in receipt of the letter. Peace was also grassed by his woman friend Thompson.

It might have been the end of Peace's dramatic life, for the police now knew that he was wanted in Sheffield, and he would have to be taken north to Leeds for trial. But according to one account, as the train neared Darnall heading north, he said to one of his guards, 'That's Darnall, where I used to live. Open the window and let's have a breath of fresh air.' One of the warders did so, and Peace leapt through the opening. One man grabbed Peace's leg and there was a struggle. The murderer kicked so hard that he lacerated the hand of the guard, and then the boot came off and Peace was free, rolling off the train at high speed. However, the criminal was dazed when the guards ran back for him, and was seriously hurt. He was recaptured, and eventually stood trial at Leeds Assizes.

He was found guilty of murder on 4 February 1879, and sentenced to death. His story was the next big sensation to fill the papers after the battle of Rorke's Drift in the Zulu War. The 'King of the Burglars', as some media called him, confessed to the Manchester killing, and the two Habron brothers were cleared.

Harry Irving expressed his interest in Peace after his long account of the adventures and career of this extraordinary rogue stirred debate in the club:

'Peace stands out physically and intellectually well above the average of his class, perhaps the most naturally gifted of all those who, without advantages of rank or education, have tried their hands at crime.' Harry concludes with a statement that would have prompted a response from Conan Doyle immediately: 'The only interesting criminals are those worthy of something better.'

Irving's first book on matters criminous was published in 1906, at the time he had just joined the club. The book was called *Occasional Papers Dramatic and Historical*, and there is a piece of particular interest here that was very topical at the time: a piece of biographical writing on a lawyer. The years between c. 1890 and 1910 brought a steady flow of such writing. Memoirs and biographies of lawyers and barristers were very current. For instance, a month after the first official club dinner at the Great Central Hotel, *The Reminiscences of Sir Henry Hawkins* was in print, complete with a frontispiece photo of the great judge and his dog Jack. Features on famous judges in *The Strand* magazine added to this literature, and Irving's *The Early Life of Chief Justice Scroggs* was a typical contribution to the genre.

What his son had called his 'penetrating analysis of human nature' comes over boldly in his account of Justice Scroggs, as it does in his best narratives of French crime. Scroggs won his office as Lord Chief Justice back in the late seventeenth century, when the powerful Earl of Danby had to restock the judiciary with King's men. Scroggs had by that time established his country seat in Essex, but had been active fighting for his King in the Civil Wars. When he took office in his first position, he made a speech that was so influential that it was copied and proclaimed in every parish across the land. Such a man would be suitable for a hanging judge later, when the infamous Popish Plot emerged. This is exactly the kind of personality study that Harry enjoyed. He concludes that the man's bad reputation, placed alongside the monstrous Judge Jeffreys, was based on something in him other than his decision-making in court: 'It is not so much what Scroggs did in the Plot trials that has exposed him to just censure [...] it is the ranting, transpontine way in which he conducted himself that has rendered him odious.'

Bearing in mind that club members included Ingleby Oddie, a man of law with vast experience, it must have been the current interest in lawyers' lives and morals that usually played a part in the group's case analysis, and Harry seems to have had a special interest there. But in his accounts of French cases, he really came into his specialism. It is helpful to recall that in the second half of the nineteenth century, French criminal stories and history had received popular appeal in the works of Emile Gaboriau, an author whose work influenced Conan Doyle, an there had also been the autobiography of

Louis Canler (*Experiences of a real Detective by Inspector F.* published in 1862), who had been a chief of the French Sureté.

What characterises Harry Irving's approach to true crime writing is his confident placing of notorious crime by the side of major historical events and personalities. In his introduction to his account of remarkable criminals he wrote, 'Do not let us, in all the pomp and circumstance of stately history, blind ourselves to the fact that the crimes of Frederick or Napoleon [...] are in essence no different from those of Sheppard or Peace.' His criminology is therefore best seen as an investigation into the microcosm of a specific community as it linked to world events. Typical of this is his account of the Fualdes case of 1817 in Rodez, in the *department* of Aveyron.

A prominent judge called Dualdes, who had been busy during the Terror, was killed by a group of men. Harry writes the account of the murder with as much suspense and tension as a fictional thriller, describing the killers deciding to stab their victim to death as he was stretched across a table, with both a child and woman in hiding as unknown witnesses to the deed. The body was hurled into the river, but word got out, and a woman was heard saying to her neighbour, 'They bled him on the table like a pig.' Arrests were made, and witnesses then reported seeing a gang of men carrying something heavy in the evening by the river. The principal villain, a man called Bancal, is explained in typical analytical fashion: 'His poverty was no doubt acute, and if his confession is to be believed, his wife had been in two minds as to allowing her own child to be murdered for 500 francs.'

The high drama in the tale is the presence of the woman in the kitchen who heard all the talk regarding the murder, and also heard the dying moments of the victim: she was Madame Manzon. Her testimony gave the prosecution all they wanted. Harry maximises the dramatic effect of his tale of dark deeds in the provinces with this note:

> Some thirteen years after the execution of the murderers, a sinister discovery furnished grim proof of the good fortune of Madame Manzon [that she had not been found and killed] [...] In 1841 in a garden that at the time of the murder had belonged to Jausion, one of the killers, there were found two skeletons and by their sides were the rotting keyboards and two hurdy-gurdies.

So died two potential witnesses who were not as lucky as Madame Manzon.

Henry Brodribb Irving served in naval intelligence in the Great War, and then in 1918, he had a nervous breakdown, or at least that is how his daughter described the illness. In fact, he had a fatal anaemia, and his death was heralded by his physical decline. He died on the evening of 16 October 1919. His son noted in his biography that Harry had corrected the proofs of his last book *Last Studies in Criminology* recently, and was 'disinclined to concentrate on any book or paper for more than a few minutes.'

Within a short period, both sons of the great Sir Henry Irving had died. Harry's son wrote, 'Whereas the valedictory salutes to Laurence had grieved for a promise unfulfilled, Harry's obituarists harped on the pity of an original talent and of an intellect rare in an actor cramped by retrospection and the assumption of his father's mantle.'

He also knew William Roughead well: the writer discussed in my introduction and the presiding spirit of all things criminous. Roughead wrote, referring to his first book in the *Notable Scottish Trials* series, that Irving:

> Fell in love at first sight with my Jessie [Jessie McLachlan, the subject of the trial] and for her sake sought an introduction to her biographer, which effected, led to a friendship greatly prized by me and subsisting until his untimely death. My account of the case became for him a bedside book – his nerves were in such circumstances of the strongest; and he told me that it was the best murder he had ever read.

Henry Irving junior provides one of the few examples of the amateur criminologists who also acted, and so had the opportunity to step into the mind of the deviants in criminal history who had been placed in popular culture as a part of popular narratives. Normally, these were in the penny dreadful publications, but there was also a boom in dramas dealing with notorious crimes on the London stage and on provincial tours. Harry will perhaps be fixed in the imagery of theatrical history in his part of Dubosco in *The Lyons Mail*. There he is in the promotional photo, with necktie and dashing suit and collar, with his curly dark hair flowing out beneath his pork-pie hat, his face in an expression of anxiety, perhaps ready to break out into a defiant scowl. Becoming the part he played was an extension of his criminous interests in motivation, of course, and each half of his creative life complemented the other.

6
George R. Sims: Justice Campaigner and Celebrity

In the twenty-first century, many people are still familiar with the line, 'It was Christmas Day in the workhouse.' But they would have no idea who wrote that piece of sentimental verse. The author was George R. Sims, and we should remember him for something much more significant: his part in the establishment of the court of criminal appeal. This writer, one of the most prolific of all the Victorian writers, was a leading light of the Crimes Club, with his own private museum collection of criminal exhibits, and tales to tell at the dinners of his associations with notable villains and famous lawyers.

Of all the members of the club, George Sims was the one who most outstandingly represents the all-round jobbing writer of the time, with skills involving writing for the theatre, popular fiction, journalism, popular poetry, and humour. Add to that his interest in criminal matters and you have someone who many at the time thought was, in many ways, a fresh version of Charles Dickens. Sims had the status of a literary celebrity too, with a humorous public image. He wrote a weekly column in *The Referee*, from 1877 until his death in 1922, under the name of Dagonet. He reached the status of an institution – one that, along with bully beef and old folk songs, somehow defined what English culture as all about.

As Dagonet, he attracted the kind of media interest that today would be accorded to a popular comedian, perhaps a *Punch* writer, or a humorist such as the late Alan Coren. In 1895 for instance, a feature on his new book of travel pieces pointed out his similarity to one the greatest American writers: 'Mr G. R. Sims is not exactly a sentimental traveller, but he is a humorist in his way, and it is a way that makes one think that Mark Twain has not a little to answer for.'

We have an insight into that public humorist in a feature in *The Idler* in 1897, in which Sims was explaining the importance of his first book

The Social Kaleidoscope. He wrote in the feature of how he came through rejection by sheer perseverance:

> I was still in the city when my first book was published. I used, in those days, to get to the city at nine and leave it at six, but I had a dinner hour, and in that dinner hour I wrote short stories and little things that I fancied were funny and I used to put them in big envelopes and send them to different magazines [...] I never had one accepted.

Nevertheless, he never stopped trying, and by 1880, he was established. He wrote that it took him thirteen years to have something printed and paid for, but in writing about his early life, he recalled that at school he was the storyteller, and he naturally talked, wrote, and performed stories. He was destined to be a professional writer of some kind. When success came, it was grand and impressive: 'The editor of *The Dispatch* wanted a series of short complete stories. I asked to be allowed to try [...] Under the title of *The Social Kaleidoscope* I wrote a series of stories or sketches.' He became a personality, and what he really excelled in was conviviality. He was what today we would call an expert networker.

Sims became a member of the Unity Club – the beginning of his many activities in clubs – as Conan Doyle did, in order to meet his peers, and of course, to be given commissions. His first play was commissioned at the Unity Club, and theatre was in his blood; he wrote that he had been a regular play-goer from the age of six to the age of twenty-four, and then he began writing for the stage. In between his writing, he enjoyed horse racing and other sports, along with boxing. He became the kind of man the Victorian public adored: someone who could be a bluff, honest, game gentleman, mixing with all classes and having strong and amusing opinions on everything.

Of all his activities and his incredibly varied life, one particularly strange phase emerges in the footnotes of biography. In 1884, he applied for the chair of history at University College Liverpool. There is no mention of this in his autobiography, but the novelist George Meredith wrote to Sims in May 1884, 'Although my name, as one practising in the fields of light literature can be of but little value in seconding you, I can at least say that I know your accomplishments and hold you to be fully competent.' Sims had multiple accomplishments, but scholarly history was not one of them. He made a great deal of money in his time, mainly from his theatrical writings. The journalist George Sala wrote, 'Mr G. R. Sims makes as much as £5,000 by a comedy or a melodrama. For all I know he may make a great deal more.' Sala wrote of Sims' 'facile and sparkling pen', and he certainly was prolific, writing across several genres.

Beneath the image of the sports lover, enthusiast of the turf, and theatrical entrepreneur, there was also a man who was zealous for social reform. This began when, as he admitted, he was in the habit of walking in the 'low' areas of every town and city he visited. He wrote that in these walks he was generally safe, but that in Naples, he took his friend Charles Warner to see 'the seamier side', and felt that he was in danger of attack and robbery.

He was born in 1847, the grandson of a Chartist agitator called John Stevenson, and he notes in his autobiography that at the time of the mass Chartist meetings in the 1840s, his other grandfather was a special constable, and that the two ancestors would perhaps have faced each other on those great occasions. His education included a time at Hanwell Military College, and at Bonn in Germany. He emerged as a student of the criminous through a long succession of close-up acquaintance with notable villains, and with the places where the criminal classes were to be found. In his autobiography, he has memories of meetings with several notorious killers of the mid to late Victorian years, and he notes that his later crusades for criminal reform and against miscarriages of justice came from these meetings, along with the clearly significant experience of walking in the Borough one time and meeting a minister who, after listening to Sims talk about the 'poetry of poverty', said that he would show him the 'prose of poverty'.

Sims' outstanding contribution to the history of crime and law is surely the energy he gave in the campaign to put right one of the most sensational miscarriages of justice in British history: the case of Adolf Beck. His friend Max Pemberton wrote that:

> An outcry arose, but it was George R. Sims who led the battalions. He had known Beck, and liked and admired him. When the *Daily Mail* heard his story, the whole of its influence was thrown into the scale on behalf of this wickedly used foreigner, and a fierce campaign began.

Sims wrote in his autobiography:

> Only once in forty years have the friendly relations between myself and the guardians of the law and order been interrupted, and that was when I took up and fought in the *Daily Mail* the case of the unfortunate Adolf Beck. For a time, but only for a little time, Scotland Yard ceased to smile upon me. Certain statements I made were regarded as reflecting upon the Yard methods.

In this case, much was to depend on a handwriting expert. The great Lord Brampton, in his memoirs of 1906, said, 'I always took great interest in the class of expert who professed to identify handwriting. Experts of all classes give evidence only as to opinion; nevertheless, those who decide upon handwriting believe in their infallibility.' That comment should have figured in the case of Adolf Beck.

Beck had had a colourful and adventurous life previous to his settling in London. Max Pemberton gives this account: 'He had been a sailor and shipbroker; visited South America and there posed as a public singer; had been wounded during one of Monte Video's pleasant revolutions and finally returned to England where he made £8,000 over a Spanish railway concession.' He invested this great wealth in a Norwegian copper mine and lost it. As Pemberton commented, poor Beck was 'one of the unluckiest of mortals'.

Adolf Beck was arrested and charged with fraud and robbery in 1896, and was sentenced to seven years of penal servitude in Portland Convict Prison. He had been identified as a certain John Smith, whose crimes reached far back to 1877. A handwriting expert called Gurrin had stated that the writing of Smith and Beck were the same. Beck insisted on his innocence, and he set his solicitor, a Mr Dutton, to campaign for his release. In 1898, after the lawyer had discovered that Smith had certain physical attributes that would prove that Beck was not Smith, he contacted Bradford police commissioner, but the head of the CID Robert Anderson refused to support the claim. Incredibly, Beck was inspected in the prison to see if he was circumcised as Smith was, and he was found not to be. But he was not released: he was simply given a new prison number, and he completed the sentence. He was released on licence in July 1901.

Fate still had suffering in store for the Norwegian Beck. The frauds on young women continued, and the police instructed a young woman to loiter close to where they knew Beck was in lodgings, to entrap him. The woman was approached by a man who then disappeared, and Beck was arrested again. He was in prison when another fraud of the same kind occurred, and the man was taken into custody. A police office called John Kane realised that Beck and the man in custody were very similar, and so after some good police work, John Smith, alias Wilhelm Weiss and other names, was actually identified as a certain Wilhelm Meyer from Vienna. The great judge Travers Humphreys wrote about the case:

> I happened to see Smith in the dock at Bow Street when Beck came and stood close to him, and I should not have described them as being much alike [...]

but one could see that Beck, if put with several men picked out of the street, would be likely to resemble Smith more than any others.

This situation, to be fully understood, needs to be put in the context of the appeal procedure in the 1890s, before the court of criminal appeal was created in 1907. This explains why Sims started his campaign when he heard of Beck's plight after the first trial, when the solicitor put the case for a retrial. As one legal historian has explained, the repercussions of the campaign were highly significant: 'The only way to reverse the public belief that miscarriages of justice were an everyday occurrence, Hebert Gladstone told the House of Commons in 1907, was by the establishment of a court capable of hearing appeals of fact, law, and sentence.'

In 1883, a certain Jane Clark was indicted at Durham Assizes for a 'nuisance', which was in this case, 'Exposing the body of a child in a public highway.' This was a Common law misdemeanour, and Judge Denman told the jury, 'I am not at all sure that this case is free from doubt in point of law.' Denman finally announced that he had consulted his fellow judges, and he arrived at the decision that Jane had indeed committed an offence under the Common law. She was sentenced to six months in prison.

On the surface, this appears to be a hard, emotionless decision, inflicting a tough sentence on a poor women who was probably half-mad with poverty and anxiety. Her mental health is not in question, it seems. The decision rested on 'a point of law'.

What had happened when Denman consulted his fellow judges was that they had met to consider 'crown cases reserved'. This meant that a group of the best legal minds in the land would meet at Westminster Hall and help the judge to sort out a fair result. It was intended to handle cases heard at the quarter sessions, and so the variety of cases considered would be diverse, and would range in their seriousness a great deal.

This was in effect a measure to deal with matters that later would be part of an appeal process, but in 1848, when the reserved cases were first heard, there was no court of criminal appeal. The only option for an ordinary person, who could not afford to pay a top barrister to start the retrial process, was to hope that the judge at the first trial would not be sure of his verdict, and so be afraid that conviction was unsafe. He would take the issue to the court of Crown Cases Reserved. In the case of Beck, what happened was that in the trial after the entrapment, Mr Justice Grantham presiding was experiencing a degree of uncertainty. As the judge's biographer explained:

Counsel had been heard on either side, and the jury had returned to court with a verdict of guilty. Nothing remained but to pass sentence, and his Lordship had already scribbled on a pad the number of years he had decided to inflict, when suddenly he glanced at the prisoner. Then, to everyone's surprise, he said, 'I will postpone sentencing until next sessions. In the meantime the police will make further inquiries.'

His instinct, with the work of Sims in the press in mind, was right. Chief Inspector Kane then resolved the matter. A commission was appointed, and Beck was paid £5,000 in compensation. George Sims had done his part in this, and so prominent was the case and the egregious error from which poor Beck suffered, that the court of Criminal Appeal was soon in the process of being created.

Sims had good reason to be intrigued by a case of mistaken identity: he had been the subject of such a thing on two occasions. The most sensational one was when Sims was away on holiday in Switzerland, and a newspaper report back home told the world that George Sims the journalist had been pushed against the Duke of Cambridge, and that the Duke 'seized the journalist by the throat ad shook him like a rat'. There followed a number of press reports with the information that the Duke was in court, alleged to have committed assault: 'G. R. Sims [...] has had the Duke arrested for assaulting him [...] Sims, who was ill and weak, was pushed up against the royal Duke, who is old but stalwart [...] Our sympathies are with Sims.' It turned out that the man in question was one George E. Simms of the *Sunday Post*.

For material at the dinners, Sims also had another prominent involvement in serious crime. This time, it was the case of Madame D'Angely. Within eighteen months of the first club dinner, there was discussion in parliament of this subject. Mr Ward put the issue that had preoccupied Sims very succinctly:

> I beg to ask the Secretary of State whether his attention has been called to the case tried before Mr Denman on 1 May and dismissed, wherein a lady, Madame D'Angely, was charged with behaving in a riotous and indecent manner in Regent Street on the evening of 24 April last, and to the fact that police constables Page 429C, and Lucas 136C, and Constable 440C gave evidence on oath that the defendant had attended Regent Street persistently for three months previous for the purpose of committing the offence with which she was charged, and whether [...] he will say what action he proposes to take in the matter.

At the time, various MPs were eager to complain about 'shadowing' by the police, as had been done to Eva D'Angely, and the result of the debate was the promise by the Prime Minister that there would be a Royal Commission of inquiry. This was to look into the question of police corruption, especially with regard to how they were dealing with prostitutes or suspected persons engaging in immoral trades. Back in 1891, a Miss Millard had been charged in Aldershot as a disorderly prostitute, but when she was examined, she was found to be a virgin. In Madame D'Angely's case, her husband had first protested that his wife was totally innocent. Sims took up the cause, and in fighting her corner, accused the police of fixing the affair and of applying 'shadowing' strategies rather grossly. In the same year as Eva D'Angely, another woman, Miss X, was similarly charged with soliciting, but what emerged from this was that she had refused to have a drink with a police officer, who had decided to make her suffer after being rebuffed.

The Royal Commission reported that the police line of thought was that 'the main difficulty in enforcing the law is caused by the [...] impatience of the public [...] whenever there has been a mistake in arresting a woman on a charge of solicitation'. We can see with hindsight why Sims' campaign was successful in highlighting the police shortcomings.

The business of prostitution had another side to it, and that also became a forest fire of social and media panic at the time – the 'white slave traffic'. Sims was also aware of that, and commented in his autobiography that his work in print helped to raise awareness of that side of the sex industry of the time. Topics as the white slave traffic and opium dens fed the sensation pages of the tabloids. The records of the activities of the Thames police in this period show that they were very much 'in support' – the white slave traffic is a case in point. In 1910, Ernest Bell published his book *Fighting the Traffic in Young Girls*, and the impact of his cases, backed up by the famous story of W. T. Stead in 1885, who had 'bought' a young girl to sell to men in need of a young prostitute, caused a moral panic. In the 1912 Criminal Law Amendment Act, there was action against offences 'for the purpose of habitual prostitution' related to procuration of young girls. A letter to *The Times* by one Ettie Sayer had told nasty tales of young English girls being lured to work in New York.

In an article written for *The English Review* in 1913, Teresa Billington-Greig set about questioning the argument that such a trade existed on the scale stated. She did research the topic, summing up the statistics supplied by chief constables with the words, 'One may fairly deduce that there is no abnormal cause of disappearance acting in the case of girls and women alone.' Yet she was prompted to write by a host of disturbing stories of young girls being trapped and exploited.

The subject persisted, and Inspector Nixon of the Thames force records one experience that suggests such an offence: his boarding of a German vessel on the Thames at Blackwall. Local officers joined him, and the girls in question were in custody. His biographer wrote that the girls' condition was not clear when found: one girl was taken ashore unconscious and dumped. Nixon went on board with Sergeant Perry, and they found a girl 'naked except for her vest. Her eyes were fast closed, her face congested. Only the twitching of her limbs revealed that she still lived'. She was taken ashore into the hands of a matron at Woolwich. The offence was 'concealing women aboard', and Nixon rather too boldly visited another ship for the same reason, alone. He found out that there were half a dozen girls due on board just before midnight. He searched all the cabins and asked direct questions; the captain could not produce the seaman's discharge book ,and was in a difficult situation. Then a woman came on board, someone known to him, working the shore pubs.

There was no certainty that this was a case of white slavery: both instances may have been simply ladies of the night aboard the ship, servicing the crews. The important fact here is that such enquiries came within the remit of Nixon and his colleagues. They were 'in support' of bigger issues, from this kind of thing, to murder and smuggling.

Apart from his crusades, such as the Beck and D'Angely press campaigns, Sims also met several notorious criminals. This included meeting the notorious Dr Whitmarsh.

The term 'back street abortion' suggests a seedy quack doctor working in a poor district of some urban sprawl, treating poor desperate women with half-baked and dangerous methods of intrusive medical work. The case of John Lloyd Whitmarsh corresponds with this term very well, except for one detail: his premises were in Brompton Road. One might have expected a rather more progressive and educated clientele, but the fact is that this man was a very dangerous character. In 1898, he found himself facing a charge of murder.

The story is really a sad one, one of thousands of similar stories about 'women in trouble' down the ages. In this instance it was Alice Bayly, who worked as a saleswoman at a drapery shop in Woolwich. Alice started walking out with a man called Edward de Nobrega, a married man, and as it turned out, a womaniser. Nobrega's wife Annie first heard of her husband's mistress when a parcel arrived at her house addressed to a 'Mr Noble'. The parcel contained some bottles. The name and address of the sender were on the parcel, so Annie went to see her in Woolwich. She learned there what she thought to be the truth, that Noble and Nobrega were the same man – her husband.

Alice Bayly first met Nobrega in Molesey five years before these events. Annie and Alice had a tearful meeting, and the wife asked outright, 'Is there anything to be ashamed of in your friendship?' Alice broke down, but she never said that she was pregnant, merely going on to say that she had not known the man was married, and that she would never willingly see Nobrega again. Annie left, and the two never met again. Nobrega and Annie had been married for twelve years and had three children. It was a common situation in Victorian marriages, with the husband often having a mistress or looking for sex with prostitutes, but this time, the business was to lead to tragedy. Alice Bayly and Nobrega had decided that an abortion was the answer to her pregnancy, and the bottles in question were a prepared medicine by Dr Whitmarsh, containing mercury. Alice had died following a visit to Whitmarsh, and the death and been slow and agonisingly painful. The poor woman, just twenty-six years old, died at Charing Cross Hospital on 10 July.

Alice's mother told the story at the inquest where Mr John Troutbeck presided; Whitmarsh was being investigated with regard to a possible case of performing an illegal operation upon the deceased. Her daughter's health was normally very good, but she had started walking out with Nobrega for some years, and on 19 June that year, she saw that Alice was ill. There were pains in her joints and she was sick. Dr Clarke of Plumstead (where they lived) came, and thought the problem was rheumatic fever. Alice felt better on the following day, but then there was a relapse. A day later she was very ill again, and she said to her mother, 'The old man done it.' She then said that she had burned the letters, and began to weep and sob, saying that she had 'gone wrong'.

Obviously, the mother pressed Alice on the identity of the old man in question, and the young woman wrote the name and address on some paper. There was another daughter in the family, called Laura, and she sent a telegram to the address given. They urgently needed to see this medical man, whoever he was. Eventually, after receiving no reply, Alice begged her sister to go to the address and tell the old man to come. She said, 'I am dying [...] he has done it and he must come and see what he can do for me.' At first he did not come, but after another day had passed with Alice's terrible suffering, he did arrive.

Whitmarsh came to the sick woman, who told him that he had killed her, but his only reply was that she would be all right in a day or two. Her mouth was ulcerated, and she showed him that; it was noted by the family that the doctor smelled of alcohol, and he merely said that he would call again. When he returned, he was worried. Alice said, 'Oh doctor what have you done to me?' Even then, all he could do was give directions for a certain type of poultice to be prepared, and then he left.

Two other doctors were called, and Alice was taken to hospital. Before she died, Alice told her mother that she had had a miscarriage. A letter had arrived at their house that week, and it was from Nobrega. He wrote:

> All my thoughts are with you, and if I do not suffer physically like yourself, I do so mentally. I sincerely trust soon to learn that you are getting on towards recovery. If you think I can do anything to alleviate your suffering or to ease your mind, do let me know through your sister, who was very kind to me when I saw her on Thursday.

It was a tragic tale. After her death only a few pawn tickets were found on her; she earned £50 a year working in retail, and never saved any money. The abortion had of course been arranged and paid for by Nobrega. She wrote a note in reply to the letter, asking Edmund Nobrega to come and see her.

Laura gave testimony, and told of her visit to Whitmarsh. It turned out that he had ignored the telegram, which was lying on a table when she arrived at his house. He eventually opened it and thought that, as Plumstead was a long way, it was not necessary to go, for he knew that other doctors would be attending to Alice. Laura then met with Nobrega, and at that meeting he said he had never heard of a Dr Whitmarsh. Alice heard of this and said, 'Oh he won't own up to that,' and admitted that she had come to know that he was a liar. Not long before, Alice had asked Laura to lend her £4, but had not said what she needed the money for. But she had been for the abortion, and had found the money somehow. Nobrega later admitted that he had seen Alice looking very ill, and had given her a sovereign to pay Whitmarsh. They had all had enough of the quack by this point, and two telegrams were sent to him, telling him to stay away.

Other people who knew Alice gave their comments. Louie Dale, who had worked with her, said that she had seen Alice in great pain, but she had still continued serving customers. When Louie asked what was wrong, Alice just said that she had been into the city with her mother and it had 'knocked her up'. Ellen West, who also worked in the shop, had known Alice for six years, and had shared a flat with her. She recalled Alice receiving a bottle of medicine through the post, and that it had been broken. She had heard Alice say, 'That fool of a man has sent me some medicine through the post and it has got broken. When I was in the city on Thursday I had a bad headache and he said he had something to help.' This all seemed like a plausible cover-up tale. The witness did remember references to a doctor living in London at Brompton Road, but she had never heard anything of Nobrega taking Alice to a chemist.

Flora Horsfall, another millinery assistant, said that she found Alice in bed, complaining of severe abdominal pains. Flora was asked to go to the shop and collect the largest bath towel available. After that, Alice had said she would be all right, but the day after, she showed Flora her mouth. 'Her teeth were black and her gums of a brownish colour,' Flora said, and apparently Alice had said, 'Oh Miss Horsfall, surely I have not been poisoned!' She told Flora that she had 'had a draught' in London the day before. Owen Dale, who owned the shop, was naturally very concerned for his employee's welfare, and she commented that he thought she had been anaemic for some time. He had given her three weeks leave on the previous occasion of her illness (after the miscarriage).

Attending that coroner's inquest was the famous detective Drew, the man who was to be notorious work his work on the Dr Crippen case in 1910. In this instance, he was simply stating what actions were being taken to link these matters to Whitmarsh. He said that there had been no label on the broken bottle, but that enquiries were being made.

The Westminster coroner's court was certainly a focus for press attention by this time; poisoning cases and anything underhand, such as illegal operations, were of course good material for scandal. Attention now turned more closely to Nobrega. This was of special interest, for it was now learned that Alice had had a miscarriage almost a year before the taking of the medicine from Whitmarsh. The legal advisers for Nobrega had this put aside while forensic matters were discussed. Dr Thomas Stevenson from Guy's Hospital described the pathology. He only found one poisonous material present in the viscera: mercury. The key point in his extensive account of the condition of the organs was that there was nothing to indicate how the mercury was introduced into the body. The facts, he said, did seem to indicate that the mercury was administered in some other way than by mouth. The poison was present in the liver, kidneys, and elsewhere.

Dr Stevenson said that, if given in the right way, such treatment and such amounts indicated nothing unusual. But the references to the bottles, the ulcerated gums, and the mercury in the organs suggested that Whitmarsh needed to stand trial in court. Inspector Drew had actually had a model made of Whitmarsh's rooms made by PC Greenwood of M Division. All agreed that this matched the statements given by Laura Ivory, Alice's sister. Surely, only fine detail – matters pertaining to the place as a surgery for abortion practice – would be relevant, and although the first reports do not specify this, it arguably must have been Drew's intention in supplying the model.

Nobrega had not been called, so everyone had to wait for more details on his involvement. Nevertheless, the coroner concluded by summing up the reasons why the case had to proceed to criminal trial:

> If they were of the opinion that the deceased died by mercurial poisoning, they must say if that was due to an illegal action. The suggestion was that it was due to an illegal action, viz. the endeavour to procure an abortion. The procuration of an abortion was an illegal action and if death occurred as a direct consequence of a felony, it was laid down in the law that it was murder.

The jury had to decide if there had been such an attempt, and if that action was the cause of the death. The coroner reminded the jury that Alice had called Nobrega 'a wicked liar'.

More substance was given to Nobrega's very unpleasant character when it emerged that, as Alice lay dying in hospital, he had remonstrated with her about her previous miscarriage, and how she had not learned her lesson. But in the end, it was said by Alice before she died that Whitmarsh had operated on her, and so, in spite of other parties all playing their part in this tragedy – including, as the coroner pointed out, the editors of journals in which advertisements were placed for these dreadful services – it was Whitmarsh who was to stand trial for murder. Whitmarsh had agreed to do the operation for £4 in his surgery over a baker's shop in Brompton Road. Laura Ivory had said in court that she overheard a conversation at Whitmarsh's place, and after Laura had said she heard a man's voice say, 'It must come away [...] I am not going to risk my neck on the gallows for you or anyone else.' The questioning went like this:

> Mr Grain (prosecuting Whitmarsh): You were not listening – it cam upon you by surprise?
> Laura: Yes, it quite frightened me.
> Mr Grain: You heard it involuntarily, as it were?
> Laura: Yes, I heard Dr Whitmarsh say what I have said, quite distinctly.

The sheer repulsion felt by anyone hearing the details of the 'operation' must always be felt in this kind of context. Alice had told Dr Clarke when he attended her that she had kept something back from him: 'On Saturday I had a miscarriage. I was eight weeks pregnant [...] I went to town and a man passed an instrument [...] I came home and the miscarriage took place.' Inspector Drew had been to talk to her in Charing Cross Hospital, and she confessed to him that she had, in desperation when pregnant on the first occasion, also taken various other substances, saying, 'I have been on intimate terms with a man whose name I do not wish to disclose [...] I found myself pregnant and took other pills, I also took some epsom salts and some gin. It did not have the desired effect.'

Alice then described Whitmarsh and the circumstances of the operation. She had paid him £4 in gold, and he had taken her behind some curtains and a screen in his rooms. The mysterious doctor was then described, so we have out first visual glimpse of the shadowy figure. Drew summarised her account: 'Whitmarsh is about seventy years of age, height about 5 feet 6 inches. with rather grey hair and a moustache.'

Alice gave a dying declaration, and Inspector Drew guided her towards saying the words that would have guaranteed the next stage of the prosecution. That was at the Old Bailey, and as well as the repetition of all the facts as heard by the coroner, there is another memoir of the end of that trial by the journalist Robert Watson, who wrote:

> At the October sessions of the Old Bailey, '98, I was present when three men were sentenced to death, two on one day. Dr John Lloyd Whitmarsh was indicted for the murder of Alice Bayly by performing an illegal operation. There was a marvellous difference between the doctors when on trial. Dr William Mansell Collins wept, mourned and fainted and finally, when sentence was pronounced, was carried down the steps of the dock.

But there was something remarkable about this case, above and beyond the actual horrendous events: it was the first time that a prisoner charged with a capital offence was able to give evidence. The Act allowing that came in this year. In fact, as Watson wrote, 'No man ever stood in the dock on trial for his life more stolidly indifferent to his fate.' The full horror of his treatment came out: mercury administered in the vagina rather than the mouth.

The jury were in confusion and disagreement. At first they had only one in favour of an acquittal, who thought that the woman was more guilty than the man. When the time for an announcement came, it was thought by some that a manslaughter verdict would be reached. But Mr Justice Bingham, directed with regard to murder, and that such a verdict was the only one possible if the evidence was believed. Bingham said, 'There is no defence in this case [...] now consider your verdict and be quick about it.'

Robert Watson wrote that he had a friend who told him that Whitmarsh wrote of Holloway, where he had been kept on remand, as 'a living hell'. It was thought that he would get a seven year sentence. But with Bingham's words in mind, that was looking like a bleak prospect. Watson reported the closing words:

> Whitmarsh, in answer to the question put by Mr Avory, the clerk of the court, 'Have you anything to say why sentence should not be passed upon you according to the law,' said snappishly and contemptuously, 'No'. It was the first death sentence the judge had passed and he read the grim formula from a book. Whitmarsh passed hurriedly down the steps of the dock as if he had been a free man.

But the reprieve for Whitmarsh was received at Holloway. The old rhyme applied, as the reprieve came quickly: 'All that I ask is a short reprieve / till I forget to love and learn to grieve.' *The Times* announced the plain facts:

> The governor of Holloway prison has received the official documents committing Dr Whitmarsh, who was recently sentenced to death at the Old Bailey, to penal servitude for life. Dr Whitmarsh [...] will now be removed to Wormwood Scrubs Prison to undergo the probationary part of his sentence.

Sims, in his autobiography, recalled that he heard Whitmarsh sentenced to death, and that the man met Sims later: 'Dr Whitmarsh told me many years afterwards, when he had served the time to which the sentence had been commuted, that he lay in the condemned cell at night and imagined he could hear the workmen making ready the gallows on which he was to be hanged.'

There is no doubt that Sims went out of his way to be close to the criminals of the day, even when they were dead, as was the case with the dramatic national sensation of the Tichborne Claimant. Sims wrote that after Orton, the Claimant, had died in his Marylebone lodgings, he 'sat alone by his side in the Marylebone mortuary and took a final look at the familiar features before the coffin lid was screwed down'.

In fact, one murderer was very well known to Sims, and he went to call on Sims before he committed his crime. This was Percy Lefroy, who had written a pantomime for the Croydon Theatre, and Sims wrote of his personal 'criminal museum', in which he had kept that pantomime script. Items from that personal museum must have been taken along to many Crimes Club dinners. Lefroy had murdered a Mr Gold on a train while he was travelling to Brighton to meet a theatre manager. Lefroy came to see Sims, and there is something very strange in Sims' memoir: he wrote that Lefroy killed himself, stating:

I made an appointment to see him again, and I promised to try and get permission for him to emigrate, that he might reinstate himself in his profession. He did not keep the appointment. Shortly after our interview he was found dead in his bed, having taken poison.

However, the records show that Lefroy was hanged at Lewes, and an eye witness account was printed in the *Daily Telegraph* on 30 November 1881. Maybe Sims' memory let him down and he confused this case with another. After all, he knew so many criminals. He wrote that Lefroy came to see him before the crime was committed, and he was about to go to meet the manager of the Brighton Theatre to try to sell his play. He told Sims that he had previously provided himself with a revolver 'in order to commit suicide if he failed to sell the play'.

It does seem strange that Sims would recall a death of that nature that in fact never happened as it was stated in the memoir. A fervent criminologist such as Sims would be well disciplined mentally, and in a practical way in order to get the facts right, but such is the nature of memory – it may distort and mix up events, so that in this case, perhaps Sims was thinking of another acquaintance who took his own life. We have to trust an eye-witness account of such a dramatic event over a memoir written thirty years after this death.

The hanging of Lefroy was observed in close detail by the unknown journalist from *The Telegraph*, and in this we have one of the most detailed accounts of a prison hanging on record (public hangings ended in 1868, but journalists were allowed to attend enclosed hangings after that). The hangman was Horncastle man William Marwood, of whom the popular rhyme was circulated: 'If pa killed ma, who would kill pa? / Marwood.'

In fact Marwood, on the day of his execution of Lefroy, was as theatrical as his client. The witness wrote:

> As we filed into the yard, I noticed that we were being one by one saluted by a somewhat diminutive man clothed in brown cloth, and bearing in his arms a quantity of leather straps. There was nothing apparently in common between the grave and the gallows and the man, and for the moment I imagined that the individual who raised his hat and greeted us with a 'good morning gentlemen' was a groom who had chanced to pass through [...] and who was anxious to be civil. But to my horror [...] William Marwood it was who thus bade us welcome.

Lefroy appeared, and his last words were, 'I hope the rope will not break.'

In the memoirs of Montagu Williams, who defended Lefroy, we have a letter written by Lefroy to his girlfriend. Its content is the stuff of popular crime at its most entertaining, with this plea included:

> Dear Annie,
> I am getting this posted secretly by a true and kind friend, and I trust you implicitly to do as I ask you. Dearest, should God permit a verdict of guilty to be returned, you know what my fate must be unless you prevent it, which you can do by assisting me in this way. Send me, concealed in a common meat pie, made in an oblong tin cheap dish, saw file, six inches long, without a handle; place this at bottom of pie, embedded in under crust and gravy.

But he had a plan B, which was for her to send, also in the centre of a small cake, 'a tiny bottle of prussic acid'. Annie did not follow instructions. She wrote, 'I feel bitterly that I have not been the friend I might have been.'

George R. Sims was the Crimes Club member who really knew the microcosms of the criminal world very closely. Other writers may have been familiar with the courts and with lawyers, and also with the literature of crime, but only Churton Collins and Sims really knew criminals personally, except for the fact that Conan Doyle, when a boy at the Newington Academy in Edinburgh, had been taught by Eugene Chantrelle, who was convicted of murder in 1878. Sims ran Arthur a close second in terms of sheer notoriety too: in his persona of Dagonet he was widely known and loved; one writer has commented, 'Such was the fame of Dagonet that a pictorial envelope addressed Mr with the drawing of a dagger and a lawn tennis net, London, reached him.' He lived for forty years at No. 12 Clarence Terrace, Regent's Park, and as he said, 'opposite the ducks'. This reminds one of the famous example of letters being addressed to 'Verdi, Italy' finding their home.

Yet to his literary friends of the club, Sims was the lively character, a first-class raconteur, who knew London intimately, and who arrived with a choice specimen from his criminal museum and a stock of memories from his meetings with infamous rogues and celebrated men of law. In Max Pemberton's opinion, Sims was 'a brilliant criminologist' to match Churton Collins. He always had something behind him that the other first members, apart from Lord Pearson, did not: his journalistic influence. He campaigned in the way that his friend W. T. Stead did in his famous purchase of a young girl to highlight the trade in child sex in Victorian society. No doubt Stead would have done more campaigning, had he not gone down with RMS *Titanic*.

Sims also figured on the margins of the Ripper case. As he noted, as a journalist in 1888, he followed the Ripper crimes 'at close quarters'. His story about the Ripper murders was that, on the night of the double murder (the last two killings), a coffee stall merchant had chatted with a customer and said, 'Jack the Ripper's about tonight perhaps.' The man replied, 'Yes, he's pretty lively just now [...] you may hear of two murders in the morning.'

Sims relates that his book *The Social Kaleidoscope* was out, and the stall keeper saw Sims' picture on this. He pointed out Sims and said, 'That's the man!' Of course, this was absurd and led nowhere. As far as Sims is concerned, he wrote with complete confidence that the Ripper had thrown himself in the Thames, and that his body was found after being in the river for a month. He added, 'But there were circumstances which left very little doubt in the official mind as to the Ripper's identity.' Possibly, he was referring here to the suspect Montague Druitt, who committed suicide in the Thames in December 1888, but there is doubt about this, because Sims wrote that the man at the coffee stall looked like Sims as he was in 1888. The picture we have of Druitt is nothing like Sims. In fact, of the three main suspects itemised by Sir Melville Macnaghten in 1894, a chief constable at the time, Michael Ostrog looks most like Sims, as Ostrog was drawn in a Metropolitan Police publication after a warrant for his arrest was issued. Yet Ostrog was detained in a lunatic asylum. There is a remarkable similarity between the two sketches, and Sims' anecdote adds some kind of weight to the argument for Aaron Kosminski being the Ripper.

Today's viewpoint on George Sims is that he was an extraordinary man; a celebrity with power and influence in the theatre and in journalism, but also a man with varied other interests, such as horse-racing and boxing. The man who stepped into the Great Central Hotel in 1904, relishing the thought of a good meal and lively company, was known to almost all. One would think that the staff probably knew him; no announcement necessary.

To add another dimension to George Sims – one that Conan Doyle would have relished – he also found endless fascination in matters ghostly. He even claimed that Adolf Beck's spirit on the other side during a psychic adventure. It is typical of the man that, among his credits as a writer, we have a translation of Schiller into English verse and comic sketches for *Fun* magazine. In an age of impresarios, and movers and shakers in late Victorian culture, he stands out as someone who mixed with the lowest class and the aristocrats of literature and culture. Even this seemingly comprehensive assessment omits one other significant oeuvre of crime writing: his creation of the female detective Dorcas Dene. She first appeared in 1897, and had further adventures in 1898.

7

Max Pemberton

The portrait photos of the club members are mostly straightforward images of literary men in suits, looking suitably dignified and professional. This does apply to Max Pemberton, but we have his picture from 'Spy', the talented artist linked with *Vanity Fair* magazine, and there we have Max the pipe-smoking, waist-coated clubman: dapper, debonair, and elegant. He is well-groomed, sporting a handlebar moustache and a bow-tie. His autobiography has the voice of a classy raconteur, a man at home in the highest circles. He was well travelled, well connected, and thoroughly at home at society dinners. He was an enthusiast for the new pastime of motoring when it arrived in the 1890s, and was essentially a writer with a flair for style and good living.

He was born in Edgbaston in 1863, the son of a businessman, with a culture of traditional rural England around him: horse trainers, countrymen, riders to hounds, and stalwart types who sometimes treaded slightly over the line of the law when sport and country pursuits called for it. He went to the Merchant Taylor's School in Suffolk Lane, by Cannon Street Station in London, and then to Cambridge, where he was one of the 'hearties' – the sporting characters – with rowing as his real passion. He was at Caius College, and a picture survives of him with the Caius First Boat in 1883, complete with boater and blazer.

His later involvement with the Conan Doyle circle and matters legal and criminal was a logical development of his first steps in such matters; that of leaving Cambridge with a law degree. He disarmingly wrote that he knew not why he achieved this, but adds:

> Looking back over the years, I can recall some half a dozen occasions when my legal knowledge (or lack of it) has been of some service to me – once when I enabled a friend to get the better of a thieving money-lender and again, when

sitting with brother magistrates in Suffolk, when I was able to suggest courses which learned judges of the High Court subsequently approved.

But he was destined at first for Fleet Street.

He began as a freelance, and he noted that every door was shut. However, he persevered and found himself part of the *Vanity Fair* team, under the leadership of Gibson Bowles. Among the talents there was the artist Carlo Pellegrini, whose drawings under his *nom de plume* of 'Ape' defined the essence of the publication. Later, Max settled to work with *Chums* magazine as well, who had approached Max with the cheery invitation, saying that they were thinking of starting a paper for boys and asking, 'Will you take charge of it at a salary of £400 a year?'

He had arrived among the glitterati of the 1890s, and in his autobiography he included a survey of some of the writers he worked with in Fleet Street, including his future club companion Bertram Fletcher Robinson, editor of *The British Weekly* Robertson Nicholl, and editor of the hugely influential *Illustrated London News Clement Shorter*. Along with these was a man he knew well, Phil May, whom he called, 'The greatest master of the "line" since the days of John Leech.' The latter was the famous artist who had illustrated Dickens and been a master of lithographic prints and wood engravings. Phil May was a Yorkshireman, who in his younger days wanted to be a jockey, but moved into journalism and cartooning later. After working in Australia he came back to London just as Max was starting out there, and in 1896, when he joined the staff of Punch, he was well known for his political portraits. The Fine Arts Society had put on an exhibition of his drawings in 1896.

Max, with friends such as these in and around Fleet Street, became a *bon viveur*, and was surely one of the most sociable men of his class and profession in the 1890s. Like Sims and Harry Irving, he was also a theatre man. This began when he wrote a libretto for the French composer Chassainge, and this opened up a knowledge of French drama in him. In London, he mixed with theatre people; one of his closest friends was Louis Austin, who was Sir Henry Irving's private secretary, so we may see just how tightly-knitted were the men around the clubs and dinner societies of that time, most of them knowing the friends and families of the others in some way.

In this society, Max became the quintessential clubman. In his autobiography, he provides a survey of the dining clubs of his time. He notes that the men of the 'nineties were fond of dining clubs, possibly as a refuge from the rigours of married life.' He knew, or was a member of, a variety of these clubs in addition to the Crimes Club. They included the Omar Khayyam Club, the Sette of Old Volumes, the Johnson Club, the Dickens Fellowship and the Tatlers. If a new club was conceived, Max would be there, as in 1896 when the New Vagabond Club had its first meeting, along with Conan Doyle. The previous year *The Times* ran a feature on 'Sunday Clubland', with the focus on an event at The Royal Institute of Painters to launch a new club, 'whose main object is to provide entertainments of a refined and varied character on Sunday evenings'. The 'feature of the club' was to be 'the reading of short papers on subjects of general interest to be followed by a brief discussion'. Unusually, Conan Doyle was not there.

Max has given one of the fullest accounts of the first few years of the Crimes Club that we have, and his comments make it clear that an implicit activity of these criminologists was in solving mysteries. His assertions are backed up by the achievements of Conan Doyle, Churton Collins, and George Sims. Max puts the case for their success very boldly: 'Assuredly, its membership can hardly be matched for variety of distinctions by any similar society and not only has it this advantage, but it has achieved great things in its varied contests with the law and with injustice.' He wrote that it was also known as the Murder Club, but if so, then that was soon dropped.

He was seen generally as a powerful and influential editor, and in later life he was busy as the manager and public voice in advertising for journalism in all its aspects. We have a glimpse of this side of him in one of *The Idler*'s round table discussions in 1895, when the circle of writers held forth on whether their work was 'artful'. Max said of editing: 'So everyone thinks that he can tell us what to put into our newspapers [...] An editor who can say no in the grand manner is unquestionably an artist.' But then he added that in any club, an editor would be seen as 'a pilferer of ideas'. He was belittling his professional abilities of course, but that comment enlightens his character: he took pleasure is disarming comments and jokes against himself.

Among the ranks of the club members, Max has to be described as the entertainer, for his antics and adventures in journalism and media events usually brought a wry smile. One example of this is his role of judge in a word-making competition run by a company that made a product called Phosferine. The challenge put to the readers was to make as many words as possible from the word 'phosferine'. A certain Miss Violet von Sachs took the firm Ashton and Parsons to court for damages after a breach of contract. She claimed that she had submitted a list of 930 words, and her sister had put in merely 794, and yet the latter had won a prize. There was Max, in court, having to explain the situation. He said that most lists had been destroyed after the prospect of litigation loomed. He told the court that the system of conducting the competition had been arranged by himself, and after consultation.

It must have been one of the great barrister Mr Justice Darling's strangest cases, and he commented that such competitions did no good, and 'led to a great waste of time'. Ms von Sachs was awarded £250 damages. Time and again, Max dipped his fingers into any scheme that appealed to me, and that offered fun or playfulness. Although it reached court, the outcome of the competition still had some farcical aspects. Max also relished being involved in any kind of drama and performance, as his friends Sims and Irving did. A perfect opportunity for some good sport with a criminous flavour was the mock trial relating to Dickens' unfinished novel *The Mystery of Edwin Drood*.

On 8 June 1870, Dickens put down his manuscript of the novel before dinner. The next evening he collapsed and died, leaving one of literature's great unfinished works. As writers have commented, Dickens never gave anyone any clues about the mystery, and not a single suggested solution has ever pleased everyone.

Dickens' unfinished mystery has attracted attention from a number of writers, all attempting to offer plausible accounts of the disappearance of Edwin, and also trying to show that John Jasper, his uncle, is guilty of his murder, or whether there is another suspect. In the novel, there is also much mystery attached to the character of Datchery, who may be Drood or one of a list of possible characters. In 1872, H. Morford wrote a continuation, and there is another book, *The Decoding of Edwin Drood* (1980), by C. Forsyte.

In 1900, Max was selected as a member of the jury in an enactment of an imagined trial of John Jasper. This wonderful dramatic entertainment was devised and presented by the Dickens Fellowship, and it was a trial of Jasper for murder. G. K. Chesterton played the part of the judge, and Jasper was played by Frederick T. Harry. In the ranks of the jury, Max sat with other writers, including W. W. Jacobs, Arthur Morrison, and Hilaire Belloc, at the King's Hall in Covent Garden. *The Times* described the publicity event with great enthusiasm:

> An attempt will be made to create the atmosphere of the period at which the story was supposed to take place, and many of those who are taking part in the trial have made a special journey to Rochester [on which Cloisterham in the novel was based] in order to reconstruct the tale. The witnesses will appear in the costume of the period, and it has been suggested that representatives of the press should also attend in appropriate dress.
>
> (6 January 1900. p. 9)

A promotional image, with best wishes, of Conan Doyle. (The Idler, *1894*)

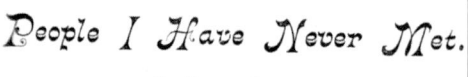

Top left: Harry Irving in his famous role of Dubosco from *The Lyons Mail*. (*Author's collection*)

Top right: Contemporary postcard of H. B. Irving as himself.

Left: George R. Sims. (The Idler, *1894*)

Above: Dan Leno at a charity cricket match. Music hall stars and authors played cricket for charity and social occasions. Conan Doyle and Mason were particularly talented in their whites. (*Author's collection*)

Above: Inspector Walter Dew, main detective on the Crippen case. (*Laura Carter*)

Above right: Alf Mason, as depicted by 'Spy'. (*Spy in* Vanity Fair)

Right: The Tichborne claimant, Orton, who Churton Collins got to know well. (*From a contemporary anonymous broadside*)

A handbill for the Lefroy case, 1881.

Above: Charlie Peace in a contemporary popular magazine.

Above right: Crippen's arrest after the telegraph message. (*Author's collection*)

Right: Cover illustration from *No. 7 Saville Square*.

TYPES DE CRIMINELS

Pl. VI

P. R. Voleur napolitain

B. S. Faussaire Piémontais

BOGGIA assassin

CARTOUCHE

G. MARINI femme de brigand

DESRUES empoisonneur

1. P. C., brigand de la Basilicate, détenu à Pesaro.

2. Voleur piémontais.

3. Incendiaire et cynède de Pesaro, surnommé *la femme*.

4. Misdea.

Left and above: From Cesare Lombroso's *Delinquent Man*, one of the dominant criminological theories of Conan Doyle's time. (*A French translation of Lombroso from the 1890s*)

An impressionistic sketch of Conan Doyle. (The Idler, *1895*)

Sir Arthur Conan Doyle. (The Idler, *1895*)

"'MRS. THURSTON'S LITTLE BOY WANTS TO SEE YOU, DOCTOR.'"

Witnesses were expected to express their own theory of the crime. The actors were thoroughly into the roles they were assigned, and as the chairman of the jury was George Bernard Shaw, there was much humour involved in the proceedings. Shaw stood up to enjoy some fun at the expense of the actor who played Mr Christarkle, saying that he was a snob. The actress playing Helena Landless, sister of Neville, the main suspect in the novel, stated that she had lunch with the mysterious Datchery. Others thought that she and Datchery might be the same person. As for the defence, the main argument there was that Drood was in fact still alive, their main witness being the woman who ran the opium den in the novel. The actress Miss Prothero made a special effort at Cockney to entertain the court.

In the end, Chesterton summed up that Mr Jasper had to be sentenced for the offence of manslaughter. Shaw and his jury created a stir, insisting that the jury had arranged their verdict over lunch. Chesterton discharged the jury. *The Times* ended, 'Thereupon the judge committed everybody present, except himself, for contempt of court, and wished a general goodnight.'

Max Pemberton's own writing received only mild praise. Reviewers tended to agree that his stories were plain and familiar; one writer commented in 1900 that Max did not sin 'by producing anything out of the common way'. He was thoroughly at home amongst other literary men, and was philosophical about the profession, as he commented in a survey of the successful writers of his day: 'The guests upon the star-scattered grass are few, though remembrance of others endures and fortifies.' One book of his that had a notable impact was *The iron Pirate*, written while he was editor of *Chums* in 1893.

Later in life, he was to have fiction regularly published, much of it by Mills and Boon, before they specialized in romantic fiction. He became a director of *Northcliffe Newspapers*, and ran the London School of Journalism. He was an inveterate letter-writer to the papers, with strong opinions on everything from military honours to charity projects.

John Hay Beith summed up Max's character very well:

> At the Garrick he always had people around him for he was very well liked and welcome at any table. He was full of reminiscences and had a tremendous memory for faces. Regarding the man he was in 1904 when he sat to dinner with his Crimes Club friends, he was not as deeply immersed in criminal investigations as most of them, but as his obituary in *The Times* pointed out in 1950, he had a serious interest in criminology, which he turned to good account in his books.

In other words, he was the one writer in the fraternity who kept his criminological interests as part of fictional works, rather than seeing any possibilities for writing true crime. This may be seen in his very first novel of 189, entitled *The Diary of a Scoundrel*.

His favourite club was probably the Savage, as he wrote that when he first attended their meetings, it was above a Turkish baths, and he described the club as 'joyous'. He stressed the status of the place in Bohemian circles, with a strong dash of theatrical flavour in its membership. That is where he was most at home, in the theatre, one has to conclude. But he loved the retailing of crime stories, and perhaps his most significant one is his account of fellow club member Arthur Diosy and his Ripper theory. This was, as Max had it from Diosy, that the maniac of Whitechapel was 'the victim of black magic'. Max wrote, 'In every case, he declared, even when one of the murders was committed under the nose of a policeman, there had been a pentagon of lights. In the street case, this pentagon had been formed of the stumps of five matches; in the houses themselves, candles had been used.'

The thinking of occult studies that interested Diosy was that this paraphernalia gave the person involved the cloak of invisibility. Other details were the presence of goat's hair and other symbolic materials. Max was convinced that the police listened and made further enquiries regarding black magic, but other club members are not so sure that he was taken seriously.

How are we then to understand and place Max Pemberton in the Crimes Club circle? He has to be seen as the instance of the convivial raconteur par excellence: the talker and entertainer. Of course, he had his Cambridge law degree, but never practiced, so his knowledge will have been sound, yet without practical knowledge from experience (as in Oddie's case), he would have had his limitations. His notable successes were in popular fiction and theatre: he had the ability to seize on the heart of a story immediately and to see its potential. There is no doubt that his vast experience of journalism would have made him thoroughly at home in a group that included Sims and Pearson.

8

BERTRAM FLETCHER ROBINSON AND *THE HOUND OF THE BASKERVILLES*

If we wanted to catch the spirit of the more sporty members of the club, it would have to be the jolly jape recalled by Max Pemberton concerning Fletcher Robinson and some friends. He wrote that Fletcher and Percy Illingworth were sharing a flat in Ashley Gardens when Owen Seaman was the editor of *Punch*. Seaman asked both of them to come to lunch with him at the Reform Club, but told each one not to tell the other. Both turned up for the meal, each in his own hansom cab, after they had refused to share a cab to preserve the supposed secrecy. As Max noted, they were 'a merry company, great athletes all and "blues" to a man'.

Robinson was, in keeping with most of his club friends, an all-rounder in an age of jobbing writers. Yet his real specialism was sports writing, and he wrote several volumes for the Isthmian Library on all kinds of sports. He was tall and athletic, good company, and thoroughly sociable. He was born in Wavertree in 1870, and then the family moved to Ipplepen in Devon, where he attended Newton College, a place with several famous alumni, including Arthur Quiller-Couch, known to all in literary circles simply as 'Q'. The headmaster at the time was George Townsend Warner.

Robinson was a writer in his early years, producing a series of essays on American writers for the school magazine, and winning a special prize for English in 1882. He read history at Jesus College, Cambridge, and there he wrote for Rudolph Lehmann's journal the *Granta*. With Lehmann, he hosted a *Granta* dinner at the Reform Club in 1893. He was active in debating societies, and clearly had high intelligence, an intense curiosity about everything, and a very bright, outgoing nature. He was always going to make good social connections and be well liked. His first book was *Rugby Football*, edited by Max Pemberton in the Isthmian Library. But he wrote fiction too, and his first story appeared in *Cassell's Magazine* in 1899.

His acquaintance with Conan Doyle began in their mutual work in the Boer War. Robinson was sent there as a war correspondent by Lord Pearson (later a member of the club also). They stayed at the Mount Nelson Hotel in Cape Town, and got to know each other on the journey home. When they stayed at the Royal Links Hotel in Cromer to enjoy some golf, the holiday became a momentous occasion in the history of English literature. Here, Robinson told Conan Doyle about the legend of the great hound on Dartmoor, a topic that goes deep and wide in English folklore, with various giant spectral dogs being recorded in the oral traditions of places as far apart as Yorkshire and Suffolk. Conan Doyle let the notion gestate in his imagination, and soon after the idea for *The Hound of the Baskervilles* was maturing. Editions of the book now have the preliminary note, 'This story owes its inception to my friend, Mr Fletcher Robinson, who had helped me both in the general plot and in the local details.'

Everyone involved in the arts today knows that, as the cliché goes, 'there is no copyright on ideas'. After the immense success of Conan Doyle's novel, naturally there were voices in certain quarters that thought that Robinson had been badly done by. This stems from the fact that the idea began by mutual agreement as a joint book. Conan Doyle told Greenhough Smith of *The Strand* that the book he described would be a joint venture, with two authors. Circumstances combined, one might say, to make commercial factors dictate that a work of that kind would be best as a Conan Doyle story, especially when the creator of Holmes realized that *The Hound* was best as a new Holmes and Watson story. For completely practical reasons, Robinson was squeezed out, but the important point here is that Conan Doyle paid Robinson the huge sum of £500 in 1901, and made more payments after that.

Paul Spiring has delved deeply into the life and works of Fletcher Robinson, and he has definitively removed any suspicion that Conan Doyle exploited Robinson. Clearly, Conan Doyle originally felt that it was a joint work, for he wrote to his mother, 'Fletcher Robinson came here with me and we are going to do a small book together [...] a real creeper.' Matters progressed and Holmes was revived. As is well known, Conan Doyle had wanted to leave Holmes behind and move on to his historical novels after the publication of the *Adventures* and the *Memoirs* of the great detective between 1891 and 1893. *The Strand* announced that Holmes was back, and that *The Hound* coincided with the theatrical version of Holmes currently on in London under the direction of William Gilette.

Conan Doyle needed to see Dartmoor of course, and he went with Fletcher Robinson. They stayed at the Duchy Hotel in Princeton, just a few miles from Dartmoor Prison (called Princetown at the time). They met a coachman called Henry Baskerville, who relished his involvement, and Conan Doyle wrote enthusiastically that he and Robinson were loving the research on the formidable terrain of the wild moors and mires around them.

Robinson also wrote of the research trips, noting that they met officers from the prison:

> In marched four men, who solemnly sat down and began to talk about the weather, the fishing in the moor streams and other general subjects [...] As they left I followed them into the hall of the inn. On the table were their four cards. The governor of the prison, the deputy governor, the chaplain, and the doctor had come, as a pencil note explained, 'to call on Mr Sherlock Holmes'.

The character of Selden, the escaped convict in the novel, is important in adding another dimension of unease out in the wild where the hound roars. The two writers at the hotel may have been told about the escape attempt in 1879, when a group of eight convicts hopped over a hedge while in a work party. After an alarm whistle had blown, a party of labourers nearby helped officer recapture the escapees. Then, very soon after Conan Doyle and Robinson were there, another escape occurred when two prisoners, Silvester and Frith, made a dash for freedom.

Conan Doyle was absolutely direct and honest in his acknowledgement of Robinson, writing at the time, 'My dear Robinson, It was your account of a west country legend which first suggested the idea of this little tale to my mind. For this, and for the help which you gave me in its evolution, all thanks.' As has often been noted, Robinson's role was as the supplier of a narrative that could be explored and developed by Conan Doyle, the most experienced fiction writer of the pair.

In spite of all common sense, matters familiar to anyone who writes for deadlines and for readers of a given genre, wild theories emerged, and we have to lament the fact that Fletcher Robinson's memory is somewhat affected by one of the oddest. In 2008, the suggestion that Conan Doyle murdered Robinson to cover up a scandal finally ended when the Exeter Diocese Consistory Court stopped an attempt to exhume Robinson's remains. The wild notion behind this was that Conan Doyle had been having an adulterous affair with Robinson's wife, along with, of course, the imputation that Conan Doyle had stolen *The Hound* plot. Robinson died of typhoid after a trip to Paris on 21 January 1907. Once again, Paul Spiring stepped in to do the work of a proper, sound historian and biographer against the groundless sensational speculations of the originators of this murder story. As the local newspaper reported, feeling was strong against the exhumation, 'Sixty objectors wrote to the diocese to protest [...] including the rector of Ipplepen, the parochial church council, and the chairman of the Arthur Conan Doyle Society, Squadron Leader Philip Weller.'

This kind of groundless assertion often leads to falsifications in the popular media, and in fact, in an episode of the television paranormal investigation series *Most Haunted,* the murder theory was again discussed. In this way, the general population, without full explanation or knowledge of the foundations of such tales, apprehends and absorbs only a fragment of the narrative. As a result, distortions and falsifications abound.

These matters blind us to the perception of the writer who sat in the Great Central Hotel at the Crimes Club dinner – a man with only three years to live: Fletcher Robinson. He had been a very busy man. In fact, the friend of Conan Doyle, Oddie, and the rest of the club had worked with P. G. Wodehouse on several short plays, dozens of short stories, a great number of journalistic pieces, and eight books. In his connections with *Vanity Fair* and *The World,* he had been in the vanguard of the new journalism for the man of fashion and adventure, which had sprung from the 1890s male romance in the novels of Rider Haggard and A. E. W. Mason (the latter a club member). Robinson was exactly right as the template for the type of British man who was fired and intrigued by the Great Game with Russia, the emergence of espionage and exploration, and the discoveries of new lands.

He was writing in that milieu, the age in which for instance, the quality journals celebrated in depth the visit of Henry Morton Stanley to Britain in 1890, and the military endeavours against the Mahdi in the Sudan. It was the great age of dangerous travel, as typified by Harry de Windt, with his journey from Paris to New York via Siberia overland, and of course, with the spirit that was to lead to the Scott expedition, and the mountaineering exploits of men and women across the world in clubs and organisations that aimed at extending frontiers and scientific knowledge.

Fletcher Robinson was immersed in that world, and of course he had reported on the Boer War for Pearson's *Daily Express* between 1900 and 1904. He had plenty of tales to tell, and he wrote across a wide spectrum in the markets of his time.

He was an amateur criminologist of course, and this interest expressed itself most prominently in his detective short stories: these became *The Chronicles of Addington Peace,* published in 1904. His detective was in the police rather than a loner like Holmes – he was within the Scotland Yard CID outfit. In a group of such men who tended to be rather more devoted to the true crime elements of criminology, he was perhaps one of the least determinedly criminous of the society, but like Max Pemberton, he would surely lighten occasions, and help the group to cohere and the occasion become memorable. In many ways, he is an inscrutable character, and his interest in crime and law is marginal, behind the sporting passions and the adventure. But he was perfectly capable of writing a thrilling story, no doubt learning some skills on plotting from people like Conan Doyle and the other natural storyteller of the club A. E. W. Mason.

We only know of one topic at a Crimes Club meeting at which Robinson was present. This was a meeting at Pemberton's house in 1906, when Max addressed his friends on the subject, 'An attempt to blackmail me.' There is a veil of mystery over what this could possibly have been. We have to speculate, as Max was only guilty of tiny peccadillos, as we all are, that any transgression he may have had is shrouded in obscurity, and whether this may have been linked to the competition scandal that went to court.

Without Bertram Fletcher Robinson, Conan Doyle would have struggled to create Grimpen Mire and the legend of Hugo and the hound so powerfully. Sadly, Robinson was the member of the club who died first, surely before he had developed fully as a writer. In fact, it is tempting to speculate that he would have more than likely gone on to write more material with a basis in the crime narratives that he was discovering with his friends and their stories of dark deeds around the table. In some of the promotional material on him, in anthologies and journals for instance, Robinson is stated as being Conan Doyle's collaborator on *The Hound of the Baskervilles*, and if we stretch that meaning a little, it is quite true.

9

A. E. W. MASON: WRITER AND SPY

Thirty five years after the first club meeting, Alf Mason (as his friend Somerset Maugham called him) attended the inaugural dinner of the junior Crimes Club, called The Black Maria Club. We know little about this, apart from the fact that the dishes at the meal related in some way to infamous villains of the past. The writers responsible for the new club were as distinguished in their time as were the original club members, and Alf Mason was still there, as entertaining as ever.

When he arrived as a new author on the publishing scene in the mid 1890s, he was, along with most of his peers, keen to participate in literary club life. He had started life as an actor with touring companies after leaving Oxford, and then, determined to succeed as a writer, he produced two novels, the second of which, *The Courtship of Morrice Buckler*, was something of a best-seller, and made his name familiar to those in literary circles who read the reviews.

At that time however, the future author of *The Four Feathers* and Crimes Club enthusiast was thirty years old, and was quite familiar with the bread line as far as his writing life was concerned. With a small allowance from his father, he had enough to live in a flat in Queen Anne's Mansions, so he was hardly living in squalor, and he worked hard and made friends. In fact, two of his friends at the time were and are extremely famous: they were Oscar Wilde and W. B. Yeats. At the time, Yeats was a struggling poet in the Rhymers' Club, and Wilde was rich and famous, it being not long before his fall from status and favour. It says a great deal about Mason's sheer charm and affability that he could chat with Wilde in expensive restaurants, while only a few years earlier, he had worked as a deck hand on a trawler and played bit parts in touring theatre companies in the provinces.

In fact, Mason met Wilde at Oxford, at the same time as he would have known another member of the drama circles there who was to be a club member: Lord Albert Godolphin Osborne. It was a small world, the milieu of letters and the stage in the 1890s. Everyone either knew everyone else who was anybody, or they knew *of* them. So it was that Mason and Wilde talked writing and life over lunch on one day, and Mason and Yeats would wander the streets, planning and sharing ideas the next. Wilde, Mason wrote, had been friendly, and had said that there was always luncheon at one o'clock at the Café Royal. Mason had also added that his friend was thinking how much the young aspiring actor-writer would need a square meal.

Wilde did more than feed the young Mason: he gave him writerly advice. Mason was working on his first novel *A Romance of Wastdale* at the time, and he told Wilde it was a story about a brother and a sister. Wilde said, 'No [...] that won't do. Everything in life has its symbol. Passion has its flower. And affection between a brother and a sister has its symbol too. But my dear fellow, it's cold boiled mutton.'

Mason was a likeable, courteous, and adventurous man. One of his friends, E. V. Lucas, wrote, 'Mason is a good talker, with many curious experiences, both his own and others, to relate, but a most stimulating listener. His laugh is famous in both hemispheres.' As his biographer, Roger Lancelyn Green wrote after the success of his second novel that 'the doors of the world of society' were thrown open to him. One particularly interesting element of the bonhomie and brotherhood we see in the club is the place of sport, and most strikingly, of cricket. Mason was a good cricketer, as was Conan Doyle, and Mason met J. M. Barrie in 1898 on a cricket field. Barrie had started a cricket team called the Allahakbarries, and in the ranks were Conan Doyle and E. W. Hornung (who married Conan Doyle's sister), amongst other literary types. Lancelyn Green noted that the matches were, in Barrie's words, 'riots of delight, good fellowship, and indifferent cricket'. In these matches, the worlds of authorship and the stage met. The great comedian Dan Leno also took part in cricket matches, and there is something about the atmosphere of those occasions that gives an insight into the Crimes Club – the spirit behind it and the atmosphere that dictated the events.

The team's name came from Barrie's asking two famous African travellers what the African for 'Heaven help us!', and so 'Allah akbar' became Allahakbarries. Mason was one of the most exuberant and enthusiastic players, as Barrie recalled: 'A. E. W. Mason, fast bowler, ran through the opposing side, though one never knew in advance whether he was more likely to send the bails flying or to hit square leg in the stomach.'

Mason was, like Pemberton, a member of the Garrick Club as well, and he enjoyed a party or a dinner as much as anyone, but he had a dynamic work ethic and could apply himself to a writing project with intense vigour and determination. At Oxford, he had seen his friend Arthur Quiller-Couch set about writing a novel to earn money and settle debts, and he saw that 'Q' had succeeded in the enterprise. No doubt that spurred him on. By 1903, he had really established himself, notably with *The Four Feathers*, which had been partly inspired by a visit to Egypt and the Sudan, where he met the great soldier Sir Reginald Wingate, and more significantly in terms of the novel, Slatin Pasha, Wingate's Austrian ally in military intelligence, who had been imprisoned and kept in chains by the Mahdi.

A picture of Mason taken in 1902 for *The Tatler* magazine presents an image that would suffice for any one of the hundreds of literary people who were able to work in large studies with vistas of London seen from their windows. By the time of that picture, he was established; no longer wandering the streets with Yeats or dining with Wilde. He had been watching, reading, and learning for some time. Unlike the other club members, he had tasted the hardships of working class labour in that short period at sea, and he had also known the poor lifestyle of the travelling player. We have to imagine the sheer level of astonishment and wonder around the table at the Great Central Hotel when aristocrats and well-heeled Oxford men listened to Mason's tales from his days in digs in Huddersfield, or pulling in a trawling net on the North Sea.

He had a good deal of humour and a touch of eccentricity about him, and this entertained his friends. J. M. Barrie for instance, wrote in a letter to Violet Meynell:

> He is loved all over the place and gets wound up by big meetings to great effect. I have been reading a bit of his next novel. His heroines [...] are always drawn from the lady he is in then in love with, and by the time I see the proofs it is always off but he keeps her in, and roars his great laugh when attention is drawn to the circumstances. He is as big a swell as ever, but his socks don't match and so all is well.

Mason had good looks, rude health, and abundant energy. At the peak of his success, when the Crimes Club enjoyed his company, his working day, as described by Roger Lancelyn Green, was typical of the author with deadlines and discipline: 'At that time his day started at eight; after breakfast he rode in the park, and returning, set to work at about eleven, writing often without a break until four or five.' He told his biographer that it took him around a year to write a book, and he described his approach to writing very clearly: 'I do not begin until I have the whole scheme absolutely fixed in my mind, beginning, middle, and end. I am a somewhat laborious writer, and write out each chapter two or three times over.'

Mason was born in Camberwell in 1865, to middle class parents. After a dame school, he was eventually sent to Dulwich College, and his love of acting found its first expression there. At Trinity College, Oxford, he was able to express himself both on stage, for the fledgling Oxford University Dramatic Society, and also in debates. His first taste of club life was at university too, as he joined the Gryphon Club. In fact, when we bear in mind that he spent a short time as Liberal MP for Coventry and played on the London stage during his student years, his future was hinted at – all except writing of course.

His professional acting career began in touring with the Compton Comedy Company, and he played the head role in Arthur Murphy's *The Way to Keep Him*. Remarkably, as he got to know Yeats, Mason was given the part of John Bruin in Yeats's first performed play – to plenty of mocking from the gallery. But one small success may lead to another, and this persistence opened up a role for him in Bernard Shaw's *Arms and the Man*, in which he played Major Plechanoff. He then wrote his first play, and earned his first payment from writing a short piece entitled *Blanche de Maletroit*, produced in 1894.

By the turn of the century, established as a popular novelist with *The Four Feathers,* and with *Clementina*, a story set in the seventeenth century, there were adaptations of his work for the stage, notably by his club friend Harry Irving. He also worked with the great actor-producer Beerbohm Tree (another amateur criminologist).

Mason's detective is Inspector Hanaud. Like Irving, and also LeQueux, he was drawn to French settings and culture. His Hanaud stories offer detective work in a justice system unlike the British, and although the character has something of Holmes in him, he is very distinctive, and the mysteries, starting with *At the Villa Rose* in 1910, are tightly done, with excellent plots and a light touch when it comes to the stories' explanatory elements.

But in terms of Mason's life as it touched on crime of any kind, unlike the lawyers and amateur sleuths of the club, his talent lay in espionage, and he figures in one of the most significant operations in twentieth century wartime spying. His path crosses with Conan Doyle again in one aspect: that of propaganda. At the beginning of the Great War, Lloyd George had become aware that a propaganda machine was required, and several prominent writers were brought into area of activity such as producing leaflets and using the press. Conan Doyle, along with Arnold Bennett, Chesterton, and several others, formed the group of potential writers at the call of the state, and Mason joined them. As we now know, Arthur Ransome and Somerset Maugham became fully-fledged spies working abroad, and Mason was to join their ranks. Perhaps unexpectedly for those who knew him, Mason, at the age of forty-nine, elected to try for the army at the front. He succeeded and was made a captain in The Manchester Regiment. But in 1915, his life changed dramatically when the man in charge of a very specific piece of intelligence work, Admiral Reggie Hall, had need of Mason's talents.

Some explanation is needed of the importance of naval intelligence at the time. Churchill himself had been well aware of the need for the reform of intelligence within the army, certainly since the Boer War. He had been clamouring for reform before the end of that conflict. In 1901, he had written, 'The whole intelligence service is starved for want of both money and brains.' In the House of Commons, he confronted the estimates made by Sir John Broderick, the Secretary of State for War, on the costs of army reform, and he spelled out the advantages of reforming the intelligence branch. Lord Haldane's cousin Aylmer told Churchill that Germany had over 200 intelligence officers, whereas England had around 20. The pressure group needed a spokesman, and it certainly had one in Churchill, who spoke of the need for 'an army of elasticity, so that comparatively small regular units in time of peace might be expanded into a great and powerful army in time of war'. He explained that for that to happen, what was needed was 'an efficient and well-staffed intelligence department'.

When it came to a diplomatic incident such as the Agadir Crisis of 1911, other aspects of intelligence work became apparent. After visiting London in May 1911, the Kaiser Wilhelm II stated that he intended to step in and claim a place in Morocco for Germany, responding to a revolt in Morocco in which tribesmen had forced French troops to move in and protect Tangiers. Germany thought the time was right to annexe a part of Morocco, and the Kaiser had a gunboat sent there. Britain issued a challenge to that, embodied in a speech by Lloyd George in which he said, 'If a situation were to be forced upon us, in which peace could only be preserved by the surrender of the great and benevolent position Britain has won [...] peace at that price would be intolerable for a great country like ours to endure.'

What this did do, in spite of Germany's withdrawal from confrontation, was create a cast of mind in the German naval command regarding future confrontation, and espionage was the first step to being prepared. The Kaiser supported a statement by his Admiral von Heringen that a clash with Britain would be welcome, and German intelligence adapted to work that would support this long-term aim. The man in charge, Tapken, started to plan actions that would lead to the Royal Navy being watched and monitored from close range within Britain, with major ports as the first espionage target.

In England, the writers of books on espionage were playing their part in the coming acceleration of intelligence organisation. Erskine Childers's novel *The Riddle of the Sands* (1903) concerns two yachtsmen who, while in the North Sea, come accidentally across naval war preparations at a place called Borkum. Childers envisaged a major plan of invasion, launched across the sea from Holland. Articles with titles such as 'The Drama of the Missing Spy' and 'Secrets of the French Foreign Office' were everywhere in the popular press, and of course the Dreyfus affair of 1894, followed by Emile Zola's famous essay 'J'Accuse' in 1898, opened up a whole new rage for literature about spies and traitors in the popular media.

It was widely known that that British sea power was still burgeoning, particularly when the development of the *Dreadnought* is considered. In 1905, Earl Cawdor became First Lord of the Admiralty. He had formerly been a major industrialist, and he was not First Lord for very long, but in his time in that position, he and 'Jacky' Fisher had a stunning impact on the navy. Fisher suggested to Cawdor that the whole fleet should be redeployed. Cawdor relished the thought of being responsible for such an achievement, and however large the task, they both warmed to it. The main fleets were repositioned, with the Mediterranean Fleet based in Malta and the Channel Fleet at a range of home ports. As the Atlantic Fleet was to be in Gibraltar, there was a clear indication to Germany that Britain was determined to retain a tight grip on key strategic positions for any confrontations that might occur. Furthermore, the positioning of the fleets was in line with Napoleonic history, a fact the Germans would have been well aware of.

Britain therefore had several fleets across the globe, and when the Great War came, as Germany had developed her navy on a grand scale, naval intelligence was clearly going to be paramount. At that point, along came Reggie Hall, reacting to initial work done by Maurice Wright, a Marconi engineer who worked out how to intercept wireless messages at long range. Wright and Captain Round developed this technology, and of course, Reggie Hall at the Admiralty knew what a phenomenal discovery this was.

A truly significant intercept was the access to what is known as the Zimmerman Telegram, in which Germany offered to return former land they had lost in the war with the United States if Mexico would ally themselves with Germany. Enter Alf Mason, working with the dashing figure Sir Hercules Langrishe, with a task – to destroy the German radio station in Mexico at a place called Ixtapalpa. The Germans were running a radio station there, using the recently invented audion lamps, created by Lee De Forest. This was a tube with a filament that was controlled by a grid. The technology made it possible to make signals from radio accessible – a device for interception.

Mason later described the situation in Mexico: 'The soldiers were in a guardroom on the ground floor, and there were thirteen audion lamps upon the first floor, and thirteen in use. [...] The destruction of the audion lamps would [...] while doing no permanent harm, preserve the neutrality of Mexico.'

What Mason did was something Baden Powell had written about in a feature he published shortly before the war on how he worked as a spy. He had pretended to be a lepidopterist, and found that a mild-looking, scholarly type with a butterfly net would not arouse suspicion out in the countryside. Baden Powell wrote:

> I was hunting butterflies [...] Quite frankly, with my sketch book in hand, I would ask innocently whether he had seen such and such a butterfly as I was anxious to catch one. Ninety nine out of a hundred did not know one butterfly from another... so one was on fairly safe ground in that way and they thoroughly sympathised with the mad Englishman who was hunting these insects.

Amazingly, Mason did exactly that, and it worked a treat. Along with a local official, he set up a dinner, at which the German officer in command talked with pride about the work his station was doing, and then, perhaps full of wine and a feeling of misplaced trust in his guests, he actually took them to the station to show off his technology. Mason and friends used this as a reconaissance, and then a second visit was arranged, at which Mason did his work of destruction. This tale provides us with exactly the right illustration as to why actors are so useful in espionage. Mason must have loved the role compared with all those desperate days playing bit-parts in touring theatre companies. The Germans on the other hand, saw him simply as a quaint and humorous tourist, and he was invited to a party at the station. His skills as an actor stood him in good stead of course.

Mason had made an opportunity to destroy the lamps, and he destroyed all of them but one. He sent a telegraph to London saying simply, 'The evidence is now complete.'

It is typical of the man that, at a dinner at The Yacht Club in London in 1919, Mason told stories about these Mexican adventures, and Arnold Bennett was present. Into Bennett's diary went the note:

> He was very good as a raconteur and evidently has a great gift for secret service, though he said he began as an amateur. Mason said that practically all the German spies [...] carried a packet of obscene photographs on their

persons. I fully expected he would laugh at the reputation of the German Secret Service for efficiency, and he did [...] Mason said their secret service was merely expensive.

He died in November 1948. His secretary Miss Andrade read to him in his final illness, and it was she who spent a great deal of time with his one biographer Roger Lancelyn Green. Green's tribute was expressed in the words, 'Most authors who achieve a startling fame early in their career with one book [...] fall away and write no better [...] But Mason's literary career shows a steadily ascending range of achievement.'

Among the amateur criminologists, he may be imagined as the one who listened, taking knowledge he could use in his fiction and drama. Yet when he did talk, it was from life: he had seen and done so much.

10
A Lord, a Knight, and a Medical Man

A survey of the many other literary clubs in London at the turn of the nineteenth century reveals something interesting about the Crimes Club: it was that, as part of its *raison d'etre*, beyond simply the reading and discussion of crimes and criminous issues, was the aim of solving criminal cases and mysteries, should such matters come along. It appears to be an aspect of the society that was implied, but never said openly. One particularly enlightening hint in this respect is that, not long after the first few meetings, Bernard Spilsbury and Melville Macnaghten joined their ranks. To have these two men, a forensic scientist and a top policeman, sitting alongside literary raconteurs and amateurs who sometimes made wrong-headed theories about crime, is an astonishing thought.

As noted earlier, Ingleby Oddie wanted the club to remain decidedly amateur and fun, and he therefore left. What captures the imagination about the club as it was from 1903 to 1906, is its mix of professional and amateur, and the sense that in its first identity, the group welcomed any line of thought, from the well documented to the scatty. Yet one cannot resist the thought that, by the time of the Great War, it was arguably a think tank for the Yard, or at least a place where the real men of law could hope to pick up something creatively useful. The detection of crime and the solving of murderous mysteries was, and still is, a hit or miss business. This was the time when criminals were being classified, defined, and sorted into categories. By 1900, Cesare Lombroso's work was translated into several languages, and his atlas of drawings and tranches of statistics were assiduously studied alongside fingerprint whorls, and by the systematic work of Bertillon (who died in 1914), the creator of forensic science, in that he gave close attention to the methods of identification, including the new science of photography.

In that context, theories and discussions could be placed on a basis of scientific rationalism, as meticulously described in the opening chapters of

Conan Doyle's *A Study in Scarlet* when Watson first encounters Holmes. The fact that Holmes is working in a science lab attached to the main work of a hospital encapsulates the new attitudes, with the difficulty in finding the right milieu for forensic work. What could have been more suitable for this species of thought than a gentleman's club? After all, for decades, such institutions had been the places where great decisions were made regarding the Empire and internal security. Nothing could have been more significant and pressingly topical than such a club, as this was the time between the 1880s social turmoil and strikes, and the terrorism of the siege of Sidney Street in 1911, when a line of police constables with rifles stood across streets in London.

That the concept of the club should have originated in the minds of two practical men with vested interests in the reform of the law, Lambton and Oddie, may come as a surprise, but the fact that it immediately attracted authors who were building reputations at a time when male adventure, the enterprise of the Empire, and the exploration of unknown regions was a dominant cultural narrative, comes as no surprise.

If we turn from the creative writers themselves to other men, we find in other club members some rather shadowy figures with mysteries of their own. One of the most elusive is the quiet member Lord Albert Edward Godolphin Osborne, son of the ninth Duke of Leeds. That Duke had married Fanny Pitt-Rivers, a Lady of the Bedchamber of Princess Alice. Lord Albert was born in 1866, and died shortly before the opening of the Great War. The family seat was at Hornby Castle in Yorkshire, and little is recorded of his early life.

Lord Albert crossed the path of other club members when he went up to Oxford, as there he was yet another who took part in thespian activities, being part of the Oxford University dramatic society, where he met Oscar Wilde and Douglas Ainslie. He was at Balliol, and matriculated in May 1885, so he would have met Mason as well as Wilde at Oxford.

We have glimpses of him as he was before he was a club member in the writings of Ainslie, principally in his *Adventures Social and Literary* (1922), in which Ainslie wrote that he took rooms in the Cornmarket where he, 'Now migrated and shared with one of my best friends, Albert Osborne.' He describes Albert Osborne as being 'very pale and fair with smooth hair. He was a most delightful companion on any adventure and invariably maintained an extraordinary calm'. Wilde apparently impersonated Albert Osborne, and Ainslie recalls this at a party:

> 'I will turn you into stone' said Pallas Athene, 'if you harken not to my words of wisdom.'
> 'Ah but I am noble already,' said Osborne, and passed on.

As other members had done, Albert Osborne joined societies as a student, his being a literary society called the Ishmaelites where, as Ainslie reported, they read papers on literary subjects. They had dinners at Bullingden, and also started a Corinthian Club with a private band, although that was of course, for heavy drinking (hence the name). But more importantly for his future life with the Conan Doyle circle, Albert Osborne was a member of Grillons, a breakfast club. Here Ainslie recalls, there were guests from the world of law, including Lord Justice Cockburn, Sir John Stephen, and Lord Arthur Russell, who would all give talks on professional topics.

Clearly, Ainslie, Wilde, and Albert Osborne were close friends. Yet in spite of Wilde's fame, and also notwithstanding Albert Osborne's friendship with Conan Doyle and the others, neither Osborne nor Ainslie figure in the standard biographies of those major figures. Douglas Ainslie, who died in 1948, established himself as a poet and translator, hardly remembered as a poet today, and referred to in reference works simply as a friend of people such as Wilde and Beardsley.

As for his friend and club member Albert Osborne, there is merely one publication to his name: *Sunshine and Surf: A Year's Wanderings in the South Seas* (1901), which he wrote with Douglas Hall. However, his name was in the papers in 1895 due to debt problems. His creditors met in August that year, and it was reported that a receiving order was made, showing that he had debts of £6, 481s. In 1889, Lord Albert had signed a promissory note for £650, but, the report said, 'By some means or other, the note had grown to its present dimensions, nothing having been paid on account.'

The case was wound up in bankruptcy, everything being owed to Thomas Kayler of Pall Mall. Two weeks later, at the court of Queen's Bench, Lord Albert was described as residing in Belgrave Square, and as a member of the New Club in Grafton Street. Most of his debts had been paid 'by a relative', but there was still the promissory note and all the accrued interest. In court, Lord Albert had to explain his situation of course, and the words used were stated in *The Times* report: 'He had never had any occupation, but for some years he was in Ceylon coffee planting. He was not interested in any property there, and for some years was entirely dependent on an allowance of £300 a year made by his father.'

We have a somewhat marginal club member, whose experience in the law was not criminal but civil: he knew what it was like to stand as a debtor before Mr Leadham Hough, the official receiver. His father the Duke had given him large sums of money to extricate him, but he was a Micawber, a ne'er do well, admitting that, 'His personal expenses had amounted to £150 or £200 beyond his income.' A compromise was found, and the Duke had saved the day.

Who then was the man who came to that first dinner? He was almost certainly still living beyond his means and relying on his father to help. We can only speculate as to what his contributions to discussion might have been. Albert Osborne strikes one as that version of the clubman who, having enjoyed the comradeship of his university fraternity, needed to prolong his life in a limbo somewhere between a vaguely artistic sense of self and the twelfth man in the pavilion, perhaps not too worried that he will ever get to bat.

Even in the huge library of volumes on the life of Oscar Wilde, Lord Albert does not figure. Had Ainslie gained more of a reputation, his aristocratic friend may have risen on the back of their friendship, but as it is, he is the club member who stands in the shadows, perhaps only too happy to listen, smile, and feel wanted.

A very different kind of dignitary was Sir Arthur Pearson, the man who founded the *Daily Express* when it began as a halfpenny paper in 1900. He was a formidable businessman, born in Wookey, Somerset, in 1866, the son of a Buckinghamshire rector. In 1914, on the occasion of the 18th annual general meeting of C. Arthur Pearson Ltd. at the Savoy Hotel, Pearson told his colleagues, 'I need not go into the figures in detail, but it is with considerable satisfaction that I would point to the fact that the profits show a material increase on those of last year.' They were doing very nicely, thank you.

Pearson's press empire at that time included *Pearson's Magazine, Pearson's Weekly* and *Home Notes*. The progress, he noted in his Savoy speech, had been pleasing: 'I am glad to tell you that the circulations of all our publications are greater than at the corresponding period last year.' In spite of competition in that period of booming popular magazine production, his publications had, 'Not only held their own, but [had] gained in popularity'.

Pearson's empire had also formed a working alliance with that other baron of the press George Newnes, one of Conan Doyle's principal publishers. The new alliance, he said, had led to considerable improvements. The two massively powerful press entrepreneurs Newnes and Alfred Harmsworth had created many of the publications that kept the club members in regular freelance work. Back in 1896, Arnold Bennett saw the two men at the Haymarket Theatre, and he wrote that they were, 'Chiefs of the two greatest popular journalistic establishments in the kingdom, each controlling concerns which realize upwards of £100,000 net profit per annum.'

At the end of his speech, Pearson commented on the one factor in his life that made Arthur Pearson stand out in terms of his nature and his work. He told his company colleagues that he was blind. He added, 'I am just as keenly interested in the progress of the company with which my name is identified.'

In fact, earlier in life Pearson had worked for Newnes, and as soon as he was successful on his own, his philanthropic nature expressed itself: he established a charity called the Fresh Air Fund, to help disadvantaged children. His eyesight problems were to serve to increase his awareness that his wealth could help others who had disabling conditions.

At the turn of the century, he was the kind of press magnate who thoroughly backed and revelled in the spirit of exploration and adventure that formed the basis of so much of his friends' fiction. One of these ventures led to the massively popular series of reports in *The Express* from the explorer Hesketh-Pritchard in Patagonia. But Pearson was a writer in his own right, producing works related to many popular subjects, and in this there came his criminological interest: graphology. Today, he would surely have been keen on forensic linguistics. His book *Handwriting as an Index to Character,* written under the *nom de plume* of Prof. Foli, was published just a year before the first club meeting. He would have been especially interested in the recent expert witnesses on handwriting, particularly in the Adolf Beck case. His opinions would have supported that some of the work being done in criminology by Bertillon and Cesare Lombroso was yet one more method by which individuals could be located and described.

It was a time when science in its application to criminal behaviour was still open to rather loose and woolly thinking; pseudo-sciences persisted. As late as 1920, Annie Oppenheim was publishing on phrenology, in work such as *The Human Face and How to Read It,* and the pre-war development of espionage opened up other disciplines that were destined to be applied to detective work, such as cryptography. In the first twenty years of the twentieth century, these all burgeoned.

As regards handwriting in forensics, the 1894 Dreyfus case had put this in centre stage. He was charged with treason on the supposed evidence of his writing a memo to a German military attaché. No less an expert than Bertillon identified Dreyfus as the author of the text submitted for study, and in spite of the novelist Emile Zola campaigning for an enquiry into what he was certain was a miscarriage of justice, it took until 1906 for Dreyfus to be absolved and released. Pearson's interests followed on work done by such academics as Wilhelm Preyer in 1895, and then Rosa Baughan, the latter being the author of the first work on graphology in English. Not long after Pearson's book in 1919, June Downey in Iowa published *Graphology and the Psychology of Handwriting.*

Apart from the case of Edalji, which entailed Conan Doyle arriving at the conclusion that the letters incriminating Edalji between 1892 and 1895 were written by two different people, there was also the miscarriage of justice in the case of William Broughton in the news. This was a story from Atlanta in 1900. Broughton was convicted of mailing an obscene letter to the City Recorder of Atlanta. In that case, three supposed experts gave evidence, which included the opinion that, if there were any contrasting and contradictory aspects on the handwriting in various texts, then this could be explained by the fact that the accused was very sharp and intelligent, and therefore could disguise his hand in different texts.

Closer to home, the two acknowledged experts in handwriting in Britain who were regularly appearing in courts, F. C. Price and Mr Gurrin (of the Beck case), were busy, and their testimony was not always sound. In a swindling case of 1899, Rex *v.* Kirby and Clifford, Price's opinion was accepted, but in Rex *v.* Thomas (1899), Gurrin's testimony was faced with that of another analyst who 'took the opposite view' of the text in question.

There is no doubt that Conan Doyle played a major part in popularising graphology generally, and Pearson was the member of the club with whom he shared this special interest in the whole spectrum of skills and expertise in criminology. In fact, if we leave aside the Beck case, there is also the Moat Farm murder, which had led to the conviction and trial of Samuel Dougal, who was standing trial just a few weeks before the first club dinner. Dougal had lived with Camille Holland at Moat House Farm in Essex, and then she had disappeared. But her cheques were still being presented for payment. Proof of forgery was needed, and although a nephew of the victim acquired such proof, there was more forgery going on.

Dougal had killed Camille and buried her body in a drainage ditch. Conan Doyle was appealed to for help, and although police had conducted a thorough search of the place, no body had been found. Conan Doyle asked the very Sherlockian question; had the moat been searched? It appears that the young Edgar Wallace, a journalist in London then, probed the police attitudes and saw that Doyle's suggestion had not been done. A local labourer helped to trace the trench that he had dug, and eventually a body was found.

In court, there were matters of forgery. As *The Times* reported, T. H. Gurrin gave evidence, and he had studied both allegedly counterfeit signatures; that of Camille, and another of an Essex JP called Bell:

> The first witness called was Mr T. H. Gurrin, an expert in handwriting, who said that the signature on a cheque for £28 15s, dated August 18, 1902, purporting to be the signature of Miss Holland, was really that of the prisoner. A signature too, on a declaration purporting to be that of Joseph Bell, a justice of the peace for Essex, relating to some Great Laxey shares, was also a counterfeit.

Gurrin was faced with a cross-examination, and his reply was that examination and conclusions as to the identity of the author were 'largely a matter of opinion based on experience'. That hint of uncertainty made no difference to the power of the prosecution, and Dougal was found guilty and hanged at Chelmsford by William Billington, whom Irving had visited in Bolton in July 1903.

The lack of scientific rigour behind Gurrin's statement is easily understood when we reflect that, for instance, an advert in a paper in 1910 had the wording, 'Gentlewoman, refined, nice appearance, desires temporary employment: only expert accomplishments graphology and physiognomy.'

There was also arguably the biggest fraud story of all the *fin de siècle* tales involving forgery: the Goudie case. In a short but dramatic film narrative in the recently discovered archive of two photographers of the Edwardian era, we see a man in a long black overcoat being escorted by two detectives to Bootle Police Station. In the grainy, crackling old film, as the commentator notes, we have the first true crime story on camera. Part of the sequence shows headlines from Liverpool newspapers, conveying the startling news that Goudie has been arrested. The film is from *The Lost World of Mitchell and Kenyon*, and in this we can see glimpses of a Liverpool long lost under the bricks and mortar of time. But the images linger: Goudie taken from his lodging house in Berry Street; children gathering, aware that some kind of celebrity has been among them. Not only was the story of Goudie the swindler the first true crime story – it ranks as one of the top three Liverpool crime tales of all time, almost as sensational, one could argue, as the Wallace case and the Fenians bombings.

What that film does not tell the viewer is that this man's activities would lead to a high-scale criminal trial at the Old Bailey, in which the legal career of that great Liverpudlian F. E. Smith (Lord Birkenhead) would be launched, and that the future Lord Chief Justice of England, Rufus Isaacs, would also be involved in the case.

Who was this man of mystery? Amazingly, he was not a major-league criminal whose name would cause hearts to stir and doors to be locked at night. He was just a poor ledger clerk with the Bank of Liverpool. His time was spent filling in accounts books and sharpening pencils. He might have passed his life that way, in obscurity, except for one character trait: he liked a flutter on the horses.

Thomas Peterson Goudie was from the Shetland Isles. He lived a life of routine in the city, staying in a lodging house for just £1 a week. In 1900, he would have seemed a quiet man, respected for regularity and hard work in the office. He was twenty-nine and well educated; his wage was reasonably good for the time, at just £3 a week. But since the mid-1890s, he had been betting and losing increasingly large sums of money. By 1898, he was in so much debt from his gambling that he worked out a simple way to defraud his employers of £100. He did this by exploiting a rich man called Hudson, who owned Hudson's Soap, and forging cheques supposedly paid out by this victim. Goudie handled the names between H and K, and Hudson was his wealthiest client. Forged cheques were written and entered in the ledger, then destroyed. As Goudie helped with the audits (done weekly), he could soon cover up this crime.

But unfortunately, he kept on gambling and visiting race courses. After a day at Newmarket races in 1900, he met with some racing touts and cheap crooks called Kelly and Stiles. It was amazingly crass and stupid of Goudie, but he somehow felt that he would tell these men of his scam. That was his fatal move. They realised they had a goose that would lay them golden eggs. Goudie was so simple that he was fooled into thinking they were high-class bookies and that he could have tips from them. As they had something on him, they could force him to bet (and thus simply put money in their pockets), and pressure him with threats to increase the level of his embezzlement from his employers.

As matters escalated, and word about this source of easy money circulated in the London criminal fraternity, two more characters entered the story. These were two blackmailers called Burg and Mances. Mances was the strong man, the 'frightener' in the racket, and he would travel to Liverpool to threaten Goudie, and bully him into involvement with their gang. Goudie had already put the massive sum of 70,000 by way of Kelly and Stiles; now everyone was greedy.

In October 1901, Goudie was found out. In just a few weeks, the greed of the criminal gang around him meant that he had stolen £90,000 for them. Goudie was cornered, and when officers arrived to quiz him, he confessed. But after going to fetch ledgers, he absconded and went to hide away in the Berry Street lodgings. Markes and Mances managed to disappear into Europe (Marks may even had committed suicide), but Goudie, Kelly, Stiles, and Burge were charged, and all was set up for the major trial at the Old Bailey.

Goudie was tracked down to his lodgings, and the barristers gathered for the fray. The judge was Mr Justice Bigham. Goudie's defence was led by F. E. Smith, and Rufus Isaacs appeared for Kelly. On the face of things, Goudie had no chance of acquittal. F. E. Smith knew that his only chance of any success was to appeal to the jury's sense of the sadness of a poor man duped by a group of evil professional criminals. After all, Goudie was facing penal servitude for life. Smith could at best hope for a shorter sentence. The clerk pleaded guilty, and he was put in the box as witness against the crooks from the racing world. Perhaps the most stunning fact in all this is that Goudie himself only received £750. The touts and blackmailers had enjoyed five-figure sums from Goudie's forging habits.

Rufus Isaacs and Marshall Hall, defending the two blackmailers, put their heads together and achieved something that Rumpole of the Bailey would have been proud of: they made it seem right that their two clients pleaded to lesser charges rather than plead not guilty. The outcome would be, if Goudie were guilty (and that was certain), a short sentence, much less than the anticipated ten years. They were right. Goudie was guilty, and F. E. Smith's speech did indeed move the jury. Smith painted a picture a pathetic little man who had been duped by ruthless hard men and leeches who bled him dry. What the jury were asked to see in the dock was not a nasty, unscrupulous con-man, but a wreck, a man broken by the harrowing experience of meeting with this tough gang. There was the added factor that Goudie had three sisters, and these ladies had been working hard for their brother to find some kind of legal aid for him.

Even Justice Bigham could not ignore all this. He passed a sentence of ten years, rather than the expected one of fifteen years. There was a story that F. E. Smith was so talented and persuasive in this speech that Sir Richard Muir passed him a note which said, 'You will be the master of all of us. No-one I have ever heard has impressed me in so hopeless a case.'

But there is a sad irony in the outcome, for Goudie died six years later, in gaol of course. But this incredible story has all kinds of interesting sidelights: the villain Burge, who served in effect only three years, partially redeemed himself by saving the life of a prison warder, showing 'conspicuous gallantry'. F. E. Smith launched his career on the case, and it emerges that his wonderful speech was in fact practised and rehearsed to perfection, and the whole piece memorised word for word.

The Goudie case attracted as much attention at the time 'as a front-page murder'. For a man who had first yielded to the temptations of gambling on the horses, with £1 bets being typical of his risk, to rise to the level of major and notorious national crook was an unmissable story for the journalists. In Mitchell and Kenyon's film, the actor playing Goudie, escorted to the cell by two plain clothes detectives, comes across as someone as dangerous as Baby Face Nelson or Al Capone. Ironically, in a twisted way, his dreams of success and fame, well away from his dull life of pen-pushing, came true. The quiet, regular clerk had become the dramatic subject of the sensational *Police News* and the penny dreadful comics. When he had first run away and lain low for a while, the central police office in Liverpool had issued posters with an image of him and a £250 reward. *The Times* gave the story massive column space. They told the tale of Mrs Harding, Goudie's landlady, shopping him to the Bootle police. Her husband Charles who was a crane-man on the docks, advised his wife to go to the police.

Handwriting and graphological analysis was at the cutting edge of criminology when Pearson wrote his little handbook. Somehow, letters always figured in his story, and in 1912 Bernard Espinasse, with Samuel and Edith Ullman, were charged with obtaining money by false pretences relating to a competition advertised in *Pearson's Weekly*. R. D. Muir led the prosecution for Pearsons at Bow Street, and he had a Mr Patterson, employed by Pearsons to run the competition, tell the court that Espinasse had been employed to select the most entertaining letters submitted from a given selection of letters. As is always the case, no employee of the company was allowed to take part.

But Espinasse had been entering under the name of Mumford, and a newsagent testified that for five years he had been receiving the letters for Mumford, and that Espinasse periodically called to collect them. The scam was completely laid open when Mrs Ullman was shown to have cashed several cheques drawn by Messrs Pearson. Detective Inspector Gough of the Yard arrived and approached Espinasse. The court report adds a little drama:

> Gough stated that [...] he saw Espinasse at Messrs Pearson's premises in Henrietta Street and read the warrant to him. He replied, 'I don't in the least know what it is.' He told him it was alleged that as an adjudicator of the competition [...] he had caused cheques for prizes to be addressed in fictitious names.

The game was up. Ullman was traced and both were soon in the dock.

Arthur Pearson later threw all his energies into charities for the blind, and also produced publications for the blind, including *Pearson's Easy Dictionary* in braille. His own blindness, caused by glaucoma, did not prevent him from carrying on with his work, as noted in his speech at the meeting of the company's top men. He also established St Dunstan's home for soldiers blinded in the Great War, which was at first in Regent's Park. These men became known as Pearson's New Blind Army. Around 1,500 men learnt new skills there by the end of the war in 1918. Pearson fell and was drowned in his bath in 1921.

In the ranks of the club at its first real meeting was Dr Herbert Crosse of Norwich, another professional working in various medical roles in his career, but most prominently becoming medical officer of health for Norwich. At the time of the club's first dinner, he was living at No. 6 Theatre Street in Norwich. He was single, living with a servant, and acting as medical adviser at the Norfolk Quarter Sessions, and from 1899 he was assistant surgeon at the Jenny Lind Infirmary, where he worked until 1929.

Crosse was born in Norwich, and then studied medicine at Edinburgh, and at King's College, London. He was at Edinburgh in 1883; a little later than Conan Doyle, who graduated in 1879.

Crosse was the secretary, and later president, of the Norwich Medico-Chirurgical Society, following his father and grandfather in the same role. His career was in step with Ingleby Oddie, for they both qualified in law later in life after having medical qualifications. Crosse was called to the bar at the Middle Temple in 1923, and joined the Old Bailey sessions, although he never practised as a barrister.

With this background, he was a valuable member of the club, being passionate and very knowledgeable on matters criminal. Not only had he experience as a police surgeon, but at one time, he was also a physician at the Grove Asylum, appointed to that post by the Norfolk Quarter Sessions. At the Grove, a few miles from Norwich at Catton, Crosse was certainly busy; we have a glimpse of the place in the death of a man called Gower in 1882, for whom Crosse's predecessor was called for an inquest. Gower had collapsed and he died of heart disease, and the inquest was held at the asylum.

Crosse was busy as a writer on criminal investigation and forensics, producing articles for the *Eastern Daily Press,* and when he was not writing, he found time to work at his many posts. He is on record as a regular witness in coroners' courts in the 1890s, as at Norwich for instance in 1899, when he reported on his post mortem examination and confirmed a death by natural causes.

He was in fact a writer who covered both areas – amateur detective and medico-legal expert. They were, and are, different spheres, and even back in 1900, the various professionals and amateurs related to criminal matters were aware of this. Sir Sydney Smith, the pathologist and Holmes enthusiast writing in the 1950s, was keen to show the difference between the two when time had elapsed and the amateurs were taking a back seat: 'The medico-legal expert or specialist in forensic medicine, is not a detective [...] It seldom happens that a crime is solved by a doctor or other scientist working in his laboratory alone.' But in the context of the club dinners, Crosse could relish his dual role: medical adviser (along with Oddie and Conan Doyle), and part-time crime writer.

In fact, with regard to the notable feature of the club members – that many had degrees in law – it needs to be pointed out that there was a feeling at the time that, a law degree, and then being called to the bar, was seen as an almost perfunctory event. H. W. Nevinson, a friend of Conan Doyle whom he met during the Boer War, commented on this. He was asked by a Master when he was in his late teens what he was to do with his remaining forty or fifty years, and Nevison replied, 'I can row, skate, climb hills, and write indifferent verses in three languages. I suppose I could go to the bar like everyone else, if I were rich enough.' The club had some members who exemplified that – but there were also Oddie and Crosse, who had studied law and been successful for personal intellectual reasons.

This does not mean that Crosse was any kind of specialist in detection of course. He was a keen amateur, as they all were at the time of the first few dinners before professional detectives joined their ranks.

Herbert Crosse died in 1941 at Brundall. Among the club members he was, with Oddie, the man to ask on matters concerning the practical side of pathology and medical evidence. Clearly, his presence at coroners' inquests developed alongside his research into forensics in well-know and in local cases.

11
Trials and Theories: Atlay and Diosy

In 1905 and 1906 there appeared two significant publications in the history of criminology; two volumes in a new series called *Notable Trials*, produced by Hodge of Edinburgh. James Hodge, son of the founder, wrote that his father 'thought that the public got little chance of knowing what actually went on in the courts, and thus the idea of publishing trials germinated; my grandfather [...] thought little of the idea, but he was from Glasgow, and so the idea went ahead'.

The *Trials* series' value to the lawyer, historian, and medical man is beyond dispute, but its greatest attribute lies undoubtedly in its interest for the ordinary member of the community, that wide range of society commonly called the general public. Harry Hodge's family had founded the company in 1874, and Harry had started publishing popular as well as learned books. The first two volumes were on Madeleine Smith and 'The Trial of the Glasgow Bank Directors', selling at 5s. By the end, the series covered the years from 1586 to 1953. From 1921, the whole list became *Notable British Trials*.

A typical *Trials* volume presents an account of each day of the trial, with lists of all legal personnel and witnesses. In addition, there are usually drawings, plans, and photographs of any important materials involved in the trial process.

The editors of the volumes were carefully chosen, and were acknowledged experts in exactly the kind of skills and literary expertise that Roughead called criminous. Much of the text in the volumes consists of actual dialogues spoken in court between lawyers and witnesses, and the aim of giving a lucid and dramatic, yet exact account, of the interplay of people and theories is fulfilled with aplomb.

One member of the Crimes Club was one of the respected experts in the Hodges' books. This was James Beresford Atlay, the son of the Bishop of

Hereford, born in Leeds in 1860. He went to Oriel College, Oxford, studying history. But like several other club members, he was called to the bar. Atlay became Registrar of the Diocese of Hereford until 1910. He established himself as an essentially legal scholar and biographer, arguably the most academically inclined of all the original club members. He edited volumes on many subjects, but his work on the famous Tichborne Claimant case stands out as a model of editing and interpretation.

In biography, Atlay wrote *The Victorian Chancellors* (1905), and a life of Sir Henry Acland, the friend of Ruskin. A correspondent to *The Times* on Atlay's death in 1912 wrote that Atlay 'had a serious bent towards serious history, and his wide reading and retentive memory, his quick grasp of facts, and his power of marshalling them, all fitted him [...] to make his mark as a historian'.

When Atlay was working on the research for his *The Victorian Chancellors* in the first few years of the twentieth century, the subject of biographical works on the higher echelons of the legal profession was experiencing a publishing boom. There was a profound interest in courtroom drama, and in the important and dramatic stories to be found in state and criminal trials. There were many explanations of the nature of this fascination, notably by R. Storry Deans, who was a barrister of Gray's Inn as well as a crime writer, who wrote that:

> There is nothing to surpass in human interest, the records of the law courts. Many a writer of fiction has founded his romances on those records; and many another has spent much ingenuity in inventing plot and incident not half so weird as hundreds to be found in the pages of the State Trials.

Peter Burke of Serjeants' Inn, wrote in a preface to another volume on the courts and lawyers, 'The authors' main object is to present a series of those incidents in the administration of justice that, from some marvellous or romantic circumstance connected with them, have created great public sensation in their day.' In contrast, Richard Harris, who wrote the life of the great judge Lord Brampton in 1904, saw the interest in legal biography as being anecdotal: 'I venture to say that there is no doubtful story in this volume.'

Atlay writes as a traditional biographer, as established by Dr Johnson in his *Lives of the Poets*, and makes an effort to give assessments of the human side of affairs, as in his life of Lord Lyndhurst, where he explains a predicament of Sir Charles Wetherell:

At this moment he was smarting under the double disappointment of seeing his claim to the vacant law offices disregarded in favour of Shepherd and Gifford, and the prospect of meeting his rivals face to face, and at the same time, teaching a lesson to an ungrateful ministry was irresistible.

As a true crime enthusiast, Atlay could not avoid including the most sensational events from his period and subject, as in the assassination of the Prime Minister Spencer Perceval. He spent most time, not on the murder, but on the political aftermath, explaining, 'The ministerial changes consequent upon the murder [...] were followed by a dissolution in the autumn,' and that, 'There was a stirring struggle in which for several days Brougham ran second to Canning.' Atlay was well aware of the attraction of biography applied to the lives of lawyers. As Lord Birkett said in reference to Jonathan Swift:

The charge against the advocate remains and was put into its most deadly form by Dean Swift [...] when he said of the bar that "they were a society of men bred up from their youth in the art of proving by words multiplied for the purpose, that white is black and black is white according as they are paid.

Also in the ranks was a man who contrasts markedly with Atlay: the dashing, red-bearded Arthur Diosy, son of Martin Diosy, the Hungarian patriot in the 1840s. Martin came to England with his family, and Arthur was born in Westbourne Grove (the area where the Studio murder took place) in 1856. As a child, Arthur would have met the great Hungarian Kossuth, who was embroiled in large-scale, supposedly criminal machinations that turned out to have little substance. Lajos (or Louis as he was known in most countries) Kossuth was a major figure in nineteenth-century Hungarian history. Hungary was then part of the Austro-Hungarian empire, the Habsburg monolith, which was to be an ally of the Germans in the Great War. Kossuth was born in 1802, and was of Slovakian origin. He later became a lawyer, journalist, and politician. He had become a national figure by 1841 when he edited an influential newspaper called *Pesti Hirlap*. His prestige increased still further when he was imprisoned for his nationalist views, and he became the main leader of the extreme Liberal Party. He moved on to the centre stage in European politics in the year of revolutions, 1848, when across the continent, radical movements pressed for reform and new libertarian values, notably more rights for those enslaved in the great empires. In that year, he became Regent-President of Hungary, but he had to take command of armies on the move, and that was not his real strength.

Kossuth tried to reach a compromise with the Habsburg powers, even using an American diplomat in negotiations, but eventually he failed in his efforts to retain power and to reach his objectives, and he became a fugitive, as so many Europeans did at the time. He first stayed in England in 1851, and from his activities then, we can understand why, when the affair of the Rotherhithe bomb factory hit the headlines, there was a lot of popular support for him among the British working-class. He was fêted by many, including the Lord Mayor of London, and he was a very talented and powerful public speaker. He also took part in a procession through London to the Guildhall. There were possibly 75,000 people watching this, so he became very well known.

Unfortunately for the Government, Lord Palmerston showed extraordinary amiability towards Kossuth, and intended to invite him to his country house. The Queen saw this as totally undesirable: here was a populist leader and demagogue who did not believe in monarchy being welcomed by her Foreign Secretary. Palmerston, blocked in this intention to speak to Kossuth, invited trade union members instead, and they read a statement that included a deal of praise for Kossuth. This played a part in bringing down the government of the day, led by Lord John Russell.

This is the background to the Rotherhithe affair and the Hale family. Obviously, the police and the Home Office were watching Kossuth closely. After all, they had a revolutionary in their midst. A link was found between William Hale, his factory at Rotherhithe, and Kossuth. But Hale was completely legitimate in terms of who he was and what his track record had been with regard to armaments: he was, in an important way, potentially part of the ordnance provision of the British Army, but Hale had never achieved this. Rockets had first been used in the field in the Napoleonic Wars, and the War Office knew all about Hale, and had worked with him. If he did turn out to be some kind of traitor or arms dealer, then that would be a shock. It all came to nothing.

Lajos Kossuth would have called on the Diosys, and Arthur Diosy knew him well. But Arthur's attentions were to language rather than radicalism or bomb factories. He began to study Japanese history and culture, and he was only thirty-six when he founded the Japan Society of the United Kingdom in 1891. Shortly before the first club dinner, Arthur was made a knight commander of the Order of Christ.

This honour is entirely in keeping with Arthur's personality and love of ritual and mystery. This order, as recalled by Sir Francis Vane, who knew Arthur and was knighted to the order at the same time, was conferred by the King of Portugal, and the honour stems from the Templars. Diosy and Vane were therefore allowed to wear the insignia of the Templars. Vane wrote that he called a meeting of his Knights: 'The resolution I put forward was to enrol associates or servant brothers to carry out active philanthropic work [...] At the same time I made direct application to the King of Portugal, the Grand Master of the Order, to allow the British knights to form such a body.' He received permission, and he then wrote that, 'Among the English knights were many of distinction – Sir Arthur Trendall, Owen the Duke of Norfolk, Sir Walter de Sousa, Arthur Diosy, Sir Albert Rollit.' He also added that the men who helped him most 'in this adventure of reviving chivalry as a practical scheme were Arthur Diosy [...] whose energy was dynamic'.

Arthur loved such pomp and splendour, with a touch of the occult perhaps. Hence his interest in the kind of symbolism he found in the corpses of the Ripper victims, as discussed in chapter four. He was not taken seriously in this business, and in fact the *Pall Mall Gazette* for December 3 1888 was harsh and sarcastic:

> Mr Arthur Diosy is aggrieved. The ingenious contributor who hit upon the nationality of the Whitechapel murderer said no-one had hit upon a necromantic motive. Mr Diosy said he told the police all about it [...] He also darkly hints that the dates of the crimes have some occult relation to magical astrology.

Virtually all recent encyclopaedic works on Jack the Ripper either have no mention at all of Diosy's theory, or mention it briefly in order to dismiss the notion of any search for the elixir of life and pentagrams. But in earlier times of Ripperology, there have been accounts and responses to such thinking as Arthur Diosy suggests.

The club met for the first time just fifteen years after the Ripper murders. At that point, any more adventurous or creative suggestion to the mysteries of the clearly symbolic and ritualistic appearance of the victims' corpses were worthy of attention. But of course, theories had been narrowed down by then, and the final reports by top detectives had marked down three major suspects. However, suggestions such as Diosy's kept the discussion open and questioning lines of thought very much alive and open to scrutiny. In the end, that can only have helped to urge more lateral thinking among experts and amateur enthusiasts.

Arthur's fascination with Far Eastern studies was very much of its time. When he was in his formative years, not only had the London stage had the massive cultural impact of Gilbert and Sullivan's *The Mikado*, produced in 1885, but also the equally influential *The Geisha*, created by George

Edwardes at Daly's Theatre by the great impresario George Edwards in 1896. *The Geisha* was a huge success, having the effect of bringing Japanese art and culture into the limelight. There was an eager buying public for Japanese prints and dolls, and even Christmas crackers were likely to have Japanese toys along with the sweets. As one writer has noted, 'Japan invaded London'. There was a Japanese 'village' in the heart of London, in Knightsbridge.

In fact, Arthur Diosy was brought in as an adviser by George Edwardes when he was planning *The Geisha*. In an 1896 issue of a magazine called *Today*, Arthur was interviewed, and he explained there how *The Geisha* was 'Japanned'. He explained that his task was to supply Mr Edwardes with 'an accurate description of the Japanese girl, her physical characteristics and ways, more especially, of the Geisha'.

He did far more than educate Britain with regard to the Far East in the context of contemporary politics and war. He explained social and cultural life, asking and answering questions such as, 'What is the social position, then, of the Japanese woman?' As an amateur criminologist, one aspect of his subject naturally attracted his attention: the state of the prisons in China and Japan. In the 1890s, there had been a steady flow of horrific reports by missionaries and travellers regarding barbaric treatment of prisoners, such as stories of offenders being kept for life in a small cage, never being allowed out, and simply fed through a small hole. Arthur was in touch with the contemporary issues, as in this explanation after the war of China and Japan:

> Several editors of English newspapers in Japan visited several Japanese gaols in the winter of 1897/8 with a view of ascertaining what kind of prison life awaited Occidentals who might be convicted by a Japanese judge [...] On the editorial staff of those very outspoken native Japanese newspapers [...] A prison editor is kept.

This official was a 'man of straw' who, if the prosecutor convicts anyone at the paper, went into 'durance vile' as Arthur put it. It was not an easy job at the *fin de siecle*, to explain the judicial processes and institutions in those distant lands.

Arthur was one of the founders of the Japan Society in 1891, and ten years later he was the vice president. A drawing of Arthur in a magazine of the time is under the heading of a series called 'Men of the Day', and the description of Arthur is that he was 'a writer and lecturer on Japan and the East, and because he has proudly supposed to have precipitated the Anglo-

Japanese Treaty, he has been called "The Japanner"'. The other comment that perhaps tells us a great deal about him is, 'He travels so much in the four quarters of this little globe that he finds it hardly big enough for his little body.'

The year before the club first met, Britain signed a naval treaty with Japan, and Arthur was prominent in the work for this alliance. French and Russian naval power in the Far East was seen as a threat by the British Government, so a protective alliance with Japan made sense. In some ways this was an extension of the Great Game of espionage which had been played between Britain and Russia in various phases since the 1830s. The treaty was signed in 1902 by Lord Lansdowne and Hayashi Tadasu. There had been a treaty of Anglo-Japanese commerce and navigation however, eight years before that.

Arthur Diosy died in January 1923 in Nice. There is no doubt that his contributions at the club dinners were bound to be startling and unexpected, for here was a man who was familiar with any number of matters that were distant from the usual Anglocentric and Empire fixated notions of being British. In his writings on Japan, he was always keen to tell his British readers that they were rather narrow-minded when it came to international politics, and to understanding cultures unlike their own. Of course, there had been a steady growth of intellectual interest in affairs in the Middle East and beyond during the Great Game of espionage with Russia, as officers studied the history and culture of distant places across India and Tibet, but Japan still remained little know in any proper, documented sense at the time Arthur Diosy wrote his books and helped to launch the Japan Society.

His knowledge and interests whetted the appetite of those members who were already imbued with the sense of adventure in their aims as writers, whether the explorations were into the darkest areas of London (as with Sims), or with the adventures of Empire (as with Mason.) In the history of the club, in spite of all his other accomplishments, his name will go down on record as the one who formulated the occult theory to explain Jack the Ripper. That is an irony he would surely have found very amusing.

12

WILLIAM LE QUEUX: LANDRU AND THE CRUMBLES BUNGALOW MURDER

Of all the various members of the club, with their diverse interests, William Le Queux may be seen as the one who was most elusive. Some members may have been specialists in some area of crime and law, others were attracted merely to the enigmas of human transgression in the cases before them, but Le Queux comes across the years as the man who wanted to write everything. The list of his works, as assembled by his most recent biographers, is so numerous that it fills four pages of very small print, each page having two columns. His name figures in reference works and histories of espionage, and yet his status in that regard is perplexingly contradictory, He was, as his biographers call him, a 'master of mystery'. If, as Chesterton once wrote, England is to be understood as the country of amateurs, then Le Queux's life and works supports that, and in the best sense, for he was passionate about so much in life, and had energy enough to heat the Houses of Parliament, if such energy could have been collected and used.

He might be imagined, at a club dinner, as the one the rest longed to quiz, to corner, and elicit the full facts of something from his remarkable life. The irony is that we shall never know the full facts. We have to make do with his wonderful fictions.

In 1925, William Le Queux published a collection of short stories with the title *The Crimes Club*. The sub-title was, 'A Record of Secret Investigations into Some Amazing Crimes, Mostly Withheld from the Public.' The actual material between the covers bears no relation to the real crimes club, but that sub-title is a piece of wish-fulfilment on the part of the author. Ironically, it describes the situation and nature of the club in 2012, as for some inexplicable reason, the club topics and activities are kept highly secret. Yet whatever the irony might be between the real and imagined club, Le Queux dedicated his book, 'Arthur Lambton, founder, Hon. Secretary and my fellow-member of the Crimes Club of London known to us as "Our Society".'

Le Queux recalled in one of his publications that he knew the Hay poisoner Herbert Armstrong, who was a solicitor, and that on one occasion, the poisoner was angling for an invitation to join the Crimes Club. Le Queux's biographer Sladen wrote:

> He was a country solicitor in Herefordshire, and when in town slept at the club. He was a man of refinement. Le Queux was just back from ski-running at Murren. He happened to remark that Our Society was holding its usual dinner that night and that he was going to attend it. 'In my profession,' said the solicitor, 'I am constantly dealing with petty crime. I would so much like to go to one of your dinners. I suppose you discuss the celebrated cases of poisoning and so on. It must be most interesting.' Le Queux replied that many unknown facts regarding great crimes were often revealed.

The case of Major Armstrong and the poisoning of his wife in the quiet market town of Hay-on-Wye is one that has been written about almost in the melodramatic manner of the television series *Midsummer Murders*. The reason for this is that the ingredients of the tale are highly dramatic and are also riddled with clichés and standard 'characters'. The Major himself was a natty dresser and charming company. He was diminutive and chirpy, and well liked in the community. His wife was domineering and from a good family. He was a Cambridge man, but was by no means upper class in his origins. To cap all this, we have in the Hay poisoning case the established storyline of professional rivalry and ambition, with ironic twists all along the way. Yet all this is somehow annoying and distracting, because after all, this is a story of a monster with a disarming smile.

Herbert Armstrong, the keen gardener, was at war with weeds. As was common at the time, arsenic was used in weed killer, and Davies the chemist was familiar with Armstrong's habits of using such a weed killer in a tube with which he targeted dandelions. At the same time he made he these purchases, Mrs Armstrong was ill, and was deteriorating. The doctor who examined her thought that she was mentally ill, and her attitudes to Herbert had included a repressive regime that may have been partly a result of her mental anguish. He was forced to stay away from strong drink, and he could smoke only in one designated room. Some writers have described her as a 'crack', and others as a 'terror' who made Herbert noticeably hen-pecked, and was observed as so by the neighbours.

By August 1920, Katherine's health was indeed cause for concern. Medical advice was followed, and she was taken away to a private asylum in Gloucester. Katherine was there for six months, but when she returned home she was ill again, and in February 1921, she died. Armstrong stood to collect £2,300 by her death, but he was still short of cash, and he owed Martin, his rival solicitor, £500, which had earlier been paid to Armstrong by a client in a land sale transaction. This situation made relations between Armstrong and Martin even more strained.

Now that Mrs Armstrong was no longer at home – and she could not object to the clothes he wore – Martin could visit Armstrong. He did, and he was offered buttered scones. The Major's words, 'Excuse fingers,' as he served the food to his guest, have since reached the status of one of those iconic statements from great crime stories – the polite and mannered words masking the fact that the scones had been injected with arsenic contained in the applicator for treating dandelions. Martin felt very ill after the tea time chat, and matters escalated. Suspicions were aroused, and a Dr Hincks was brought in. The Martins also received a box of chocolates, delivered by post; a present from Armstrong. Sure enough, Mrs Martin, who ate a chocolate, was violently sick. Putting two and two together, Martin made a case for attempted murder, and thoughts turned to Mrs Armstrong and how she may have conceivably died.

Armstrong was now investigated, and the medical men started a process that would lead to the exhumation of Katherine Armstrong. The moment is a very dramatic one. The great forensic scientist Sir Bernard Spilsbury made the journey from London to Hay on 2 January 1922. What had raised suspicions even more was the fact that Armstrong was in the habit of keeping small quantities of arsenic in screwed up parcels of brown paper. He would keep these in his pockets and in his desk drawers. When first questioned by police, they were aware of this, and of the fact that he had regularly bought arsenic from Mr Davies. Davies, Hincks and Martin must have had long and exploratory conversations about Armstrong before action was taken.

Bernard Spilsbury had conducted the investigation of Mrs Armstrong's corpse under a tent in the churchyard, and he had taken away several specimens for analysis. It then came to the process of investigation, and eventually the charge of murder against Armstrong. In April 1922, the trial opened at Hereford Assizes. Sir Henry Curtis-Bennett defended Armstrong, and Mr Justice Darling presided. For the prosecution, Sir Ernest Pollock led for the Crown. Armstrong was on demand in prison at Gloucester, and every day of the trial he was driven to Hereford and back. The trial was a momentous one for the great Judge Darling. He was seventy-three, and it was his last murder trial. Curtis-Bennett was a very astute man, and a skilful speaker in court. All this made for this being one of the great criminal trials – and this escalated the status of the affair in the annals of murder in Britain.

Spilsbury's evidence was totally convincing and very impressive. The chemist told the court that just before Mrs Armstrong came home from the asylum, the Major bought arsenic, and it seems that the chemist was remiss in that he perhaps did not mix the arsenic with charcoal as he was supposed to do. Some coloured white arsenic was found on Armstrong's person, and then a second search of his desk revealed another arsenic parcel trapped at the back of a drawer – something that and been missed in the first police search. The stage was set for the conclusive evidence of Spilsbury. He told the court:

> From the amount of arsenic which was present in the small and large intestines, it is clear that a large dose of arsenic must have been taken – I mean, a poisonous dose, possibly a fatal dose – certainly within twenty-four hours of death; and from the amount of arsenic which was found in the liver – over two grains – and from the disease which I found in the liver, it is clear that poison must have been given in a number of large doses extending over a period, certainly of some days, probably not less than a week.

The centre point of sheer sensation and puzzling interest was the fact that the packet of arsenic had been discovered at the back of the desk drawer in Armstrong's office. The defence, led by Curtis Bennett, appear to have used this as a gambit. One opinion is that it was placed there by the defence, but that is a very cynical allegation. More likely is the possibility that Armstrong recalled that it was there and he told his defence team. The packet was two-faced though: Lord Darling thought the discovery was very damaging evidence, and both sides waited with bated breath for Armstrong himself to take the stand. What happened was that the court was asked to accept that Armstrong had the habit of poisoning each dandelion in his garden individually, with a tool having a fine point.

The defence had to find a way to explain away that odd fact – not only that Armstrong used the tool with the fine point on the weeds, but that small holes had been found in poisoned chocolates that were surely the result of the use of that same tool.

Curtis Bennett tried his best in his last speech to the jury, but nevertheless, according to those present, such as Filson Young who later wrote about the case, the general feeling was that Armstrong would be acquitted. This was wrong. Bennett actually went for a walk while the jury were out, and he expected to come back to a not guilty verdict. But Armstrong was found guilty and sentenced to death.

Such was the man who could so easily have been taken along to sit with the Crimes Club by Le Queux, but the meeting gave his a good topic for discussion when the time came.

The fictional Crimes Club consists of a far more cosmopolitan and dashing set of characters than in the real club; the people and plots are closer to James Bond than to the kind of enquiries made by Conan Doyle or Churton Collins. What is of real interest is the insight the book gives into the creative mind of its author. William Le Queux was a truly remarkable and outstanding man of letters, his life being unique and intriguing in many ways. Despite his interest in crime, and his hundreds of books covering novels, non-fiction, and short story collections, his name has been mostly referenced with regard to the spy mania in the years immediately before the First World War and during the war years. Some explanation of this is needed to pinpoint the place of Le Queux in his most notorious role before we look at his work in crime reporting and investigation.

In 1917, the writer D. H. Lawrence was staying in Zennor, Cornwall, with his German wife Frieda. They stayed for a time at the Tinner's Arms, and then rented a house called Higher Tregerthen. There was a good deal of suspicion from the locals, for here were a couple, staying by the sea on an isolated stretch of coastline, and the woman was a German. Rumours began to circulate that the couple were signalling to German submarines. Stories abounded, including rumours that there were smoke signals from their chimney, or that there was a supply of petrol for the submarines below the adjacent cliffs. People thought they heard German songs being sung in the house. After all, they reasoned, the route for the Atlantic convoys was close by. The couple were stopped and searched as they carried shopping home. They were not the only temporary residents in the area, and others, like Lawrence, had been rejected for conscription, or had somehow avoided it.

In his letters, Lawrence wrote that he was 'innocent even of pacifist activities, let alone spying of any sort, as the rabbits of the field outside'. It all led to a military exclusion order, and they had to leave. Had the locals known that Frieda was actually Frieda von Richthofen, a relative of the red baron fighter pilot, there may well have been even more trouble. This episode in Lawrence's tempestuous life was a template example of the spy fever that swept the country during and before the Great War. Perhaps the most typical example of this irrational paranoia was the accusation that Frieda was signalling by using clothes on her washing-line. The mass media were largely to blame for this, and they built on the fears already in existence in literature. As far back as 1871, Colonel G. T. Chesney had written *The*

Battle of Dorking, in which there is an imagined Franco-Russian invasion of England. The novel created all kinds of spin-off stories and sales were huge, with 80,000 copies sold. Then in 1906, William Le Queux published *The Invasion of 1910*. Here was something new: an account of something just a few years ahead, and by the Germans, the nation with the new Empire vying for supremacy with England. The shock comes from the mundane domesticity of the setting, as in this passage in which there is a report of the advance in Suffolk:

> In a moment the superintendent had taken the operator's seat, adjusted the earpiece, and was in conversation with Ipswich. A second later he was speaking with the man who had actually witnessed the cutting of the trunk-line. While he was thus engaged, an operator at the farther end of the switchboard suddenly gave vent to a cry of surprise and disbelief.
> 'What do you say, Beccles? Repeat it,' he asked excitedly. Then a moment later he shouted aloud, 'Beccles says that German soldiers, hundreds of them, are pouring into the place!'

A play called *An Englishman's Home* ran for over a year, and was also filmed in 1914. The enemy, though not referred to as Germans, wore spiked helmets, and so the reference was obvious. Early spy films involved the Royal Navy, partly due to the furore over the building (or shelving) of the *Dreadnoughts*.

Le Queux is particularly interesting, because he became involved in espionage, though in an amateur way, and he made a number of statements on the potential threat from Europe on Britain's domestic security, although often he was a propagator of myths. He even claimed to have contacts in Berlin, and that he had been supplied with a list of British traitors there. He wrote that there was a secret group in Germany called the Hidden Hand. Although he had no proof, he insisted that the traitors on the list included very prominent people in Britain, including politicians and writers. What he did achieve, which was a serious matter with important repercussions, was to team up with the distinguished soldier Lord Roberts to organise a make-believe invasion. With the help of the *Daily Mail,* they turned the affair into a fiasco that generated universal fears regarding the vulnerability of English shores and defences to attack and invasion. It was a classic example of the journalistic coup of creating a terrifying 'might be' situation in order to make the British Government act, as in recent times when a journalist might board a train with a mysterious parcel and not be stopped and searched by anyone.

Le Queux went his own way in his romantic and playful world of spying. This sort of activity at home in England was mainly of the provocative variety, such as imagining Germans arsenals and spies in disguise as ordinary workmen. But what is sure, is that his warnings and fabrications did catch the attention of James Edmonds, and via him, the Committee for Imperial Defence.

There were certainly German agents in England, and they were there to buy information, make sketches from observation, write reports, study communication systems, and particularly, to ascertain the true nature of British naval power. Naturally, there were spies in the field as well, and the propaganda machine made it clear what was happening to them. A typical story printed in the popular press, was that of a tale told by an American Ambulance Field Service volunteer:

> Early one morning a soldier appeared in a trench [...] he started chatting with some passing poilus [soldiers in the French infantry]. He told them he was inspecting the lines and they showed him around their trenches [...] He wandered around the woods with his new-found friends, who showed him the positions of many guns. As night came on, he ... left his friends and went to the trenches [...] he told the sentry he had orders to inspect the barbed wire [...] The man never returned [...] there is little doubt that he was a German spy.

Magazines such as *The British Magazine* showed graphic photographs of German spies being executed by firing squads, or lying by a roadside, dead and tied to a stake.

Le Queux, if we take a realistic, commercial angle on the spy mania, simply exploited a current market for fiction. Nothing sells like a murder story – except a spy novel at a time of paranoia. It was typical of this complex, mutil-faceted writer that he tackled the subject of espionage, and it is certainly right to defend him by maintaining that such fiction, or semi-fact, was needed at a time when war was imminent.

But there is another perspective too, and this in fact shows that Le Queux did indeed play a part in the Committee of Imperial Defence, which was concerned with matters related to the possibility of invasion. In 1907, Lieutenant-Colonel James Edmonds was appointed as Director of MO5, the first fledgling intelligence section. Edmonds believed the spy stories in the press. He created a campaign of propaganda, and in that project he enlisted the help of Le Queux. As Thomas Boghardt has written, 'As the similarities between Edmond's memoranda and Le Queux's stories suggest, Edmond's evidence of German espionage was partially based on Le Queux's input.'

Then Edmonds went to report to the War Office, with Le Queux's outline integrated into his own plan.

Le Queux really came into his own with *The Invasion of 1910*, with graphic accounts of imagined panic across the shires, such as: 'The mills would shut down [...] The city of Bradford was [...] in a state of ferment. In the red, dusky sunset, a Union Jack was flying from the staff above Watson's shop at the corner of Market Street, and the excited throngs, seeing it, cheered lustily.' Then, as the tides turns in the imagined desperate conflict, 'By the invasion Germany has, up to the present moment, gained nothing. She has made huge demands, at which we can afford to jeer. True she has wrecked London, but have we not sent the greater part of her fleet to the bottom of the north Sea?'

The subject of spies at the time also raises the question as to how far writers tried to link the most compelling and topical elements of spying into crime writing. One example is the development of cryptograph.: Ciphergrams had a certain air of romance and adventure around their use, and Herbert Yardley's book *Ciphergrams* has chapters that could have been taken from Homesian spin-offs: 'The Airplane Cipher', 'The Lady with Nine Cats', and 'The Man with a Hundred Faces'. But his supposedly real-life tales are indeed persistent mysteries. In one chapter, he discusses, 'the Strange Murder', which purports to refer to the murder of a certain Roy Hartwell, who was 'the typical man about town, whose escapades were frequently featured in the press. His flat was the scene of many drinking and gambling orgies'.

Roy Hartwell was supposedly discovered one morning in an arm chair with a bullet hole through his head. There was allegedly a piece of paper with a cipher on it in his pocket. I have not been able to discover any reference at all to that case. I strongly suspect that the book is a work of fiction, or at least quasi-fiction. This genre, with a further dash of adventure and mystery, was Le Queux's territory.

His life would surely have remained a mystery for modern readers had it not been for Chris Patrick and Stephen Blaister, whose book *William Le Queux, Master of Mystery* opened up for us the marvellously unreal and extraordinary life of this most elusive club member. Even *The Times* obituary in 1927 left a great deal to the imagination, and merely tempts the reader to search for facts. The tribute notes that he was a writer of sensational stories, a traveller, a student of criminology and of the secret services of continental powers.

He was born in 1864, of French descent, although even that is questioned by Patrick and Blaister. What does seem to be true, is that he was sent abroad for his education, to Pegli in Genoa, and then on to Paris. His future life as a journalist was naturally enhanced by his multi-lingual abilities. He went to Paris at first to study painting in 1881, and it seems that this was funded by an inheritance. However, all his life there appears to be a series of paradoxes and shifts from major cosmopolitan experience to small-scale domestic ones. Hence he first worked in Paris, but in 1883, he washed up in Eastbourne and tasted his first experience of criminal law. He was a junior crime reporter on the *Eastbourne Gazette*, and then moved on to work with the *Middlesex Chronicle* until around 1890.

From 1890, he was a London journalist, working at first with *The Globe*. Like Dickens earlier in the century, he worked as a parliamentary reporter and discovered how useful that work was for networking. A year later he was made foreign editor, and he also made a start on his career as a novelist. At the time he met with the Crimes Club members and joined in, he was occupied with the spy fiction, and with questions of national defence, but he was also very much involved with the criminal world. Once again though, there are questionable facts from his autobiography *Things I Know*, which appear to be far from substantiated. He was supposedly a friend of the great barrister Marshall Hall, and this is said in *Twenty Years of My Life* by Douglas Sladen, but Patrick and Baister cast doubt on this. They rightly point out that there is no mention of Le Queux in the detailed biography of Hall by Edward Majoribanks (published in 1929).

But a crime reporter he was. He claimed to have met several notorious criminals, as well as minor thieves. He would have known about the latter from his police court reporting. In his autobiography, he mentioned his place in the Crimes Club:

> Who goes spying must often keep queer company, associating with swindlers, adventurers, escrocs [swindlers], and undesirables of all sorts. The criminal world is at least exciting. To a student of crime and its psychology it is, of course, of intense interest. As one of the oldest members of the Crimes Club of London, I have always taken an especial interest in the criminally inclined. Curiously enough, I seem to possess a magnetic attraction for criminals. Why, I cannot imagine.

Of all the criminals he claimed to have met, or cases he reported on from close quarters, three stand out: George Joseph Smith, Henri Landru, and Patrick Mahon.

Smith was the notorious 'brides in the bath' killer, a man according to Marshall Hall, with a frighteningly hypnotic gaze. He was a charmer with women, and somehow they agreed to marry him, in spite of his philandering and his tendency to live dual lives under false names. His preferred mode of taking life was poisoning his women in baths, in order to take their money. He married Bessie Mundy in 1910 after he found out that she had £2,500 in the bank, but this was protected in a trust, so he left her and moved on. The trust may have saved her life, but they met again, and amazingly, he was forgiven. He realised that, in spite of the trust, he would inherit the money if he was left as beneficiary in her will. It was time to buy a bath and do away with her. In spite of suspicions, he inherited the money and moved on, meeting his next victim, Alice Burnham, in October 1913. They married, and in Blackpool he found a place with a bath suitable for his purposes. Alice was found dead in the bath, of course.

His final victim was Margaret Lofty, whom he met using yet another false name. As his third wife was dying upstairs, George was playing 'Nearer my God to Thee' on the harmonium downstairs. But he was found out after being arrested for bigamy. Investigations led to exhumations of corpses, and he was charged with murder. His trial began at the Old Bailey on 22 June 1915.

Le Queux was there for the trial. The Crimes Club would have been intrigued by the fact that this was a serial killer with a trajectory. A multi-staged process worked on the victim, from taking the woman to the doctor, having drugs prescribed, to the death by apparent drowning. Le Queux witnessed one of the most dramatic pieces of court evidence when Sir Bernard Spilsbury demonstrated that drowning in the type of tin bath used by the victims was not possible, hence there had to be the application of drugs. Spilsbury used a woman assistant in the bath to show that, without her head pressed down, she could not slip and drown. In fact, the woman almost did – when Spilsbury pushed her head. The story goes that Le Queux and Sims both tried out the bath during a lunchtime break.

As for George Joseph Smith, he was hanged by John Ellis at Maidstone on 13 August 1915. In court, he had said at one point, 'You may as well hang me at once, the way you are going on [...] go on, hang me at once and be done with it.'

With the case of Henri Landru, one of France's most brutal and amoral serial killers, we have a very different, and much closer, involvement by Le Queuex. We have a photo to show that he was there, investigating the case at the house at Gambais in the forest of Rambouillet.

Landru was born in Paris in 1869, and was often in prison in the years just before 1912, when his father committed suicide. After that, dapper little Landru, well groomed and presentable, knew how to profit from courting and flattering women, promising marriage and plotting to take their money. But unlike Smith's victims, Landru's women disappeared, and then he would assume another name and identity and move on. Like Smith, his preferred method of murder was poison, and he had a base; a country house called The Hermitage at Gambais. When a relative of one of his wives came looking for her, she realised that two men with different names were one and the same person – Landru.

Landru had been mobile, having a knowledge of cars. He would appeal to lonely women – and this was in a time of war of course – and charm them. As F. E. Smith said of the case, if he betrayed the trust of his victims, they would be helpless because, 'To publish to the world their losses would also reveal their shame and their folly.' He wanted everything his victims had, even their furniture. He was found out when this relative saw him by accident in the Rue de Rivoli, and followed him. She saw him go into a shop, so she asked there if they had his name. Her triumph was complete when the shop told her that they had his name and his address.

The rogue had even placed an advert in the papers, declaring that a 'widower with a comfortable income desires to meet widow with a view to matrimony'. There was no messing around with politeness or euphemism in Landru's world. But when the police descended on The Hermitage in Gambais and investigations began, something very nasty emerged. The house and garden were thoroughly searched, and they were led by reports from locals that there had been noxious smells coming from The Hermitage.

Landru was committed for trial in 1921. In the investigation, Le Queux wrote that he was very much involved: 'As one interested in criminology, I was invited by the Chief of the Surete to assist the police and the medico-legists in their investigations.' He also recalled that, working in the excavations for evidence, and expecting the worst, they found under the concrete:

> A number of small pieces of charred bone [...] burned hairpins, two steel stay-busks, bone buttons, and other objects. The search had been exciting enough, and we were all keen on examining most critically each handful of earth and stone. But those were the discoveries that eventually brought Landru to the guillotine.

Those events happened in 1918. The trial began in 1921, and Le Queux followed it closely, writing extensively on the case.

In one newspaper, Le Queux was given the highest intensity of promotional puffing, making him seem like a top expert, a Holmesian figure indeed:

He here recounts how, from the secret police dossiers which were completed after the trial, and to which he has been afforded access, and also from notes which the assassin wrote in his cell two days before his execution, he has pieced together the amazing hidden chapters of the career of the lover of over 200 women.

Le Queux had actually met Landru during his time in custody, and he wrote that he met the killer at the location of his horrendous murders. But that hardly seems possible. It seems very unlikely that the police on such an enquiry would allow a journalist access to the prisoner. Though what cannot be denied is that a photo exists, showing Le Queux bending over an edge of the garden at The Hermitage, notebook in hand. It doesn't look staged or false, and the fact that his knowledge would be useful cannot be denied.

Many years after the crimes, a note was discovered written on the back of a drawing in a frame, and it said, 'I did it. I burned their bodies in my kitchen oven.' Apparently, when there was no hope left, and he was destined to have his head separated from his body by Madame Guillotine, it was given to a lawyer.

Le Queux also reported on the famous and excessively repulsive Crumbles Bungalow murder of 1924. This was a case he knew well, featuring the terribly brutal and callous murder of Emily Kaye by her boyfriend Patrick Mahon, in a lonely bungalow on Pevensey Bay. Mahon had dismembered Emily in what should have been a lovers tryst. He was a married man who, like Landru, charmed his victims, and like the French serial killer, Mahon tried to slice the corpses into manageable pieces. But he had placed a locker room ticket from Waterloo station in a jacket, and his wife found it. She thought this was maybe a bag with something suspect in it, related to her husband's gambling habits. But when police retrieved the bag, there were body parts and lots of blood.

The bungalow was searched, and once again, the biographer Sladen wrote that Le Queux was there. That seems doubtful, but he was certainly reporting on the case for the press. Sir Bernard Spilsbury, in his usual determined way, worked night and day to reassemble as best he could the scattered body parts of Emily Kaye. As commentators have pointed out, after all that forensic work, the great scientist could not say how Emily had died, but he could say how she had not died, therefore the case for the defence, relying on Mahon's lies, collapsed. According to Sladen, Le Queux was invited by Spilsbury to look at the horribly gruesome scene of the killing and mutilation. Le Queux, perhaps uncharacteristically, refused. Of the many apochryphal Le Queux tales, this is one that maybe rings true.

William Le Queux died on 13 October 1927 at Knocke, in Belgium. His life was packed with incident and adventure, and there is no doubt that, throughout his multiple genres in which he produced a huge number of works, there is a mixed biographical thread of fact and fantasy. *The Times* obituary made the most of his larger than life claims, such as his statement that he was 'the first wireless experimenter to broadcast from his station at Guildford in 1920-21'. The few hundred words contains a range of experience and achievement that baffles the mind, and makes the man seem almost superhuman, but the summing-up is interesting: he 'qualified himself for writing sensational stories by wanderings in various countries, and by his studies of criminology and of the secret service systems of continental powers'.

The obituary mentions his 130 books, and undoubtedly depicts an eccentric man of extraordinary abilities and imaginative potency. It points out that in his unreliable memoir *Things I know* (1923), we have entertaining anecdotes of secret missions and 'interviews with monarchs'. The piece hints at a wonderful character with abundant life, a born raconteur, who perhaps did not trouble too much over facts and research.

In fact, in the months after his death and *The Times* obituary, there was a string of letters in the paper recalling his blunders, misinformation, and his excessive zeal in generating sensational tales. One correspondent, M. Heron Goodheart from Genoa, wrote, 'In one book [...] he makes his hero travel to London, with a secret despatch belt around his waist. On his arrival in London he hurries to the Foreign Office and interviews the "Chief of the Night Department".' M. Goodheart even pointed out that Le Queux once described a mountain, 'Mighty Corcovado reared his snow-crowned crest.' Then Goodheart points out:

> A reference to the map shows that the height of this mighty mountain is 2,313 feet. The snow-line in the tropics is just within, being I believe, 15,000 feet. We have to add, when did we worry too much, in fiction, about such details? In William Golding's *Lord of the Flies,* apparently Piggy's spectacles, which are used to start a fire and attract a plane to save the marooned children, are the wrong kinds to have such a usage. This is all nonsense in a way, and no-one wants to see a good story crushed by troublesome fact.

In the end, as Matthew Tindal wrote back in the eighteenth century, 'matters of fact [...] are very stubborn things'. Whatever the case was with Le Queux, he was there around the table with stories to tell, and he had met and seen a number of notorious scoundrels and monsters, we can be sure of that. Some of his criminal connections appear to have been incidental, and others were met with during the course of his professional life. But in every case, he not only had opinions, but as every god journalist should do, he made the most of all the material that came his way. In a sense, he has suffered the fate of those writers who write too much, too easily. Arguably, he was so immersed in the world of the popular press and mass publishing, that he always had too much to write about, and too little time to achieve it all. Yet he had a good try at that, and must never have known was boredom was.

Where in Chesterton's words, Conan Doyle had supplied the poetry of London in a new way, by enhancing criminal investigation into a special version of male adventure, Le Queux had kept breezily to the exotic and the far-fetched. Conan Doyle had made what Chesterton called a good detective story: 'In its nature a good domestic story [...] steeped in the sentiment that an Englishman's home is his castle, even if, like other castles, it is the scene of a few quiet tortures and assassinations.' Le Queux had explored and maximised the full range of settings, styles, and genres available to a mystery writer. If that tendency rather weakened the case for him as a gentleman criminologist, then there is no problem. His stories, fact, fiction, or a mix of both, are still compelling and dynamic.

Conclusions

To conclude first with a broad perspective: the years from *c.* 1890 and 1910, when in the latter year, Our Society was established and its membership multiplying, there were massive events in the history of crime and law in Britain. The most outstanding milestones were as follows: the Criminal Evidence Act of 1898; the establishment of borstals by 1902, and their widespread establishment by 1908 with the Crime Prevention Act; the option for the accused to speak in his or her defence at trial in 1898; the arrival of the first probation service in 1907, and in that same year, the creation of the court of criminal appeal. Add to these the introduction of the Fingerprint Bureau at the Yard in 1901 and the creation of the Secret Service Bureau with Vernon Kell and Mansfield Smith-Cumming in 1909, and the significance of the context for the amateur enthusiasts becomes clear.

The 1898 Criminal Evidence Act was nothing less than a revolution in court drama. It allowed the accused to speak in his or her own defence, rather than have the advocate speak and cross-examine witnesses as the main ploy for the defence. As Travers Humphreys said, the Act 'revolutionised the style of advocacy adopted by the counsel for the defence in criminal cases'.

Moreover, we can take another perspective. Film had arrived in those years. As noted in the chapter on Conan Doyle, Mitchell and Kenyon had started their cinematic business in the 1890s, and in 1901, their film *The Arrest of Goudie* brought a true crime subject to the screens for the first time, although from 1896, there had been films in Ireland and France, and again, a criminal theme was there early on, with a film version in 1911 of the great murder classic *The Colleen Bawn*. As research has recently shown, Dan Lowrey at the Dublin Star of Erin Theatre of Varieties, attracted huge audiences – 7,000 people in the first week of the films.

In other words, the club assembled on the cusp of the new mass media too: something with all popular themes in its brief, including crime and gruesome murder.

My story of Our Society began with its beginnings, and the nature of the club, and I included in that summary an account of William Roughead. After knowing each other's work for many years, he and Conan Doyle finally met in 1925 when Roughead went down to London – a trip he made very rarely. He wrote that he was a guest of the Crimes Club, and that he was introduced to Conan Doyle. Roughead's health was toasted, and he noted that Sir Charles Russell gave a talk on the Wilde case. He wrote to his friend Edmund Pearson to tell him that it was the most interesting evening he had ever spent.

Twenty years after its first meeting Our Society was very much the same as it was when it introduced set talks, rather than desultory talk. By the early 1920s, only Conan Doyle, Pemberton, and Lambton were left from the original group. Churton Collins's son describes its popularity: 'It became so successful, that within two or three years the waiting list had assumed alarming proportions.' He adds that the aims of the society had been 'ludicrously misrepresented' by a journalist 'who had never been present at any of its gatherings'. That kind of thing is the price paid for making it known that 'the strictest secrecy was the cardinal principle of the club', as Collins' son explains. Clearly, the development of the club was not without disagreements in the first ten years or so, as it suffered a transformation in its aims and its activities.

If we have to assess the achievements of the club in those first few years, it has to be allowed that, although it was essentially a brotherhood of friends and professional peers with common interests, and no remit to have any impact on wider affairs, it did have definite triumphs from men in its circle, across the wide spectrum of law in all its contexts. Conan Doyle was exemplary of course, being a real detective whose advice and expertise were in demand across the globe. Following close behind in terms of real achievements in applied investigations, was Churton Collins. In spite of his occasional errors, Collins was a real investigator and researcher, who visited prisons and notable offenders in order to work out theories. It is hard to find another literary critic who turned his analytical skills to solving crimes. Arthur Lambton, although not outstanding in criminal investigation, certainly had an impact on the reform of the law with regard to inheritance. Then of course, we have the elusive and puzzling William Le Queux, and his crime reporting. There is no denying that he was close to major crimes and the participants in investigations, particularly with Landru and the

Crumbles murders in mind. There is no doubt that he investigated, and spoke on the crimes and the major criminals he had met: the only issue is how far he stretched the truth.

As to George R. Sims, he is surely an enigma. His autobiography makes high claims for the fact that he knew virtually all the criminals and police involved in the most notorious London crimes in the last quarter of the nineteenth century. Yet in spite of his assurances, his statements are not always trustworthy in that regard. He was always a reporter, making the most of a good story, and adding high claims for the importance of all encounters and experiences in his undoubtedly very full and exciting life.

The others were either scholars or men about town, with a penchant for sensation and a genuine curiosity about crime. But there was a foundation of one major interest beneath virtually all the members from 1903 to 1905, and that was drama. The theatre was a part of almost all their lives, and crime narratives on the stage, as well as on paper, were immensely popular in the 1890s and the early years of the new century. The Crimes Club (and the Medico-Legal Society) came along at the moment when the mass media were stepping up crime reporting, responding to the significant advances being made in both policing and in the nature of crime. Like Sherlock Holmes himself, the club emerged in step with the advent of international espionage, terrorism, and assassination, and of course, with the science of detection.

The club was formed in a *Zeitgeist* that was trying to express and mediate the revolution in criminology that was taking place. At the basis of all this was technology applied to forensic process. The talk at the club dinners could range from the telegraph, used for the first time to trap a killer in the Crippen case, to the advanced ballistics practised by Robert Churchill in his lab behind Trafalgar Square. Churchill's biographer Macdonald Hastings summed up the situation in the world of detection *c*. 1900: 'It was the specialists outside Scotland Yard – men like Sir Bernard Spilsbury, the pathologist Sir William Wilcox, the toxicologist Dr Roche Lynch [...] who began to transform Conan Doyle's conception of a super-detective into reality.'

Conan Doyle was the man who arguably played a significant part in making the profession of detective something with glamour and panache. There had been a detective force at Scotland Yard since 1842, but even with the advent of such roles and responsibilities as infiltration of anarchist groups, royal protection, and all the work under the aegis of the Special Branch, it was still shadowy and a little morally suspect even by 1900. After all, for decade, the popular image of the detective had been one related to the fact that the job was two-faced, and somehow dishonestly underhand.

With this in mind, we can see the creation of Sherlock Holmes as an account of why and how the private detective may be more skilled and intellectually equipped than the detectives at the Yard. To some extent, the Crimes Club, as it developed away from Lambton and Oddie's initial conception, reinforced this view. Holmes's reasoning is more acute than the professional counterparts. More than anything else in the work of crime detection, he represents an individual in complete control of all the processes of such police work, from initial questions and the scene of crime, to the imprisonment of the suspect.

However, matters are not quite that simple. The Yard man was beginning to ascend in status and reputation in the early years of the twentieth century. In Fletcher Robinson's *The Chronicles of Addington Peace*, his inspector is from Scotland Yard. Then we have *Stories of Scotland Yard* by Vivian Grey, published in 1906, with its very complimentary and positive portrayal of the professional detective. The Edwardian years, for the contrast between gentleman detective and professional Yard man, were a watershed.

In fact, it is possible to reverse the viewpoint and suggest that, before Holmes was invented, there were men around in the Special Branch who, although their work was not widely known, achieved remarkable things in the art of detection.

Detective work was moving into the political arena twenty years before the first club dinner. It was only logical that leaders would come along who were very different from the military men and 'through the ranks' personalities such as Williamson, the future commissioner. In other words, there was a need for a spy network that would operate apart from the detectives, while obviously needing their help on occasion. The spymaster who emerged was a strong personality with an eccentric streak in him: Edward Jenkinson, a man who loved working in disguise, and who had a penchant for cloak and dagger adventure. By 1884, James Monro was heading the CID, following Littlechild, and he was becoming increasingly aware that Jenkinson was going to be difficult. The spymaster insisted on working in his own way, with information kept back from the CID. He saw himself and his network as being separate from detectives, and this was a growing rift as the years went on.

Jenkinson had emerged as a prominent figure in this respect after being under-secretary for police and crime at Dublin Castle after the Phoenix Park murders of 1882, in which the chief secretary for Ireland Lord Frederick Cavendish, and his secretary Thomas Burke, had been stabbed to death in that Dublin park. In London, in his new position of power, Jenkinson began to develop a network of double-agents known as 'spooks', and real agents, wherever he thought there was a possibility of a bomber-group being formed. This meant planting agents in such places as Mexico, Paris, and New York. Later, it also meant that he would need links with Russia, as by 1885, there was a strong possibility that the old machinations of the Great Game of espionage based on the Russo-British rivalry for control of the Levant and India would be renewed.

But after a long series of bomb-scares, myths, and fabrications that cost a great deal of money, Jenkinson was sacked. Arguably, the only real achievement of his reign was to show that detectives were perhaps the best types of personnel to work on Royal duty, due to a bomb-plot against the Queen in 1887, the year of Jubilee. Jenkinson had gone by then, but his eccentric and whimsical use of secret communications and ruses had shown a way to operate beyond the normal limits of police work. At least he had shown that terrorism has to be tackled in ways very different from what he called 'plodding police methods'.

When Jenkinson left, James Monro found himself in charge in 1887 of both arms of the detectives at the highest level: the CID and the special Secret Department as it was then known. Monro opened a new section of the CID, with seasoned detectives Littlechild, Pope, Melville, and Quinn at the head. Monro also had a new second-in-command: Robert Anderson, a man who had been working well with intelligence sources in the States. The famous spy Henri Caron, alias Thomas Beach from Colchester, was part of the string of agents. This advance in police work was extremely significant: it raised the question of how much should the police know about political activities? After all, it was an age of increasing anarchist movements and growth of militancy in left-wing and Empire groups. Jenkinson had not worried about that too much. He had had Abberline of Ripper fame working for him at one point, checking numbers of immigrants arriving in London. But now all that undercover stuff, in the control of one rogue boss such as Jenkinson, would have to stop. The new outfit would have to report to the Home Secretary regularly.

The vindication of the new secret office came with the uncovering of the Jubilee plot of 1887. The Fenians wanted to place a bomb in Westminster Abbey, to be exploded during Queen Victoria's attendance at the thanksgiving service there. Monro's new men were stunningly professional in their detective work, and what they did impinged on espionage. Monro was aware of a man called Millen, assigned to create this bombing; the agent Beech had done some excellent work in that respect. What we then have are two parallel operations of first-rate detective shadowing of suspects. The men in London who were to plant the bomb were living with assumed names, but were tracked down and followed. Monro even had an officer assigned to meet Millen in Paris, under pretence of being 'an interesting invalid' who would chat up Millen and watch him.

Detectives then observed and tracked a man in London known as Melville, who turned out to be John J. Morony, a significant figure in the Fenian *Clan-na-Gael*, the American branch. Following that, a certain Harkins was followed and questioned, along with a Mr Callan. The capture of the latter typifies the drama of this episode in detective history. Before the police arrived for him, Callan, said his landlady, had thrown something down the toilet. After a search of the drains, the police found dynamite. It was a magnificent triumph for Monro and his men. But there is an interesting coda: in his memoirs, Anderson claimed that Millen had been a double agent, and that he had been feeding information to London for some years, even in the regime of Jenkinson. Whatever the truth of this, the important point is that at the time of the Jubilee, Monro did not know who the conspirators were until the help came from beyond his Special Branch.

This kind of story surely lies behind the way we juxtapose the Holmesian amateur and the Yard man. The stock view of Conan Doyle's Inspector Lestrade is, although surely reinforced by the Basil Rathbone film versions, one of a man lacking in any kind of impressive skills – in fact, a bungler at times and a plodding blockhead at worst.

The Crimes Club definitely became a reflection of these changes in attitude, and of the importance of the Sherlock Homes inspired amateur. But they never claimed to be a brains trust of criminal studies. We have to express some sympathy with Ingleby Oddie, who resigned in 1909 when the meetings ceased to be for pleasant conversations with friends, and nothing more. The clue is surely in the word 'club' – always a term applied to a group gathering for leisure and relaxation, and good conversation. In contrast, the medico-legal members were always a 'professional society'. That is a very different thing, usually with a chairman and even a president. Almost certainly it has publications, such as transactions or a journal. The Crimes Club merely expressed itself in hot air, not in print.

It would have been easy at the turn of the nineteenth century, with the influence of physiognomy and criminal types in mind, to satirise criminology as it was then perceived. G. K. Chesteron did just that, in an essay titled 'A Criminal Head', and there he writes to have fun at the expense of the new science:

> In a popular magazine, there is one of the usual articles about criminology; about whether wicked men could be made good if their heads were taken to

pieces [...] I always notice however, a curious absence of the portraits of living millionaires from such galleries of awful examples.

Yes, the Crimes Club would be open to some teasing, for they talked and wrote in a world of flux with regard to the formation of criminology as a science.

The secrecy and exclusivity has naturally created the kind of curiosity that will logically see the club as a vague concept, somewhere between a gentleman's cigar and brandy affair and an extension of student (mainly Oxford) camaraderie. It is the kind of image that creates the mix of mystery and satire one often finds in references to Masonic lodges. If discussion goes on behind closed doors, and the topics are on crime, then popular conclusions will either be that everything is rather harmless and boyish, or that there are questionable reasons why topics are secret.

The opposite viewpoint might still insist that such a group is a think tank, and that top Scotland Yard and MI5 personnel attend in order to absorb some highly cerebral theory that could relate to national security, or to the patterns of deviant iniquity perpetrated by the latest mutations in serial killers. Of course, the maintenance of exclusivity also preserves the mystique, and that is something that Arthur Lambton never wanted. He saw that a good conversation, full of anecdotes and humour, was what the appeal should be. Ingleby Oddie had suggested to Lambton in Naples, as mentioned earlier in the chapter on Lambton, and Oddie had suggested 'a coterie of crime experts', so he was not necessarily thinking of simple conversation. That was Lambton's version. So perhaps from the origins, in a conversation on holiday in Italy, it was destined to be a secret society. My thought on this would be that Lambton had in mind very much what George Orwell did when he wrote, 'Your pipe is drawing sweetly, the sofa cushions are soft underneath you, the fire is well alight, the air is warm and stagnant. In these blissful circumstances, what is it that you want to read about? [...] Naturally, about a murder.'

To end on a positive note: if we look to the actual applied work of some of the club members, then we have evidence that amateurism did have a place in police work – and in a context beyond the mere use of the expert witness. The presence of Conan Doyle made its identity a mix of impressive criminological thinking (evident in their investigations and theories) and the brilliance of applied medical knowledge. As noted in the profile of William Le Queux, there was a sense – fictional and sensational – that 'Crimes Club' suggested a group of men equal to the mind of a Moriarty, but any thought of that was in their fun, their sheer pleasure in refining countless hypothetical lines of thought around that continually fascinating structure of the narrative of a crime: offence and victim, investigation, chase and arrest, trial, aftermath. That has the five acts of a Shakespearean tragedy, but it is also a ready-made drama from the lives of real people in the stories presented and discussed at the club dinners. The real energy and organising principle behind the criminous perspective on true crime is that of investigation into human beings. We see it in Harry Brodribb Irving's deep interest in Roughead's Jessie Mc'Lachlan, and it is also there in our infinite fascination with murder.

Acknowledgements

There are many people to thank for help in the research for this book. The work has entailed plenty of digging for material in obscure places. Particular thanks go to Darren Armstrong at the Norwich and Norfolk Millennium Library, staff at the Brynmor Jones university library, University of Hull, and to Kate Walker for productive discussion. For some of my drawings in the illustrations, thanks are due to Laura Carter.

Special thanks go to Peter Costello, whose book on Conan Doyle first alerted me to the Crimes Club members in the first few years of its existence.

For occasional topics in relation to railways, my thanks go to historian Brian Longbone, who helped me to imagine the impressive creation of the hotel at Marylebone where the club members first gathered.

Bibliography and Sources

Note:
As is usual with books of this nature, requiring a great deal of information to be gathered from fragments and ephemera, my sources are many and varied. The following is a select bibliography, but it covers everything referred to in the text, including works discussed, and other related works that may have been touched on, albeit marginally at times. But I have considered these to be important enough to include, to assist other historians and researchers in their task. The Crimes Club as it was *c.* 1903-1910 has been an aspect of Conan Doyle's life that has been passed over in the main biographies, and so material on most of my subjects' lives has been found in long-forgotten memoirs. Fortunately, these fragments of memory tend to lead to many other sources. There is no mention of the Crimes Club in three recent biographies (published between 2008-2011), and a search of the indices offers no mention at all of several of these club members. The focus of the book is notably on merely a few years in Conan Doyle's life, and so wider reference has been needed to bear upon those years, and the impressive biography by Andrew Lycett has been indispensable. Equally, without the work of Paul Spiring, little would have been available on the impressive but elusive Bertram Fletcher Robinson.

Access to some references regarding trials has been made easier by the Penguin reprints of earlier writings on some major cases, so that Eric R. Watson's account of the George Smith trial (written in 1915) for instance, is reprinted.

The less visible members, standing in the shadows, are seen largely through others' eyes, and in asides. To gather their stories, some speculation has been required. I was aware from the first conception of the enquiries here, of Conan Doyle's words in 'The Norwood Builder': 'You mentioned your name as if I should recognise it, but I assure you that, beyond the obvious facts that you are a bachelor, a solicitor, a freemason, and an asthmatic, I know nothing whatever about you.'

Primary Sources

The following texts are the editions used. I have listed only those works discussed in my text. Dates of first publication, where necessary, are in brackets:

Works by Conan Doyle, Arthur (editions used or cited)
A Study in Scarlet (1887) (BBC Books, 2011)
The Hound of the Baskervilles (1901) (Penguin, 2011)

The Mystery of Cloomber (1895) (Dover, 2009)
The Return of Sherlock Holmes (1905) (Penguin, 2011)
The Captain of the Pole-Star (Various dates in periodicals) (Hodder and Stoughton, 1940)
Memories and Adventures (Greenhill Books, 1924)

Works by other Crimes Club Members
Atlay, J. B., *The Victorian Chancellors* (Smith, Elder, 1906)
Diosy, Arthur, *The New Far East* (Cassell and Company, 1896)
Irving, H. B., *A Book of Remarkable Criminals* (Cassell, 1918)
Irving, H. B., *Occasional Papers* (Bickers and Son, 1906)
Lambton, Arthur, *My Story* (Hurst and Blackett, 1924)
Le Queux, William, *No. 7 Saville Square* (Ward Lock, 1920)
Le Queux, William, *The Crimes Club* (Nash and Grayson, 1922)
Le Queux, William, *The Invasion of 1910* (Ward Lock, 1906)
Mason, A. E. W., *At The Villa Rose* (Hodder and Stoughton, 1910)
Mason, A. E. W., *Witness for the Defence* (Hodder and Stoughton, 1913)
Oddie, S. Ingleby, *Inquest* (Hutchinson, 1941)
Pemberton, Max, *Sixty years Ago and After* (Hutchinson, 1936)
Sims, George R., *Among My Autographs* (Chatto and Windus, 1904)
Sims, George R., *Anna of the Underworld* (Chatto and Windus, 1916)
Sims, George R., *Ballads and Poems* (Neville, 1883)
Sims, George R., *My Life: sixty years recollections of bohemian London* (Eveleigh Nash, 1917)
Sims, George R., *Prepare to Shed Them Now: the ballads of George R Sims* (Hutchinson, 1968)

Works on Crimes Club Members
Adlard, John, *A Biography of Arthur Diosy* (Edwin Mellen, 1991)
Beerbohm, Max, *Letters to Reggie Turner* (Rupert Hart-Davis, 1964)
Browne, Douglas G., and Tullett, E. V., *Bernard Spilsbury: His life and cases* (Harrap, 1951)
Carr, John Dickson, *The Life of Sir Arthur Conan Doyle* (John Murray, 1949)
Chesterton, G. K., *Autobiography* (Hutchinson, 1936)
Chesterton, G. K., *All Things Considered* (Methuen, 1908)
Collins, L. C., *Life and Memoirs of John Churton Collins* (John Lane, 1912)
Dark, Sidney, *The Life of Arthur Pearson* (Hodder and Stoughton, 1922)
Green, Roger Lancelyn, *A E W Mason* (Max Parrish, 1952)
Holroyd, Michael, *A Strange, Eventful History* (Vintage Books, 2009)
Irving, Lawrence, *The Precarious Crust* (Chatto and Windus, 1971)
Irving, Lawrence, *The Successors* (Rupert Hart-Davis, 1967)
Lycett, Andrew, *Conan Doyle: The Man who Created Sherlock Holmes* (Phoenix, 2007)
Patrick, Chris and Baister, Stephen, *William Le Queux: Man of Mystery* (The authors, no date)
Sala, George Augustus, *The Life and Adventures of George Augustus Sala* (Cassell, 1895)
Spiring, Paul R., *Bertram Fletcher Robinson: A Footnote to The Hound of the Baskervilles* (MX Publishing, 2011)
Watson, E. R., (Ed.) *Trial of Adolf Beck* (William Hodge, 1924)

Watson, Robert Patrick, *Memoirs of Robert Patrick Watson* (The Colmore Press, 1899)

Other Printed Sources
Baden-Powell, Robert, 'My Adventures as a Spy' in *Fifty Amazing Secret Service Dramas* (Odhams Press, 1920)
Barrie, J. M., *Letters of J M Barrie* (Peter Davis, 1942)
Barrie, J. M., *The Greenwood Hat* (Peter Davies, 1930)
Behrman, S. M., *Conversations with Max* (Hamish Hamilton, 1960)
Bennett, Arnold, *Journals* (Penguin, 1954)
Birkett, Norman Lord, *Six Great Advocates* (Penguin, 1961)
Cecil, David, *Max Beerbohm: a Biography* (Constable, 1964)
Charteris, Evan (Ed.) *The Life and Letters of Sir Edmund Gosse* (Heinemann, 1931)
Chesterton, G. K., *Alarms and Discursions* (Methuen, 1910)
Chesterton, G. K., *Father Brown* (1911) (Penguin, 1981)
Cohen, Herman, (Ed.) *The Criminal Appeal Reports* (Stevens and Haynes, 1909)
Cortazzi, Sir Hugh, *Britain and Japan 1859-1991* (Routledge, 1991)
Gregory, Kenneth, *The First Cuckoo* (Allen and Unwin, 1976)
Humphreys, Travers, *Criminal Days* (Hodder and Stoughton, 1946)
Le Couteur, Wilson, *The Great Outposts of Empire* (Federal Houldershire Lines, 1907)
Nevinson, H. W., *Running Accompaniments* (Routledge, 1936)
Smith, Sir Sydney, *Mostly Murder* (Odhams Press, 1959)
The Law Reports: The Public General Acts, 1926 (Eyre and Spottiswoode, 1926)
Vane, Sir Francis, *Agin the Government* (Sampson Low, 1929)
Williams, Montagu, *Leaves from a Life* (Macmillan, 1890)
Yardley, Herbert O., *Ciphergrams* (Hutchinson, 1920)

Secondary Works

Books
Alcan, Felix, *L'Homme Criminel Atlas* (Ancienne Librairie Gumer, 1887)
Bartley, Paula, *Prostitution: Prevention and Reform in England 1860-1914* (Routledge and Kegan Paul, 2000)
Birkenhead, Earl of, *Famous Trials* (Hutchinson, 1923)
Bloom, Ursula, *Curtain Call for the Guv'nor* (Hutchinson, 1954)
Boghardt, Thomas, *Spies of the Kaiser* (Palgrave Macmillan, 2004)
Bold, Alan (Ed.), *Bawdy Beautiful: The Sphere Book of Improper Verse* (Sphere, 1979)
Bonham-Carter, Victor, *Authors by Profession* (The Society of Authors, 1977)
Browne, Douglas G., *The Rise of Scotland Yard* (Harrap, 1956)
Canler, Louis, *Autobiography of an Ex-Detective from 1818 to 1858* (Ward and Lock, 1862)
Chesterton, G. K., *The Defendant* (R Brimley Johnson, 1901)
Chesterton, G. K., *The Uses of Diversity* (Methuen, 1920)
Cline, C. L. (Ed.), *The Letters of George Meredith* (OUP, 1970)
Colquhoun, Kate, *Mr Briggs' Hat* (Little Brown, 2011)
Cook, Chris (Ed.), *Britain in the Nineteenth Century 1815-1914* (Routledge 2005)
Cook, Matt, *A Gay History of Britain* (Greenwood, 2007)

Cook, Matt, *London and the Culture of Homosexuality 1885-1914* (CUP, 2009)
Costello, Peter, *Conan Doyle Detective* (Robinson, 2006)
Davies, Hunter, *A Teller of Tales* (Sinclair Stevenson, 1994)
Delany, Paul, *George Gissing: A Life* (Phoenix, 2009)
Eddleston, John J., *The Encyclopaedia of Executions* (John Blake, 2002)
Fido, Martin, and Skinner, Keith, *The Official Encyclopaedia of Scotland Yard* (Virgin Books, 1999)
Foot, M. R. D., *Secret Lives* (OUP, 2002)
Gaute, J. H. H., and Odell, Robin, *The Murderers' Who's Who* (Pan Books, 1979)
Greene, Hugh, *Further Rivals of Sherlock Holmes* (Penguin, 1976)
Guy, William A., *Principles of Forensic Medicine* (1844) reprinted as *Victorian CSI* (History Press, 2009)
Hastings, Macdonald, *The Other Mr Churchill* (Harrap, 1963)
Hastings, Selina, *The Secret Lives of Somerset Maugham* (John Murray, 2010)
Hattersley, Roy, *The Edwardians* (Abacus, 2006)
Hodge, Harry (Ed.),. *Famous Trials 2* (Penguin, 1948)
Hyde, H. Montgomery, *The Trials of Oscar Wilde* (Dover, 1973)
Irving, Ronald, *The Law is an Ass* (Duckworth, 2000)
James, Trevor, *There's One Away: escapes from Dartmoor Prison* (Orchard Publications, 1999)
Kingston, Charles, *Famous Judges and Famous Trials* (Stanley Paul, 1910)
Lane, Brian, *The Encyclopaedia of Forensic Science* (Headline, 1992)
Moss, Alan, and Skinner, Keith, *The Scotland Yard Files* (National Archives, 2006)
Murray, Paul, *From the Shadow of Dracula: A life of Bram Stoker* (Pimlico, 2005)
Orwell, George, *Decline of the English Murder and Other Essays* (Penguin, 1965)
Pattenden, Rosemary, *English Criminal Appeals 1844-1991* (OUP, 1996)
Riggs, Ransom, *The Sherlock Holmes Handbook* (Quirk Books, 2009)
Shpayer-Makov, Haia, *The Ascent of the Detective: police sleuths in Victorian and Edwardian England* (OUP, 2011)
Smith, David James *Supper with the Crippens* (Orion, 2005)
Sugden, Philip, *The Complete History of Jack the Ripper* (Robinson, 2002)
Sutherland, John and Fender, Stephen, *Love, Sex, Death and Words* (Icon Books, 2011)
Sweet, Matthew, *Inventing the Victorians* (Faber, 2001)
Teichman, Jenny, *Illegitimacy* (Blackwell, 1982)
Whitbread, J. R., *The Railway Policeman* (Harrap, 1961)
White, Chris (Ed.), *Nineteenth-Century Writings on Homosexuality* (Routledge, 1999)
Whittington-Egan, Richard, *Speaking Volumes* (Capella Archive, 2004)
Whittington-Egan, Richard, *William Roughead's Chronicles of Murder* (Lochar Publishing, 1991)
Wolmar, Christian, *Fire and Steam: how the railways transformed Britain* (Atlantic Books, 2007)
Wood, J. Hickory, *Dan Leno* (Methuen, 1905)

Periodicals and Newspapers/ Reprints in Chapters
'The Hanging of Percy Lefroy at Lewes' *Daily Telegraph* 30 November 1881
The Medico-Legal and Criminological Review Vol. II Part IV. (Medico-Legal Society, 1934)
'Conan Doyle and the Mystery of the Bullet-Proof Uniform' *Police History Society*

Journal Number 13, 1998, pp. 37-38

'George R Sims at Home' Special correspondent, *The Times* 27 August 1892

'Idler' interviewer, 'A Chat with Conan Doyle' *The Idler* August1894- January 1895 VI, pp. 341-349

Annal, Dave, 'A Problem in the Family' *Your Family History* June, 2012 pp. 22-25

Doyle, Arthur Conan, 'My First Book' *The Idler* August 1892 – January 1893 Vol. III, pp. 633-640

Hopper, Keith, 'Irish Slides' Review in *Times Literary Supplement*, 16 November 2012

Lawrie, Alexandra, 'Browning in Hackney' *Times Literary Supplement*, 20 January 2012

Waller, Philip, 'Sims, George Robert' *Oxford Dictionary of National Biography* (OUP, 2004)

Watson, Eric R., 'George Joseph Smith' in *Famous Trials* 2 (as above)

Archives

The George R Sims Collection: The Rylands Library, Manchester. GB 133 GRS

This is a collection of Sims' printed and manuscript works and also music scores. These were donated by David Mayer in 1995-6. The archive comprises: manuscripts, hard-bound typescripts of dramatic works, play scripts in typescripts, manuscript musical scores, correspondence and scrapbooks. As the note at the site comments: 'Also reflected in his journalism was a keen and long-held interest in Jack the Ripper murders and Sims developed his own theories on the subject.' As noted in the relevant chapter, his main suspect was Kosminski. Of all the Club members other than Conan Doyle, he represents a writer outstandingly in need of a reappraisal; he made things happen in the law as well as writing about crime.

Digital Sources/Internet/ Visual sources

'Forcible Feeding' letter by H. B. Donkin *The Times* 18 December 1909, p. 12

'The Murder at a Studio' *The Times* 6 June 1906, p. 3, Times Digital Archive

'Studio Murder' *Washington Post* 1 July 1906

'The Condition of Holloway Prison' *The Times* 30 August 1901, p. 6

www.lprinfo.com/history-handwriting-analysis.html

www.casebook.org/press_reports/washington_post/060701.html

www.orderstjohn.org/templars/eoc1890s.html

The Lost world of Mitchell and Kenyon (British Film Institute, 2004)

Index

Armstrong Case 131-132
Atlay, James Beresford 125-126
   The Victorian Chancellors 125
Authors' cricket team 10

Beerbohm, Max 13, 66
Bennett, Arnold 11
Broadmoor Asylum 5
Brown, Dr Gordon 62

Carr, John Dickson 30
Carlton Club 9, 26
Cherrill, Fred 14
Chesterton, G. K. 11, 21
Collins, John Churton 45-57
   criminology 47
   defence of Doyle 46
   Ireland's Eye mystery 48-50
   Merstham Tunnel case 51-52
   Ripper murders, 48
   Wakley murder 54-56
Costello, Peter 9, 36
Crimes Club 11-13
   early days 26
Criminal Appeal, Court of 5-8
Criminal Evidence Act (1898) 145
Criminal Records Bureau 16
Crippen Case 59-61
Crosse, Dr Herbert 122-123

Dalston Case 28-29
De Quincey, Thomas 13, 18
   Murder Considered as one of the Fine Arts 13

Dew, Inspector Walter 59-61
Diosy, Arthur 62, 126-131
   Far east specialism 128-130
   Jack the Ripper occult theory 128
   and Kossuth story 126-128
   and Templars 128
Doyle, Sir Arthur Conan 33-45
   A Study in Scarlet 28
   The Return of Sherlock Holmes 30
   as a clubman 34
   conception of Holmes 36
   interest in 1860s cases 36-38
   situation in 1903
   Stonyhurst 38-39

Edalji case 39-40
Edgerley, Dr. 6
Espinasse fraud 121

Farrow murder 14-16
Fingerprint Bureau 13
Frood, Herbert 22

Galton, Francis 14
Goudie fraud case 118-121
Great Central Hotel 9, 21, 22, 73

Harmsworth, Alfred 10

Idler, The 11
Irish Crown Jewels case 41-44
Irving, Henry Brodribb 66-75
   interest in French criminals 69-70
   stage career 69

visits the hangman 68
Irving, Sir Henry 9
Ives, George 10

James, Henry 17
Jefferson, James 5-7

Kell, Vernon 16-21

Lambton, Arthur 20, 25-21
Lawrance, Judge 6
Leeds Assizes 5
Legitimacy Act (1926) 32
Le Queux, William 131-142
   his fictional crimes club 135
   Landru case 140-142
   spy mania

Lombroso, Cesare 12
   L'Uomo Delinquente 12

Macnaghten, Commissioner 60
Mason, A. E. W. 104-111
   spying in Mexico 108-110
Medico-Legal Society 23
Moat House Farm murder 117-118

Newnes, George 10
Notable Scottish Trials 19

Oddie, Samuel Ingleby 10, 58-65
   Brinkley murder 63-64
   Crippen trial 59-61

Osborne, Lord Albert Edward
   Godolphin 113-115

Pearson, Sir Arthur 115-117
   interest in graphology 116-117
   Pearson's magazine 115
Pemberton, Max 93-98
   and *Edwin Drood* trial 96-97
   clubman and writer 94-95

Robinson, Bertram Fletcher 99-103
   partnership with Doyle 100-102
Rojas, Francisco 14
Roughead, William 17-20

Scotland Yard 23
Sims, George R. 7
   Dagonet 76
   Lefroy murder 90-91
   Madame D'Angely case 81-2
   Ripper theory 92
Slater, Oscar 40-41
Spilsbury, Sir Bernard 23
   Whitworth case 83-88
Strand magazine 12

Vicars, Sir Arthur 43-44

War Office 22
Wilde, Oscar 104-105, 113

Yeats, W. B. 104-105